anywhere but here

stories

anywhere but here

stories

Tim Bugansky

J.B. Solomon Editions
Alliance, Ohio

J.B. Solomon Editions

Alliance, Ohio

jbsolomon2007@yahoo.com

www.myspace.com/jbsolomonunlimited

Library of Congress Control Number: 2007927656

ISBN: 978-0-6151-4548-8

"Presence" was originally published in *Luna Negra*.

Cover Photo: Tim Harrison

Author Photo: Kim Eggerton

Front Cover Design: Tim Harrison and Kim Eggerton

Back Cover Design: Kim Eggerton

For my mother

contents

gorillas in our midst

"The gorillas are coming!"

That's what my father says as he bursts through the front door and runs past where I am playing with my building blocks on the floor of the front room. He is early for lunch, I realize, for my stomach has not yet started to rumble and the smell of tortillas and hot chile peppers is not yet escaping from the kitchen.

My father has not stopped to remove his work boots and place them on the front porch beneath the hammock. He does not take off his sweaty shirt and hand it to Juana like he normally does. He does not stop to pat me on the head and survey what I have been building on the floor. He leaves his hat on, too, and rushes right past me. He is in a hurry.

"The gorillas are coming!" my father says again.

Juana watches him pass her. She seems confused. She asks him something in Spanish. I do not know Spanish except for the numbers and colors, so what Juana says to my father sounds like a chirping bird to me. He says something back to her. He sounds different than Juana when he speaks in Spanish, like a grunting pig, but I still do not understand the words. So I just stay on the floor with my blocks and wonder when the gorillas will arrive.

My father has disappeared into the back of the house. I sit on the floor and Juana stands above me. I wonder why she has not gone back to the kitchen to finish lunch. My mother has been out back in the garden, but she now comes into the house after hearing my father talk about the gorillas. She wears dirty garden gloves. In one hand she holds a little shovel, in the other a bunch of weeds.

"I want to see the gorillas," I say to my mother. And I do want to see them. I have never seen gorillas the whole time that I can remember being in Guatemala. Quetzal birds and parrots and a boa constrictor that we accidentally ran over one day in the Jeep. But no gorillas.

"Not that kind of gorillas," my mother says. The way she says it makes me wonder if I should have known better than to ask to see them in the first place.

My father has returned from the back of the house. He carries his shotgun and a box of shells. Through the screen door I watch as Ricardo, the plantation manager, pulls up in front of our house in his Land Rover. I wave to him but he does not wave back. He says something in Spanish to my father as my father leaves through the screen door and gets into the Land Rover beside Ricardo. They pull away and head in the direction of the plantation's front gate.

My mother looks sick.

depths of detachment

W hen Erik awoke Monday, it was to the dawn of October. He had tried to stay up late the night before, waiting for the 30th to become the first and winter to come one step closer to setting in. But he'd fallen asleep somewhere between the eleven o'clock news and the twelve o'clock movie and the month had changed right under his nose.

Waking up on the living room couch, though, he knew instantly September was gone. The scent of leaves that drifted in through the open bay window somehow smelled more like October, more dead and decayed. The early-morning evangelist – the one who came on and went off the air before most anyone was even awake to notice – was talking about death. Death was imminent for us all and in Jesus lay the path beyond death. Jesus loves, Jesus forgives, Jesus saves. Believe in Jesus and death is merely a speed bump along the interstate to eternal salvation. Disbelieve and roast in the fires of everlasting hell.

It was still dark out; the clock on the wall read 5:30. From out in the kitchen he could hear the clatter of dishes.

Erik's mother had been doing the dishes for two weeks. For fourteen straight days she had methodically washed, dried, and replaced them. Wash, dry, replace. Wash, dry, replace. Every cup, saucer, plate, bowl, and utensil had made the journey from the cupboard to the sink and back. Not to mention all the pots and pans, plus the crystal and China. And when everything was spotless, the cycle would begin again.

She didn't speak to him. Not that she had spoken to him all that much lately, anyway, since his father's trips had been getting longer and longer. But now it seemed as though she were a mere ghost; an unstable specter trudging about in silent lethargy, condemned to an eternity of washing dishes. She never cooked – at least not for him, and in those two weeks he had never seen her put a morsel to her own lips. He prepared his own meals. There was a plus side to this arrangement, though: He never had to clean up afterwards.

A week into her trance he made a futile attempt at communication. He had been peeling an apple at the counter when her unspeaking presence next to him became suddenly unbearable. He whipped around and grabbed her by the shoulders, catching her mid-rinse.

"Don't you understand?" he almost screamed. "Don't you understand he's never coming back? Never again? He's *gone*!" His entire body was coiled with tension, yet she remained limp and lifeless in his grip. She stared blankly at him for a moment, as though he were as much a ghost to her as she to him. Then she turned slowly and rinsed.

That was the last time he tried to speak to her.

He got up and unraveled himself from the quilt, upsetting his popcorn from the night before. The Tupperware bowl tumbled from its precarious position in between two couch cushions. The puffy white kernels spilled from the bowl and scattered across the carpet. Like so many stale white leaves bouncing in the wind, Erik thought to himself as he walked through the debris.

He crunched past the couch and toward the kitchen. Ahead of him, at the sink, his mother scrubbed and rinsed one final plate, then set it in the drainer. This done, she let out a long, soft sigh, one of the strange sorts that were the closest she came to speech anymore. It was a hybrid kind of sigh, one that seemed to express two different emotions simultaneously: a sense of longing (for his father, he supposed) and a sense of regret at not having more dishes to wash.

The sigh lasted as long as it took Erik to walk the length of the hallway. Then it was done but, instead of beginning to dry the dishes, she slumped over, letting her head hang and her shoulders droop and her hands sink further into the dirty water, exhausted from her self-inflicted punishment.

Opening one of the cupboards, Erik retrieved a box of Frosted Flakes and then took a bowl and spoon from the drainer. The cereal clung to the sides of the still-damp bowl. There was no milk; they'd run out the week before. From the side of the blue cereal box, Tony the Tiger smiled at Erik and gave him a big "They're Grrreat" thumbs-up. Tony obviously didn't know that the boy had a mother who couldn't stop doing the dishes and a father who was never coming home again. And on top of this they were out of milk.

Erik ate quickly, even though it was well before 6:00 and by this time he knew that he would not be going to school. The dirty bowl and spoon went in the sink; his mother immediately saw to it that they wouldn't remain dirty for long.

Hurrying back down the hall, he bounded up the steps to his room. It was still early – quarter to six – but he wasn't feeling tired. Getting up early didn't really bother him; he didn't sleep much anymore, and was beginning to doubt whether or not he would ever be able to a get completely sound night of shut-eye again in his life.

His things were all still under the bed where they'd been stowed three weeks before, everything he'd bought at the flea market with his fence-painting money. There was the big army surplus backpack with the bright pink "Nuke the Commies" iron-on patch adorning the top flap, a hatchet, a coil of nylon rope, a Swiss Army knife, fishing line and hooks, the green tarp, and a box of matches. Supplies he'd purchased to have handy just in case. Just in case of *what*, he hadn't known at the time; but at night as he lay awake in his bed listening to the ceaseless clinking of dishes below him, he'd felt a sense of security knowing that if he ever wanted to leave, he could. All he had to do was pack.

Stuffing the items in the backpack, he added a towel and a heavy blanket off his bed. The Ziploc bag that held the rest of his fence money found a spot, too. He put on some jeans, a T-shirt, a faded sweatshirt, and a windbreaker, then plucked two books from his bookshelf: *Huckleberry Finn* and *The Old Man and The Sea*. He'd read the first so many times he'd lost track, and he'd been meaning to get to the second for as long as he could remember. Erik was only a freshman, but he liked to read. Sometimes it was all he *could* do – it seemed there was no one human he could converse with, so he might as well listen to words on a page.

Downstairs he grabbed a skillet and a kettle from underneath the stove, a coffee mug from above it, and his cereal spoon – now clean – from the drainer. From the cupboard he took a box of Bisquick, the jar of Folgers crystals, a bag of raisins, a jar of peanut butter, two packages of beef jerky, and a canister of Quaker oatmeal. These all went in the backpack, as well. As an afterthought, he took the Frosted Flakes from where he'd left them on the table and stuffed them in the backpack, too. He wasn't surprised to find that Tony was still smiling.

Shouldering the bulging olive drab pack, he was out the front door in an instant. His mother hadn't seemed to notice his departure. The last time he saw her she was still bent over the sink, her arms hanging listlessly in the basin.

His bike was lying in the front yard. He righted it and hopped onto the dew-dampened seat. In a moment he was pedaling madly down the road, heading toward the lake.

•   •   •

Dusk came quickly to the little cove. The sudden decline in sunlight took Erik by surprise, and he nearly lost his balance and tumbled from his lofty perch. The treetop lurched with the sudden shift of his weight, but he managed to catch himself and regain his position. His back securely lodged against the trunk and one leg on either side of the protruding branch, Erik tried to return to his book but it was difficult to concentrate. Daylight was fleeing quickly and he found it harder and harder to follow the exploits of Huck and Jim.

Below, the trio of ducks took off from the water's shadowy surface. They had been paddling leisurely about all day long; now, though, there was a sense of urgency to their flight, as though they were anxious to outrace the sunset.

Through leafless patches in the branches above his head, Erik could see ghosts of the evening's first stars. A slight breeze picked up off the lake, and the remaining leaves fluttered and trembled, now revealing, now concealing, now revealing the faint heavenly glimmer.

Erik remembered Huckleberry Finn saying, *We had the sky up there, all speckled with stars, and we used to lay on our backs and look up at them, and discuss about whether they was made or only just happened.* He remembered nights during the summer when he sat up on the roof of his house, cloaked in darkness and starlight, staring up at the stars and thinking about his father.

He'd left one morning in June, Erik's last day of school. The boy had been sitting at the breakfast table with his Frosted Flakes when he felt the hand gripping his shoulder from behind. Never a hug, never a hand*shake*, just a hand.

"So long, champ," his father had said in a tone of voice which implied that this time it might be longer than usual.

"Bye," Erik replied, trying to appear interested in the eleven essential vitamins and minerals listed on the side of his cereal box. However, he could tell something was different. He couldn't help but notice the tone of voice, and he suspected that the slamming of the door was probably the last he'd be hearing from his father.

Still, though, he would ascend to the rooftop to sit beneath the stars. At first he went merely to wonder where his father was, as though he might find some hint or insight woven into the nighttime sky. A small part of him clung to the hope that perhaps his intuition had been wrong, that maybe his father *was* coming back, and that somehow by looking at the stars Erik would help him find his way.

Later on, though, Erik became resigned to the fact that his father was gone for good. The boy fled to the roof merely to escape his mother and the atmosphere of brooding that pervaded the house. Now, instead of offering any sort of consolation, the stars only worsened his outlook. The infinite void of space made Erik feel more alone than ever.

We had the sky up there, Huckleberry Finn had said.

Erik was back on the ground now. In his hands he held the open book and read these lines over and over. *We had the sky up there ... and we used to lay on our backs ...* He read and he remembered late-September evenings spent shivering on the roof. He remembered desperately not wanting to go to bed; not wanting to endure the constant clatter of dishes but knowing he'd have to, sooner or later.

Suddenly, Erik had cast the book onto the fire and was watching pieces of it float upward toward the heavens. Moments later he was on his bike, riding back up the path in the direction of the road.

•   •   •

If it hadn't been for the neon sign lit up in front of the restaurant, Erik would've passed the place right by. And even the sign wasn't completely reassuring. Three letters were burned out, making it read, "Ed's B_r an_ G_ill." But a faint, distorted light was visible through the frosted front window, and the area surrounding the squat, dilapidated board structure smelled strongly of grease. Erik was hungry, and he was about halfway around the north end of the lake, giving him a good ten miles back to camp.

So he guided his bike into the gravel parking lot. Stones sprayed and bounced and the bike skidded in a wide arc. He dismounted and let it fall to the ground with a rattling thud.

The inside of the bar was dark and hazy. Thick cigarette vapors hovered above the floor and clung to Erik's clothing the moment he entered. The bar was almost as dark on the inside as it was outside. A single light bulb, bare and uncovered and attached to a frayed electrical cord, was suspended from the ceiling. Looking at it hanging there on the end of the cord reminded Erik of a human eyeball, shrunken and pale with thin strands of optic nerve trailing out the back. The luminescent eyeball hung above a ramshackle pool table; the table's green felt was moldy and moth-eaten and assumed an unearthly pallor in the light bulb's bleary glow.

Smoke and grease were the predominant odors of the room. The smells intermingled, combining in a massive assault on his senses. The acrid smoke brought tears to his eyes and caused him to erupt in a coughing fit which he tried unsuccessfully to muffle. The grease-smell felt heavy and oily in his nostrils. He could almost feel his arteries clogging with each breath.

From where he stood at the doorway, he was directly facing the bar. It didn't look to be the sturdiest structure in the world; Erik questioned whether its warped surface could support too many more rounds of drinks. Five stools lined the bar. Only one was occupied. On the far right stool, a figure was hunched over facing a row of empty beer bottles. The man was wearing a grey hooded sweatshirt with the hood up. The hood formed a reverent little peak at the top where his head was tilted downwards.

Behind the bar stood a big bald man wearing a grease-stained apron. He was polishing a glass when Erik entered the building. Hearing the door slam shut, he looked up, saw Erik, and with one meaty finger silently beckoned the boy to approach. Erik did so hesitantly, sitting down on the far left barstool, furthest from the hooded patron.

"So, what'll it be?" the bartender boomed, planting both hands on the countertop and leaning in toward Erik. His voice was magnified by his series of countless chins, and on his breath lingered the odors of beer and decay. His cheeks, red and puffy and grizzled with stubble, shook when he talked.

Momentary fear gripped Erik. For the briefest instant he considered bolting for the door but decided against it. Intuition made him think better of it, and hunger sealed the decision. Instead, he swallowed hard and looked at the wall behind the bar. Alongside a glowing Stroh's clock was tacked a chalkboard listing the specialties of Ed's B_r an_ G_ill. A network of cracks crisscrossed its surface, fragmenting the words into a myriad of pieces.

Erik barely glanced at the board before stammering, "Uh ... grilled cheese sandwich ... bowl of chili. And, uh, a cup of coffee. Please."

"A coffee drinker, eh?" the burly man sneered, in a manner which suggested he regularly chopped up coffee drinkers and made chili out of them. He turned momentarily and reached behind him, producing a mug and a coffee pot. He filled the mug and set it before Erik, then returned to the stovetop located behind the bar.

Erik took a hesitant sip of the coffee. It was lukewarm and bitter and so strong it seemed to grate against the sides of his mouth. He set aside the mug and cast a sideways glance at the man at the opposite end of the bar. His hood was still drawn and he still sat hunched over, facing his row of beer bottles. From where he sat, Erik could count the bottles: six empty ones at the back edge of the bar and a half-full one which the man was working on now. In between every slow, methodical sip, he would set the bottle back down on the counter and retrieve a cigarette from somewhere within his sweatshirt. This he would light up and smoke with the feverish intensity of a soul starved for nicotine. His hands shook madly and he drew on the cigarette with short, hissing, rapid-fire inhalations. About halfway through, he would stab it out in an ashtray and take the next slow sip from his beer. The entire time that he watched this endless cycle, Erik never saw the man's face; from his vantage point it looked like the very hood itself was devouring the cigarettes.

"Y'know, it ain't nice to stare." The bartender's interjection shocked Erik and he lurched around to see his food sitting before him. The bartender – whom Erik fancied to be the Ed mentioned on the sign out front – was shaking his hog-jowled head to and fro and sneering at the boy.

"So tell me," he said, drawing a beer from a tap behind the bar, purposefully letting it get too full and slop loudly onto the floor, "what brings a kid like you to these parts?" He took a noisy slurp from his glass.

Erik shrugged, his mouth full of greasy grilled cheese. "I dunno. Fishing." He took the final bite from his sandwich, then looked down at his empty plate, surprised to find he'd finished the grilled cheese so quickly. He picked up a spoon and started on the chili. As he drew his mouth nearer to the bowl he saw that the man at the end of the bar was still on his frantic smoking spree. By now, the ashtray was spilling over with the butts of half-consumed cigarettes.

Erik was nearly finished with his chili before Ed said anything further. "Fishing, huh? I used to do quite a bit of fishing myself. Me and my buddies, every Friday night we'd load up a cooler fulla brews and take my ol' outboard out on the lake. Damn, we sure had a hootin' good time. Can't say's we caught all that much, though." He shook his head and his jowls wistfully followed suit. "Them days, though, they're long gone. All finished here?"

Erik nodded as Ed removed the plate and bowl. He forced himself to down the rest of the coffee; he had to force himself even more not to retch. Sliding the empty mug across the counter, he looked down the bar again. This time, the man was looking back.

From within the shadowy depths of the hooded sweatshirt, Erik could see the glowing red tip of the man's cigarette. Slowly, a pale white hand with slender fingers and jutting tendons reached up and pulled the hood down. The face that stared back at Erik seemed a composite of Jesus and the grim reaper. It was white to the point of translucence, with wandering blue veins, stringy brown hair, and a rambling beard to match. Gaunt cheekbones jutted from the sides of his drawn face. His eyes were barely open, and were so sunken within their sockets that they were all but invisible. The undersides of the sockets were lined with purple-black rings.

Slowly, painfully, with none of the feverish intensity of before, the Jesus-reaper removed the cigarette from his parched blue lips. With his opposite hand he pointed across the three-stool gulf that separated him from Erik. In a raspy, barely audible voice, with wisps of smoke trailing from the corners of his mouth, he hissed, *"There are bodies in the depths of the deep dark lake."*

Then his head sagged and he withdrew his pointing hand to his mouth to stifle a series of hoarse coughs that racked his throat and rattled phlegm somewhere deep within his body. Thin strands of hair danced to the rhythm of his choking fit, and the veins on his head and the tendons on his clawlike hand stood out with renewed intensity.

Gradually, the fit subsided and the man painfully raised his head to stare at Erik once more. A crooked grin slowly wormed its way across his pale face. Suddenly, before Erik's eyes, it seemed as though the details of the translucent face were replaced by those of his father's. The eyes were closed, though, and the flesh was gray and mottled and appeared to be slightly decomposed. *He's dead.* The thought sprang into Erik's mind unexpectedly; he was taken aback, and continued to stare dumbly at the new face that now occupied his field of vision. Then, just as surprised by his words as he had been by his thoughts, Erik whispered aloud, "And I don't care."

In an instant Erik had bolted for the door. By the time he remembered he had not paid for his food he was outside and on his bicycle and pedaling like mad across the causeway and didn't care anymore about eating or paying or *anything.* He was just suddenly afraid, so very afraid.

As he pedaled he glanced back over his shoulder at the bar, growing more distant by the second. He thought he could hear the pale man's haggard cough traveling across the water.

The entire trip back, the whole ten miles, the man's words fueled his flight. *There are bodies in the depths of the deep dark lake.* The saying had an eerie rhythm to it, and it reverberated inside his head, propelling him through the inky blackness of the night.

Back at camp he was exhausted but could not sleep. He drew himself closer to the fire while the words rushed through his head. *There are bodies in the depths of the deep dark lake.* And sometime during the night the fire died down and Monday withered with it, giving way to the first shards of dawn.

putting pepe to rest

Pepe the German shepherd had killed a bull by ripping out its throat. For that crime he had been chained for life to an orange tree at the little house in the country. Now he had escaped and rampaged through the chicken coops. Only two of the fifty chickens were still alive, and this time Pepe had no chance for redemption.

The abuelo had come to the apartment the previous night with a burlap sack in hand. Splotches of red soaked through the material. "Chicken," the abuelo had said, handing the bag to my host mother.

She peered inside. "But it is only pieces," she said. "It's all in shreds, it's all bloody and mangled."

"I know," the abuelo nodded gravely. "Pepe got loose. Only two chickens survived. I saved whatever meat I could from the dead ones. Tomorrow I will take the shotgun to the farm and I will put Pepe to rest. Do you wish to come, Timoteo?"

The question was addressed to me, and I nodded in reply. The next day after school I went straight to the abuelo's house. He sat at his kitchen table with a hunk of bread, a piece of cheese, and the shotgun. He alternately nibbled on the food and rammed a cleaning rod down the gun barrel. Then he ran an oiled rag over the exposed metal. The weapon gleamed blue-gray.

He wasn't my grandfather, but I called him "abuelo" anyway. I called my host mother "Mamá" and my host father "Papá" and my entire Argentine exchange family "mi familia." It did not seem difficult or strange. The words were in Spanish, so they did not hold the same significance as "Mom" or "Dad" or "family." It was even easier to do with the abuelo. Everyone has two grandfathers, after all; I imagined he was the one I had never met.

I was the only one who enjoyed going with the abuelo to the country during the week to do the chores. Everybody else – my host parents, siblings, cousins, aunts, and uncles – went only on weekends when the abuelo would prepare sumptuous midday feasts for the entire family. Sometimes we numbered two dozen or more. We sat together around the long tables in the dining hall behind the house, devouring course after bountiful course. There were salads of onion and roasted sweet red peppers; legs of lamb and thick slabs of beef cooked over a wood fire; enormous cauldrons of stew, slow-simmered garbanzos, spinach, bacon, and peas ladled into bottomless bowls; giant frying pans heaped with liver and onions, red and tangy-sweet with paprika; little loaves of fresh bread laid on the tabletop alongside the eating utensils; endless bottles of wine, cold and white in the summer, soul-warming red in wintertime. We ate until we could eat no more. Then we dozed on the grass outside if it were warm, or lingered languidly around the tables inside if it were not.

Everybody came on the weekends to enjoy. The abuelo and the caretaker did all of the work at the farm, though. I had helped with what I could since coming to the family. In the summer we had tended the garden together, picking the small red *guindilla* peppers and threading twine through their stems so they could be hung to dry against the side of the house. We plucked oregano and basil leaves from their plants and placed them to dry in buckets atop the sun-soaked picnic table.

Now that it was winter we killed an occasional lamb or pig. Once in a while we made sausage with the help of the abuelo's brother and the butcher who lived down the lane from the farm. Soon it would be time to kill both a pig and a cow to make salami. Whenever there was milk, the abuelo made cheese. I helped to remove the cheeses from the molds, cover them with herbs and oil, and spread cloth over them to ward off the flies while they aged.

On the way to the farm we stopped at the edge of town to buy shotgun shells. "There are shells in the house at the farm," I said. "In the cupboard next to the wine."

"But they are old and they may not fire perfectly and Pepe might suffer," he said.

"But the shotgun is old, too," I pointed out.

"I have cleaned it so well that it is better than new," he replied. "I cleaned it last night and twice this morning and once before you arrived, and now you have seen me clean it again."

The abuelo didn't want Pepe to suffer. He loved the dog, even though he had killed a bull and destroyed forty-eight chickens. For the rest of the drive to the country that day, he told me about Pepe. For me Pepe was synonymous with the farm and the orange tree to which he was chained. I had never seen him separated from either one.

He had received Pepe five years ago from the same butcher down the lane who helped to make the sausage. When the sausages had cured that year, the abuelo passed by the butcher's house with an armload of them for a gift. In return the butcher plucked a puppy from the litter that scurried around the yard and presented it to the abuelo.

The abuelo talked about how Pepe had killed the bull. Pepe was in the pasture and was trotting past the bull when the bull suddenly swiped at him with his horns. The side of one horn collided with Pepe's thigh, and the dog sprawled to the ground. He instantly returned to his feet and struck, lunging with bared teeth. The bull bellowed and collapsed onto its knees, its throat gushing crimson. It wasn't clear if the bull had hit Pepe out of malicious or playful intent. To hear the abuelo speak of it, Pepe seemed to have been the innocent party. He recounted the dog's actions with pride, and I wished that I had seen it happen.

"It wasn't Pepe's fault," the abuelo said. "The bull struck first. He is a brave dog, *un perro bravo*. He is proud and he had to defend himself. But what he did was very savage. I could not leave him unchained after he did that."

I suspected that any other dog would not have been treated as favorably the first time around. Now, however, there was no choice. "One must die so another may live," the abuelo would always recite while we sharpened the pig-butchering knives. "*Así es la vida*. Thus is life." And now Pepe had to die so that another might be spared in the future.

"One never knows what Pepe might do to a person," the abuelo said. "He would not mean to, but it may just happen. I do not believe that he meant to kill the chickens. It just happened. He is a brave dog. It is a shame that his bravery got away from him."

We had arrived at the farm. The abuelo got out of the car and walked purposefully to the orange tree to which Pepe was once again chained. He was a huge dog. I was always impressed by his massive frame, his enormous snout, his furry, club-like paws. Yet his face was innocent and angelic. He always smiled a toothy dog-smile, his tongue hanging lazily out of the corner of his mouth.

"Has he tried to escape?" the abuelo asked the caretaker, who had seen us arrive and was emerging from the house.

The caretaker shook his head. "Not a single problem," he said.

"He would not try. He is a good dog. He knows he has done wrong."

The abuelo knelt beside Pepe and said something into his floppy ear. From his coat pocket he withdrew a bone and presented it to the dog. It was a chicken leg. Pepe's tail thumped loudly with gratitude as he chomped on the bone. In an instant it was gone and the abuelo was unhooking the heavy chain from around his collar.

"Do we need a rope?" I asked. "To lead him?"

The abuelo shook his head and spoke again to Pepe. Then he started off in the direction of the field. He beckoned to Pepe; the dog obediently rose to his feet and followed the old man.

I was left standing by the orange tree, holding the shotgun and the new box of shells. The abuelo motioned at me to load the gun. I did so, popping in a shell and snapping the single-shot chamber closed. I searched for a safety, but the gun did not have one. Then I followed the two of them at a safe distance, taking care not to let Pepe see the gun.

We passed the empty chicken coops. Their wooden sides were battered and bloodstained, and feathers littered the ground. I reached the gate that led out to the field, where the abuelo and Pepe had stopped. The abuelo reached out his hand and took the gun. I made a move to open the gate for him, but he opened it himself and raised his palm to stop my further advance. The matter was between the two of them now.

I watched as Pepe trudged faithfully after the abuelo into the open field. He could see the gun now but did not run away. They proceeded a few paces, then stopped abruptly. The abuelo turned to Pepe and bade him sit down. Then the abuelo walked around behind the dog and placed the barrel of the shotgun firmly against the back of his neck.

There was a muffled roar and Pepe's lifeless body crumpled to the ground.

We dug the grave together. The abuelo seemed unfazed by the whole task. He worked briskly, focusing on the job at hand as though it were any other farm detail. He had not enjoyed killing Pepe, I am sure, but he did not reveal his emotions. He was more reserved than usual, though. Normally he would be chattering away about the animals or the weather or the sausages curing in the barn. I could tell he was thinking about something.

"I believe I will stop by the butcher's house later," he finally said. "I think he has some puppies to give away."

departures

S he arrived bearing a box. It was to hold the last of her books, the last of her possessions that occupied what until just the week before had been our shelves in our apartment in our life together.

Outside, the last of the season's leaves were barreling up and down the street, tossed to and fro by the indecisive November wind.

I had been awake for hours, pacing the small apartment, gazing intermittently out the rear window at the litter-strewn back lot: the abandoned refrigerator whose crippled door hung by a single hinge; the eleven wooden pallets, splintered and impaled with rusty nails; the deflated basketball that hobbled lamely about when the wind grew especially fierce.

"Figures you'd have that CD playing today," she said, referring to the sound of the stereo in the background. She forced a smile. "You know I could never stand it."

I glared at her. Her cheeks were flushed from the cold. Her face glowed in stark contrast with the sparse gray light that stole into the room.

"What's the matter?" she said. Even now she tried her hardest to be soothing and understanding. "What's wrong?"

I was angry that it was she who was moving out, she who was taking her things and leaving me with possessions that could never again truly be mine, since they had for a time been *ours*. The fact that she was leaving – and leaving me behind – also seemed to concede to her the final word.

But I couldn't imagine her staying in *our* apartment, either. I couldn't imagine her bringing other men there, those men looking into the mirror where I had once looked, those men sitting on the same toilet, those men drinking water from the same tap, her yielding herself to someone else, their haphazardly scattered clothes entangling on the floor while their scents intermingled in the air and their limbs and hair and lips intertwined in places that had once been ours.

It was this inability to ever be satisfied for which she was leaving me: my propensity to loathe unconditionally, which butted heads with her need to love unconditionally.

I had known much earlier than she that things would never work out between us. But I wanted so much to have someone to forever be present, another being upon whom to deflect my hatred of myself. I felt most alive when I killed her with insults.

My silence disquieted her. The forced friendliness on her face was crumbling into panic.

"What's the matter?" she said. "Please. What's the matter?"

She wanted to be friends. That was another thing I loathed about her: that she was willing to forgive and refused to dwell on the past. I inhabited a world of double standards. I hated her for realizing that. I hated her for refusing to abide by the double standards, for simply treating me kindly and hoping for the same in return.

"Wh—" she began again.

"Why can't things be different?" I practically screamed at her.

She considered for a moment, though she had not been taken aback when I finally spoke.

"Things could have been different," she said. "They could have been different and they could have been better."

But she didn't blame me. No, she would not grant me that pleasure, that opportunity.

"Nothing makes you happy," she said. "I tried. God knows I tried."

"Why? Why the fuck bother?"

"Because you made me happy. Once upon a time you helped me to like myself. And I was just trying to repay the favor," she said. "It took me a long, long time to admit to myself that I couldn't – and that it wasn't my fault that I couldn't."

Her tone – calm, rational, nonjudgmental – goaded me.

"What the fuck do you think I am?" I said. "Some kind of child?"

Before we moved in together, I would wait at night for her to call me. If she didn't call, I was so angry that I would stay awake the rest of the night. If she did call, I usually found something to fault: why hadn't she called the night before, what was that tone in her voice, didn't she know I had to wake up early the next day.

"I'm human, too," she said. "I have a life and feelings of my own. I try to tiptoe around the things that make you insecure. But you don't extend me the same courtesy. You barrel right into my insecurities. You take them and throw them at me and stomp the whole lot of it into the ground. You stomp me into the ground."

While she spoke, she had been plucking her books off our shelf, depositing them into her box, which she'd set down next to the stereo, as though picking apples from a tree. Her movements were graceful, despite the anxiety creeping into her voice.

I wanted so much at that moment to hug her. I wouldn't let myself, but I couldn't allow myself not to touch her, either.

I intercepted her hand as it reached for the final book. I clutched her wrist until her grip slackened and the book tumbled to the floor.

"What are you doing?" she said.

Still clutching her wrist, I pushed her to the ground. She tried to sit up, but with my left hand planted firmly on her breastbone I held her pinned to the ground. The buoyancy and optimism she tried so hard to maintain oozed out beneath my fingers.

With my right hand, I reached over to the stereo and turned up the volume.

"You're right," I said. "You always did hate this CD. But maybe you just weren't listening hard enough."

One of the speakers was at the end of the bookshelf. Right next to her head. She whimpered as I turned the volume up. And moaned as I turned it up louder still.

The ground began to pulsate. Her face decomposed into a mangled pile of teeth and tears.

"No ..." she sobbed. "Stop it. Stop it. Stop it. Stop doing this to me. Stop doing this to yourself."

Even now she couldn't be selfish. Even now, when the volume was as loud as it could go and she was squirming with discomfort and her eyes were spilling torrents onto the floor.

I let her go. Sobbing, she clutched at the carpet, as though she were a baby and it a blanket.

And I left her there. And I left, plunging without a jacket into the frigid embrace of the world.

rumors of revolution

The mother has no sons. The older of her two boys went off to university four months ago. He wrote one letter, then he wrote no more. He disappeared one night from the flat he shared with three other boys from the village. Two of the others are gone, as well. The third returned home, but only in the thick of night did he dare tap on the mother's window and bid entry to her home. He shivered as he sat at the table, despite the steamy air of the tropical night. *I do not know why they did not take me, too. Please believe me*, he said. *I did not hate the others. They were my friends. Since childhood when we played soccer together in the lot behind the basket factory. It is all so crazy. One does not know whom to trust. The world has gone mad. Please believe me.* She believed him and gave him a cup of coffee and a cigarette to calm his nerves. He smoked feverishly, purposefully, as though trying to suck reason into his soul and make sense of the world.

The younger of the mother's two boys, at sixteen the baby of the family, slipped up the mountain path one night to join the rebels in their dens. In the morning, she read his note twice before burning it and scattering the ashes in the garden out back. He was always good with a rifle, her baby. He shot birds and wild pigs and carried them home for the supper-pot. Now he lived in the hills and moved by night. Now he shot at things other than animals. Of this she did not think. She wondered instead if he got enough to eat.

The family is but two now, yet the mother cooks for four. She fries four plantains, stews enough meat for herself, the boys, and her husband. She boils rice for all and still bakes dessert. But she only picks at her plate and her husband barely eats, either, despite his long days in the mine. After dinner there are pans of untouched food filling the places of her sons at the dinner table. At night the father stares sullenly at the tabletop, his foggy sleepless gaze splintering the wood. The mother washes and dries the dishes five times. She rehearses what she will say if the police come. *The eldest? I do not know, officer. He went off to the capital and writes us no longer. Stolen away by life in the big city. Too good for the country, now. Or stolen by some woman. It is probably that. And the baby? He never loved us. Good for nothing, he was. At least the eldest worked, though he may have disliked it. The younger hated work with a passion and avoided it at all costs. Would rather drink aguardiente and sleep the day away. I do not know where he is. Probably dead-drunk in a gutter somewhere or on some ship with louts like himself. No, I do not see them anymore, officer. Nor do I wish to.* It pains her so to rehearse this. She hopes never to utter these lies.

The town speaks in whispers of what is happening in the world. One must be careful, though, upon whose ears the whispers fall. Shutters close earlier these days. The plaza is empty except for stray dogs and vagrant drunks. Only ghosts and shadows walk the streets at night. Rumors of war creep into the houses, slowly at first. Then buzzing swarms of them descend like the inevitable mosquitoes that follow a summer rain. A village across the mountains was raided the other day. Only the chickens survived. The houses were torched and smoke billowed skyward, twisting its way over the peaks to the mother's village on the other side. A girl going to another town came across a fleshless skeleton buried up to the skull in a throbbing termite mound. The white skeleton-teeth beamed a ludicrous smile.

Please believe me. The tension mounts within the cloistered houses of the village. *The world has gone mad.* Neighbors trade suspicious glares and mistrustful silences. The darkness grows more menacing. The nights are eternal. Endless. *One does not know whom to trust.* A mother washes the dishes for the fourth time that night and thinks about two sons she will never see again.

all units, all for naught

T he fire turned out to be a disappointment. The firefighters had arrived in time, and it appeared the situation was well under control. Roger stood up close near the smoking building, reporter's notebook in hand, his camera slung around his neck. He gestured with his hands as he spoke to the official in charge.

I stood back with some of the neighbors, watching from a distance as the fire crew put the finishing touches on the blaze. One man went up in the bucket and began methodically dousing the entire structure. Meanwhile, yellow-suited men inside the three-story tenement building knocked out the upper-floor windows. I watched as one shoved an axe handle through, sending shards of glass cascading to the ground. He poked his helmet-clad head out of the empty window pane and gave a thumbs-up to the crew below. Smoke billowed from the shattered window behind him, framing his body in a thick, wispy white haze. Some of the smoke curled out of the window opening and around his masked face like ethereal fingers reaching from a black unknown.

"Crack house, that's what it was," one of the onlooking neighbors standing next to me asserted to another. "'Nother crack house fire. I'll be goddamned if that's not the third one in the past two months."

"Yep," the other grunted in affirmation.

The wrapper from a Snickers bar, carried by a gust of wind, skipped from the litter-strewn street and found its way to the vacant lot where we stood. I shivered and shoved my hands deep in my pants pockets. I'd left the newspaper office without putting on my jacket. I stood wearing only a T-shirt, at the mercy of the late-autumn Ohio wind. Another gust sent the candy bar wrapper spiraling skyward and drove a chill through my body. I followed the wrapper with my eyes until it disappeared up among the heavy clouds, then shifted my gaze to the tenement house: a weather-beaten, aluminum-sided structure with smoke pouring out of its third-floor windows. The building stood framed against the stark gray November sky.

Up close near the tenement, Roger had put away his notebook and was snapping a few photos with the Nikon. He took one of the man up in the bucket, then one of a firefighter upstairs knocking out another window. Roger performed this task with little interest or enthusiasm, merely going through the motions. Even from the distance at which I stood, I could tell he was disappointed.

•   •   •

Roger had been on his feet almost the instant the call came over the scanner. He cast a low whistle at the sound of the all-units request. With one surprisingly adept motion, he grabbed his faded overcoat and the battered Nikon that lay half-buried beneath the journalistic rubble of his desk.

"All units!" he exclaimed, with more excitement than I'd ever before seen him express in my three part-time months at the newspaper. Then he added, with a glance across the room in my direction, "Wanna come?"

Issued from the mouth of a brooding man who rarely had anything to say to the regular news staff – much less me, the minimum-wage high-school stringer – this offer took me by surprise. I faltered a second, glancing around the empty late-afternoon newsroom, into which a muted November half-light spilled through the partially drawn blinds.

The only other staff member present was the social page editor, a tiny woman who was surrounded by, more than seated upon, her high-backed swivel chair. She and the chair were dwarfed on all sides by stacks of wedding announcements and write-ups of the recent happenings of the various clubs and societies around the Reliance area.

"Come on," Roger prompted, already on his way out of the newsroom. "An all-units fire doesn't happen every day. It's close, too – we can walk." He seemed to derive certain pleasure from the notion of trekking crosslots through downtown Reliance to view the fire, as though there were a sense of rugged adventure associated with it. There was also a strange hint of urgency – almost a pleading tone – in his voice, and I couldn't help but wonder what captured his interest so much about the fire.

Momentarily weighing the situation, I decided that I'd had enough of reworking press releases for the time being. The prospect of getting paid to watch a fire seemed far more appealing than the latest public-service spin put out by the State Farm Bureau or the Governor's Commission on Fair Business Practices.

As I caught up with Roger, he turned and remarked again, "All units! Gotta be a big one." He heaved open the front door and held it for me. Ducking beneath his outstretched arm, I glanced up and caught a strange, far-off gleam in his eye.

"All units," he whispered to himself in a detached, barely audible voice. And then we were outside and heading toward the fire.

By the way Roger chattered as we made our way through the side streets and across the litter-strewn vacant lots that lay between the newspaper building and the fire site, we would encounter a building engulfed in a solid wall of flames, with four dozen men locked in a perilous, life or death battle to extinguish it – as well as the chance for a picture which, by the standards of the *Reliance Record*, would be considered gripping documentary photography and would certainly find a place on the front page.

I had difficulty matching his pace as we headed toward the fire. His was an old, ambling, time-worn gait that almost resembled a mutated hopping, but he nevertheless covered territory quickly. He lurched with a strange ease across the unkempt and uneven terrain, maneuvering adeptly out of the way of potholes and broken glass and piles of trash. He managed his sizable belly quite well, given the circumstances, appearing almost graceful in the process. His overcoat flapped slightly with each gust of wind.

We neared the sight of the fire, though, and he faltered. Looking skyward he paused for a moment, blinked in disbelief, and sighed: "White smoke." I followed his gaze, encountering a white column twisting upward from behind a row of faded brick buildings.

•   •   •

Standing in the vacant lot across from the fire site, I fixed my gaze on the building. It was a ramshackle structure, typical of those to be found in downtown Reliance. Gaping holes were casually scattered across the outside walls, exposing rotten plywood underneath the aluminum siding. The lot on which it sat was mostly dirt, with patches of weeds and scrubgrass here and there. Vacant shingle-spaces dotted the roof like missing teeth. The front porch was sagging and warped and not at all stable-looking.

"I heard they was fixin' to condemn it," said one of the men beside me.

There were three of them in a little group, all apparently from the neighborhood. Each wore a heavy flannel shirt and a stocking cap pulled low over his ears. They trodded in place, stepping from work boot to work boot and rubbing their hands together in an effort to rid themselves of the cold. I tried my best to stay warm, at the same time keeping my eye on the subsiding activity of the firefighters and listening to what the three neighbors had to say.

"Crack house, that's what it was, I tell ya."

"Mebbe so, but they was still fixin' to condemn it."

"Bullshit. Jack Butcher's cousin was gonna move in there next week. Apartment B, second floor, I think it was."

"All I know is ain't no apartments on the *third* floor. They's supposed to be remodelin' it right now. Got four 'partments on each of the first two floors, and they was gonna put four more on the third, divide it up and run water and electric and put down carpet and all."

"I thought you said the place was a crack house. All the people that live there involved in the operation? They got the li'l kids pushin' dope?"

"No, the whole thing ain't a crack house – somebody 'uz just usin' the third floor as one since there wasn't nobody livin' there."

"How do you know?"

"Buddy of mine was helpin' fix it up, doing the third-floor drywall. He said they found a whole labat'ry up there. Sleepin' bag and some cans of food, too. He never seen no one, though." The man who had spoken paused momentarily to retrieve a can of Skoal from his back hip pocket. He packed the can with a swift motion, then popped it open and stuffed his cheek with tobacco. "Been police come by a coupl'a times askin' questions and such, askin' who lived there. Come by my house the other day. I tol' 'em ain't nobody livin' up there onna third floor, but rumor had it there was somebody workin' up there from time to time, so to speak. I ain't seen the police around here since. Prob'ly got better things to do." With this he spat forcefully, casting a gob of Skoal-saliva to the cold, hard ground.

"Hell, what the police gonna do about it, anyway? They don't care. They wanna bust some crack houses, they can talk to anybody in the neighborhood. Anybody and his uncle can name a half-dozen or so right off the bat."

"Who owns this place, anyway?"

"J.T., I imagine. Hell, he owns half of downtown Reliance. Regular slumlord. Yes, I b'lieve this is one of his."

"Coulda been for insurance. J.T. done it before, from what I hear; hired some guy to torch a coupl'a his rentals that were fixin' to be condemned. Quick money, it was. Course, put some people out of a place to live, but what does he care?"

"I wouldn't put it past J.T."

One man emerged from a house down the street carrying a six pack of Old Milwaukee. He strode over to where we were standing. Ripping one of the cans away from the plastic rings, he passed the rest of the six-pack on to the other three men standing near me. They each took a can for themselves, then one dangled the remains of the package in my direction.

"Beer?" he offered. "It'll take the chill off." It was the first time any of them had addressed me. I hadn't even been sure they knew I was standing there.

"No, thanks," I declined with a polite wave of my hand. The man shrugged and set the remaining two cans on the scrub-grass floor of the vacant lot.

"My cousin was just about to move in. Next week, he was – apartment on the second floor," the newcomer offered in between sips of his beer. He motioned at the smoldering tenement. "Now it don' look that way, though."

•   •   •

Roger had finished with his photos and was once again talking with the official in charge. I was just about to move closer to the house to attempt to warm myself a bit when I saw him nod, shake hands with the fireman, then turn and walk in my direction. He looked despondent and downcast, and moved with none of his previous agitated excitement.

Joining me, he confirmed what he'd already speculated before: the firefighters had arrived early and doused the flames before they had a chance to spread. The white smoke indicated the absence of a live fire; black smoke would have meant trouble.

"Looks like there's minimal structural damage aside from that third floor," he said. "Lots of smoke damage, though. They don't know what the official cause is. The inspector will come through next; I'll be able to call in the morning to see what he finds.

"Just a little more time and they wouldn't have been able to contain it as quickly. If they would've only gotten here a few minutes later, it would've been different." He seemed genuinely sorry that things hadn't turned out for the worse.

Together, we slowly walked away from the fire scene. I had no trouble matching pace with Roger this time. He almost plodded, shuffling his feet as if he had no intention of really going anywhere.

"These aren't even worth developing," he said, motioning at the camera. "Just took them for good measure."

The wind picked up again. It was harsh and crept stealthily up the sleeves of my T-shirt. I thrust my hands deeper into my pants pockets and wondered why I hadn't worn my jacket. My ears burned from the cold.

Roger looked at me then. "How about some coffee?" he inquired. The resigned look on his face indicated that he was in no hurry to return to the newsroom.

•   •   •

"Denny's, a reporter's best friend. Learn to love it," Roger advised as we passed through the front door. "Open twenty-four hours. Unlimited coffee – and good coffee, at that. Ample smoking section, too, which is hard to come by these days. Long gone's the time when you could have a cigarette right there in the office." Pausing, he produced a pack of Lucky Strikes and lit one up. "You don't smoke, do you?" he inquired of me.

I shook my head. "Nope."

"But you do drink coffee, right?"

I nodded, enlivened by the thought of hot coffee on a cold November day.

"Good," he said with a wry smile. "You're halfway there."

We took a booth next to the window. Roger left on his overcoat. He smoked and stared at the outside world, but also continued to talk to me. "So, you want to be a reporter?" His words took me by surprise. There was no tone to his voice; it was more of a flat assertion than a question.

"Yeah, I guess," I replied, not knowing what else to say.

I expected him to next ask me why, but he didn't. Instead he mused, "People like to see their names in print. That's where this paper gets its business. The *Reliance Record*. We devote more space to the Cub Scouts than we do to public affairs."

The coffee came then. I wrapped my hands luxuriously around the steaming mug.

"Just one question," Roger said, ripping open a packet of sugar and sloppily stirring it into his coffee. I looked at him and waited.

"*Why* do you want to be a reporter?"

There it was. I weighed the inquiry, wondering what kind of response he was expecting, not wanting to disappoint yet not wanting to lie. "I like to write," I said finally. "I really enjoy writing."

"You call this writing? Really, how hard do you have to think for the stuff they have you do? Tidying up press releases, covering a football game once in a while, attending the occasional city council meeting?" He paused, stabbed out his dying cigarette, and promptly lit another. "You probably work ten times harder on the essays you have to write for school. I'll bet those make you think a lot more than anything you get paid to write for us. This job is a lot closer to stenography than it is to creativity."

"Honestly?" I said in reply. "You're right. I guess I don't have to work very hard at this stuff. But I like to write, all kinds of writing—"

"And I know you're young," he interrupted, "but to be frank with you, it doesn't get that much harder. The writing's all the same. Sure, you get more big stories thrown your way, but in a town like this, how big are they, really? They're only as big as the paper lets them be. You figure if you screw up there can't be that much that can happen to you. Besides, journalism like this is all the same – same strategy, same formula, same old shit. You get pretty good at it, actually. I'm an expert at the ten-inch house-fire story. I've got a sheaf of 'em with my byline on top; essentially say the same thing, all of 'em. I can write the things in my sleep. Same goes with the council-considers-new-ordinance story, the residents-oppose-development story, the landmark-restaurant-closing story, the high-speed-car-crash story, the local-boy-does-good story. All little moments of life, little pieces of humanity, but reduced to formulaic pieces of clichéd bullshit."

He sighed, and it seemed as though the sigh were half meant for me, with the other half reserved for himself. He folded his hands and stared down at the tabletop. His clasped fingers appeared permanently inkstained, and the nails were rough-hewn and dirty.

"But when you think about it, being an expert in something like that doesn't mean anything," he went on, "because there's only a certain amount you can do, a certain amount of space you've got to work with. Creativity hardly figures into the equation. Occasionally with a feature story you can really cut loose, but good feature story opportunities at this paper are few and far between. 'Moose Lodge Installs New Officers,' 'Pumpkin Queen Finalists Announced,' things like that – that's more our speed."

"But I like to write," I pressed again. "And anyway, I don't want to work at a paper like this forever. I want to work big-city dailies, then eventually go freelance, write magazine articles and short stories. Things like that. I'd even like to write novels."

"I was like you once. I wanted to do things. Lots of them. But somehow I ended up here." He drained his coffee cup and motioned to the waiter for a refill. Then he fished within the folds of his overcoat for another cigarette. "It's strange. With this job, you don't really have an impact on the world, yet in the world of the well-connected people of this city, their little encapsulated bubble, your job means everything. You legitimize their position in the universe."

"But isn't that the purpose of a local paper?" I asked innocently, not wanting to offend him yet interested in what he had to say. "I mean, people can read *The New York Times* for that other stuff, but ..."

"But the *Times* won't cover their school board meetings for them. I know, I know. You're right. But still, I find it a little depressing. Don't you?" he looked at me from above the tilted rim of his coffee mug. I had no idea what to say. I'd never really considered the thought before; I'd just been thankful to have landed a part-time job that matched my career interests. As far as I was concerned, it beat flipping burgers any day.

"Reliance is dying," he continued. "There isn't that much positive news anymore. All of it's negative – drugs, crime, gangs, unemployment. Which would make good articles, but we don't do that kind of stuff. There's no more factories. The steel mills all packed up and left. There's rumors about an auto plant coming some time in the future, but those rumors are as old as the ones about the proposed highway exit that's supposedly going to bring businesses to town."

He rubbed his eyes, stretching out the puffy bags beneath them before going on. "Wal-Mart opened up outside of town; and sure, it created some jobs, but businesses down here are closing left and right. It's only a matter of time before there's no downtown at all. But hell, maybe that's for the better. You've seen what it's like down here." He drew deeply on his Lucky Strike and exhaled slowly through his nostrils. "Do you realize that this city has fewer people than it did in 1923?"

I shook my head.

"Meanwhile, look how much the country as a whole has grown." He grunted and bowed his head slightly.

"When you work as a reporter in a town like this, you learn a lot. A lot about the petty corruption and stupidity and in-fighting that goes on behind the scenes. And there *is* that kind of stuff going on here. The politicians and business leaders in this city don't amount to anything on the scale of real-life importance; they're nothing but chicken scratchings. But in their own minds, in

their own little world, they're everything. The city at large is going to hell and
they're locked in their own behind-the-scenes power struggles. Just like Nero
and Rome. Not saying they could refurbish the whole city, but goddamn, they
could at least quit their squabbling once in awhile, long enough to open their
eyes and take a good look around them.

"But you'll never read that in the *Record*. It's not our style to be critical
like that. That's what really gets me – there's some constructive things that this
newspaper could be doing to correct the situation. And if not correct it, at least
draw some attention to the problems. Sure, there's no evidence right out in the
open that the mayor's taking bribes, or that half of city council answers to a few
business interests ahead of the general interests of the community, but
everybody knows about it. All it would take is some research and a little
investigation. A few well-placed questions, for chrissake. But we don't operate
that way.

"You see these problems and you want to do something. *I* want to do
something. I know I may not come across as such, but I consider myself fairly
compassionate. I really like this city; I remember when it used to be something,
when downtown was the place to go. You could walk along Main Street and
window shop; you could stop in a diner for a cup of coffee and a slab of pie.
There used to be three or four – diners, that is – and the owners knew the
customers and the customers knew where they could always go for a friendly
word and a piece of gossip.

"Anymore, there isn't anything. No more diners, only Denny's. And
the owner tells me he's about ready to shut down. And as for shops, well, you
know downtown – there's a few, but they're nothing worth bragging about. A
dilapidated barber shop, a couple beer joints, and a few dusty antique stores.
Nothing like it used to be. Downtown is dying. Reliance is kicking the bucket.
And nobody cares. Hardly anyone even reads the newspaper anymore. There's
gotta be things that can be done, but what's the use, you know? What's the use?
It seems like all the time I'm so tired.

"And it'll only get worse. The paper, I mean. The *Record's* family-owned, for now. But eventually one of the big media companies will get around to buying it. They'll give it a facelift, make it look more slick and professional. But it will be just as vapid and ridiculous. Probably even more so, because right now it may be amateurish, but it's still a community newspaper. Once it's corporate, we'll have to go to all kinds of bullshit meetings where executive types will talk about efficiency and the bottom line and advertising revenue and shrinking news holes. They'll parade statistics before us and unveil new three-word slogans they paid some West Coast branding company hundreds of thousands of dollars to come up with. And we'll be 'producing content' for our 'consumers' and 'delivering profitability' to the 'shareholders.' For now, it may be a piece of shit, but it's *our* piece of shit."

He finished his second cup of coffee and set it down on the saucer. It made a resigned clink. He stared at the bottom of the empty mug, as though there he would find some answer to his own rhetorical question.

"So goddamned tired," he repeated. He shook his head, threw some money on the table, and promptly stood up. "Might snow this weekend if it keeps this up. You covering the playoffs?"

I nodded. I could tell that the question had been posed out of politeness, that his mind was elsewhere and he really didn't expect an answer. he didn't seem to notice my response, and we walked back to the office in silence.

My belly was warm from the coffee, but the wind – increasing in ferocity and smelling more like winter – gnashed into my hands and face with its cold teeth. Evening darkness was slowly setting in as we made our way back through the newsroom door.

•   •   •

Before that day, I never knew Roger kept a bottle of Scotch in his bottom desk drawer. But when we got back to the newsroom, I watched from my own desk as he fished it out and took a good-sized swig. He made no effort to conceal the action, and from across the room the social page editor harrumphed with disapproval before returning to her wedding announcements. Roger seemed unconcerned.

They tell me that when he died of a heart attack about a year later, the bottle was still there – although by then, I suppose, it was a different bottle. White Horse, Fine Old Scotch Whisky. It rested sandwiched between a stack of blank reporter's notebooks and a sheaf of faded news clippings from the previous thirty years.

And me? I finished high school and worked full-time for the paper the following summer. After college I traveled around for a while, saw the country, worked my share of different reporting jobs. I had a few short stories published here and there. Even did some freelance magazine writing on the side. But somehow I found my way back to Reliance, to the now corporate-owned *Record*, and to a desk in the back corner of the newsroom. Denny's closed; it still has yet to be replaced by anything. Crack's still kicking, but these days it's been joined on the street by meth. Heroin, even – *heroin* in *Reliance*. I took up smoking, tried to quit twice and failed, then gave up trying altogether. Even though I mainly cover the police beat now (with the occasional city council meeting), I've still got some literary aspirations. There's this book I've had in mind for a long time that I'd like to write. I can't seem to get it started, though. I find this depressing on occasion, but I try not to worry. I'm young still, and there's lots of things I'd like to get done.

Sometimes, though, I can't stop myself from thinking, *But what's the use?* You know?

courting the african queen

I will forever associate being an exchange student in Argentina with a bar full of beer, body odor, and bravado. And with the misunderstood and much-maligned jungles of Africa.

The entrance to the seedy little bar was awkwardly low and narrow, wedged between the butcher's and the bicycle shop. At first I almost missed the door, it had been so long since I'd been there. Like all Argentine drinking establishments of similar caliber, it bore no sign to identify it from the outside. And the street was thick with shadows; I would have walked right past had it not been for the sweat-smell and muted light spilling out through the bar's open door and for the low sounds of conversation emanating from within.

A total of three men occupied the nameless tavern: two patrons and the bartender. All three greeted me in Spanish as I entered.

"*Che*, where you been? *Tanto tiempo que no nos vemos*. Long time, no see." The first voice originated at the end of the dilapidated countertop, from the thin unshaven man dressed in faded grey corduroys and a button-up short-sleeved shirt.

"*¿Como te va, Alfredo?* How's it going?" I acknowledged him with a nod.

I took a seat at the other end of the bar, on the corner next to Juan, the plump round-faced lawyer who was outfitted in his usual slightly worn three-piece suit. As soon as I was seated he turned to me, grinned a toothy hello, and posed the same question.

"*Tanto tiempo*. Long time. Where you been?"

The *cantinero* approached from the other end of the bar and addressed me with a friendly nod. "You still an exchange student?" he inquired, lazily wiping out a glass.

"*Sí.*"

"Rotary, isn't it?"

I nodded, to which he made a slight cluck of disapproval. "*Lleno de ricos*. Full of rich guys. *Mucha plata*." He rubbed his thumb and forefinger together momentarily in a symbol of material wealth, then resumed wiping glasses.

I had to smile at the lighthearted heckling that characterized my trips to the bar and, moreover, my experiences with the country in general.

"I was in Rotary once." It was Juan who said this.

"Back when you were respectable?" inquired Ernesto, the bartender.

"Yeah, way back then. Seems like only yesterday."

"*¿Y ... qué pasó?* What happened?"

"I never went to the meetings. And when I did, they said I drank too much wine."

"*Carajos. Pelotudos ricos rotarios*. Assholes. Rich Rotarian bastards." Ernesto spat in mock disgust, humoring Juan and simultaneously winking in my direction.

"*No me importa*. Doesn't bother me any," Juan said dismissively. "Being respectable can only get you so far in life."

I ordered a Quilmes. Ernesto retrieved the beer from the cooler, flicked off the bottle cap and poured a glass full with smooth, practiced nonchalance. He had a bushy black mustache and wore a wine-splotched off-white apron. It seemed to me as though the wine stains were in the exact same places they'd been when I'd last dropped by over a month before.

"So where you been?" He returned to the original question as he plunked the liter bottle on the counter next to my full glass.

"I did a lot of traveling in December. Went to Cordoba. Rosario, too. Spent three days in Uruguay. Plus, I went to see my *novia* a lot." I faltered a little upon mentioning this. I hadn't been going to bring it up. Just leave it unsaid and sit and drink my beer and think about her and get slowly drunk and listen to the three of them babble on about nothing as though they knew what they were talking about, perhaps occasionally adding a word or two myself. That way I might be able to distance myself from the reality of it all. But it slipped out, quite possibly in subconscious self-defense, because to such Argentine men time spent with a woman is the only justifiable excuse for time *not* spent with them and in the company of other robust men like themselves.

"So why aren't you in school now?" said Alfredo from against the wall, a few decibels too loudly. He was slightly drunk.

"*¡Boludo!* Blockhead, it's almost midnight," I answered, a bit relieved. Maybe they wouldn't pick up on my comment after all. "Besides, it's January. School's out for the summer."

He looked a little sheepish, but quickly recovered and retorted, "Well you might as well be in school now. After all, you never went when you were supposed to. You were always here with us."

I shrugged. "Why should I have gone? I already graduated back home. Anyway, the kids are all *boludos*. All they do is screw around. They don't want to learn."

"And you *do* want to learn?" Alfredo raised a skeptical eyebrow. But the question was in jest.

"I want to learn Spanish, and I can do that just as well while traveling or with you guys as I can sitting in school. The teachers never come, anyway, so we just end up playing soccer or trying to get things stuck in the ceiling fan."

"You make me so proud. The Yankee exchange student likes to spend time with me." Alfredo grinned sloppily and returned to his drink.

"You've got a girlfriend?" It was Juan, ignoring Alfredo's rantings and returning to what I'd said before.

So it hadn't slipped by. I figured it wouldn't. What the hell. Might as well talk about it. If it started to get too bad I could always get them going in another direction. That was always easily done in a conversation with many Argentines, not to mention Argentines who happened to be drinking.

"Had." I nodded and took a long drink of beer.

"Had?"

"Yeah. She went home earlier today. I just got back from the airport."

"She wasn't from Argentina?"

I shook my head, drained my glass, and filled it to the top again.

"Where was she from?"

"South Africa."

"*¿Sudáfrica?* Your girlfriend was a *negrita*? A little black girl?" Juan seemed almost shocked.

"No, she wasn't black."

"But she was African?"

"Yes. *South* African."

"So why wasn't she black?" cried Alfredo in exasperated disbelief.

"Not all South Africans are black, *pelotudo*."

"They should be. They live in Africa, after all."

"He's been courting the African queen. *La reina africana.* What was the name of your tribal princess?" Juan had discovered a golden teasing opportunity.

I faltered momentarily, but ended up revealing it anyway. "Theresa."

He tried the name out a few times, rolling it over his tongue. "Theresa, Theresa. *La negrita Theresa, reina de la selva africana.* Little black Theresa, queen of the African jungle."

He said it again, considered the sound of it, and then chanted it a third time. "Little black Theresa, queen of the African jungle." The 'r' in her name came out short and clipped, making the word completely different than the slurred English pronunciation: "Tay-RAY-suh" instead of "Tuh-REE-suh."

"Little black Theresa, queen of the African ..." Alfredo joined in.

"She wasn't ..."

"I know. You said."

"And it wouldn't have mattered to me if she were. And she didn't live in the jungle. She lived in *Johannesburgo*." I liked the way the city's name reverberated in Spanish. It sounded full, strong, important, much more so than in English. I reflected on this a moment then ordered another beer.

"You're not allowed to drink, are you?" Ernesto posed this question as he turned toward the icebox.

"No. At least that's what Rotary says. It never stopped any of us before."

He chuckled, paused teasingly at the edge of the cooler. "Rotary doesn't care, do they?"

"No. They don't give a *carajo* about anything. Give me another Quilmes."

"You drank that first one fast." The comment carried no hint of condemnation, though; it was just a simple observation.

"Because he's a *verdadero argentino* now. A real Argentine. He's one of us! He knows how to drink!" expounded Alfredo from against the wall, shaking his glass of whiskey and sending half of it to the floor in the process.

"I won't drink this one so fast. *La quiero recordar*. I want to remember her."

Ernesto was reaching into the icebox for my second bottle when Juan interrupted him.

"Quilmes? Why drink beer? You need to forget her in style, with a *buen vino argentino*. Ernesto, put back that beer and bring my friend the Yankee exchange student a bottle of your finest red wine."

"No, I want to get drunk slowly. I want to remember. Wine will get me drunk twice as fast as beer." I wanted a slow, lingering drunkenness that I could prolong well into the morning, thinking and remembering and emptying myself of it all. I wanted to walk slowly, heavily home and fall into bed and be enveloped by a deep forgetful sleep devoid of thoughts or feelings or consciousness. And when I woke up maybe the memories would be gone with the elusive dreams of my weighty slumber.

"But wine has more class. It's cheaper than beer, too. I'm surprised you're going to drop that much on *cerveza*. You always were a bit of a *pijotero*, a little tight with your money," Juan said.

"*Andáte al carajo,*" I shot back at him. "Go to hell. A lot of room you have to talk. What's that you're drinking, anyway?" I pointed at the bottle which sat in front of him on the bar. "Santa Ana? You call that a good wine? That's shit – almost as bad as the *mierda* that comes out of a box that they sell in *el supermercado* for fifty cents a liter."

He shrugged his shoulders. "I'm just drinking," he defended himself. "I'm not drinking to the memory of my lost African girlfriend."

"Why doesn't Rotary want you to drink? If you're going to learn about Argentina, you've got to drink a little *cerveza* now and then," Ernesto mused as he filled my glass with Quilmes. He smiled. "A little *cerveza*, a little *vino*, a little *champaña* – it all adds up to a lot of culture."

"He should know a hell of a lot by now!" shouted Alfredo. "He's drunk himself full of culture!" The glasses jumped on the counter as he assertively pounded the wood with his clenched fist.

I shrugged and addressed Ernesto's question. "Because they're all *hinchapelotas*. A bunch of anal-retentive stiffs. I don't know. It's just a rule. But nobody follows the rules and Rotary knows it and they really don't care. They don't let us have girlfriends, either."

"Much less black girlfriends …" Juan laughed into his glass of cheap red wine.

I let the comment slide this time, keeping in mind the absolute fascination that many Argentines I'd met had with black people, as well as their pride in being what they considered a progressive, diverse, enlightened society – even though the few blacks I had ever seen there were Brazilians or American tourists, and these only in the capital. Usually, in the country diversity often seemed like nothing but a deluded state of mind.

"Have you ever been with an Argentine girl?" Juan inquired curiously.

"Not yet …"

"*¡Boludo!* What are you thinking, not getting any Argentine women? You're surrounded by some of the most beautiful women in the world, and you chose some *huacha*, some little tramp from out in the middle of the jungle. The least you could've done was to have a girlfriend here in Mercedes while you had your *africana* there in …"

"Liniers."

"… in Liniers."

"But you speak Spanish well." Ernesto's observation seemed to come from out of nowhere.

"What's that have to do with anything?" I asked.

"You've only been here what, five months? By how you talk, I would've thought that you'd had at least one Argentine girlfriend."

"I'd probably speak a lot better if I would have had an Argentine girlfriend."

"Serves you right for choosing a South African *novia*. Now you can find yourself an Argentine girl. Best way to learn Spanish. With the tongue and all." Juan laughed as he poked his wine-sodden tongue in my direction.

"I don't know if I want a girlfriend at this point. Maybe just a *transa*. Someone who doesn't want any kind of commitment."

"You can find one of those, too. *Muy fácil*. Lots of *chicas rápidas* here. Easy girls are all over the place," Alfredo offered helpfully.

"Yeah, you want to meet Alfredo's sister?" Juan said, chuckling at his own joke.

"*¡Andáte al carajo, pelotudo hijo de puta!* Go to hell, you goddamn son of a bitch!" Alfredo retorted savagely.

"*La concha de tu puta hermana.* Your whore-sister's crotch," Juan shot back.

"How much time do you have left?" asked Ernesto, ignoring the tangent into which the other two were plunging.

"Until July. Six months."

"*¡Un montón!* An eternity! Plenty of time for *chicas*," Ernesto said. "But why'd your girlfriend leave already?"

"She'd already been here a whole year. She came last January. Their school year is different than ours."

"She'd probably been with studly Argentine men, plenty of *fuertes hombres argentinos*." Abandoning his insult-trading session with Alfredo, Juan hoisted his drinking hand and forcefully shook it in the air, sending droplets of cheap Santa Ana red wine cascading onto the bar surface.

"I don't know. I didn't ask."

"How was her Spanish?" Juan asked.

"She spoke well."

"There you go! She must've had an Argentine boyfriend. Probably had one on the side while she was with you. She was smart. Did what you should've done."

Ernesto placed a couple dishes of salted peanuts on the bar. "You never said anything about a girlfriend before."

"You guys never asked me."

"How long had you been going out?"

"Since October. I met her when we all went on the Rotary trip to Bariloche." The beer had made me more talkative, I noted. I was revealing information of my own accord now.

Juan grinned knowingly. "Bariloche. Uh huh …we all know what the kids here go to Bariloche to find. *Amor libre, encuentros anónimos.* Free love, anonymous encounters. Lots of coo-chee coo-chee down in the mountains of the South."

"I wouldn't exactly call it anonymous. We were all traveling together, after all. It's not like I met her in some disco on a Saturday night and never saw her again."

"No, even better. You got to bring her home with you." He paused and thought for a moment. "At least Rotary's good for something. Helped you find a nice little *africana* to play with for a few months. I really couldn't say what else they do for the exchange students. Nothing, in my realm of experience. Back when I was in Rotary I saw the little *intercambios* like you only twice a year. They put them on display once at a meeting when they first got here, and once again right before they left. Sometimes they'd learned a little Spanish, sometimes they went home as *ignorantes* as when they came. Can't say I ever sat in a bar and drank with any, though."

"Exchange student," mused Ernesto with a slight chuckle. "What are your friends doing now? Back home, I mean."

"They're all in college. Most of them, anyway."

"Studying, I imagine."

"Probably. Once in a while, anyway. At least, I'd hope so."

Exchange student. I, too, had to chuckle at the irony of what he'd said. The whole nature of being an *estudiante de intercambio* implied studying, yet none of us ever studied. Here I was in Argentina, former high-school honor student (Centuries ago, it seemed!), current Rotary exchange student, getting drunk to the memory of a South African girlfriend gone forever. And just look at who was sharing the experience with me. The whole situation had a strange sort of inexplicable irony which I found very amusing. The alcohol was taking effect. I drained my glass and ordered another liter of beer.

Dropping some peanuts into the next glass, I watched them float around on top for a moment, and crunched a few down with the next mouthful of beer. "*Riquísimo.* Delicious," I said out loud. After two liters of beer the act seemed to hold some entertainment value.

"You learned that here. Nobody else in the world does that," indicated Alfredo excitedly. His patriotism was roused.

I agreed with him, although I was sure there were other people in the world who also put peanuts in their beer. Lots of people in America probably did it, for all I knew.

"Two best things about Argentina. The women, and peanuts in the beer." Alfredo took an enormous gulp of whiskey.

"French women are more beautiful," Juan offered casually. "French women are divine. Argentine women are all *putas feas* next to the French. Beside those *mademoiselles*, ours are nothing but ugly whores."

"But Argentine women can cook," smiled Ernesto.

"So can French women. But French women look gorgeous while they do it."

"*Bueno*, I'll give you that. But you still have to admit that *mujeres argentinas* can cook like few others."

"*Some* of them can cook. Not my wife, though. She makes absolute *mierda* out of everything she touches. Complete and total shit. She tries to cook but I always end up having to go down to the *rotisería* anyway. Doesn't bother me, though. I'd rather eat a big hunk of grilled *asado* over the *mierda* she tries to cook any day. Absolute *mierda*. *Mierda absoluta de la puta madre*."

I tried to imagine the absolute shit of the mother whore that Juan's wife tried to feed him for dinner, but as abruptly as he finished his statement he veered off on another tangent. "Why didn't you ever bring your girlfriend here? I've never kissed a black girl before."

"She wasn't black ..."

"I know. Only *jodiendo. Un chiste.* Just screwing with you. It was a joke." He opened his arms in a feigned request for forgiveness.

"Why *didn't* she ever come here?" inquired Ernesto. "You're a jerk — you never introduced us to your *novia*."

"To this place? Why would she have wanted to come here?"

"*Tenés razón.* You're right," admitted Juan. "The only reason I come here is because no other bar will serve me."

"And you got kicked out of Rotary ..." I teased.

"Did she ever come to Mercedes?" Ernesto veered back in the direction of my *novia.*

"No. What's there to see in this city? It's the asshole of the world. Out in the middle of the *pampas*," Juan said.

"It's not that bad," countered Ernesto, with little conviction.

"The hell it isn't!" said Juan. "You're just uncultured. This place reeks of *basura*. It smells so much like garbage that it draws flies. Big black buzzing flies."

"*¡Callate!* Shut up. You're just pissed off because they kicked you out of Rotary." Alfredo's pride in his city had stirred him out of the silent, semi-drunken stupor in which he'd been mired for the last few minutes.

"*Andáte al carajo.* Go to hell," Juan shot back.

"Have you ever met a black person?" I ignored the other two's squabbling and addressed the question, posed out of sheer curiosity, to Ernesto.

"Come to think of it, no. Only Bolivians."

"Same thing!" came another shout from Alfredo at the far end of the bar.

"I have," said Juan. "I almost married one."

"Really?"

"*Sí.* Theresa, she was called. Lived in Liniers. Had *tetas* like this." He indicated with his hands and smiled slyly at me.

"*Pendejo.* You asshole."

"Why'd you want to come to Argentina, anyway? It's a terrible country. The economy sucks, the politicians suck. They rob you blind. I'd rather be in the United States than Argentina." Ernesto had his back turned when he said this.

"It's better than Bolivia!" Alfredo almost fell off his barstool as he hollered to make known his opinion regarding his nation's international standing. He momentarily collected himself, then inquired of me, "Where are you from again? Wyoming?"

"Ohio."

"I thought so. That's close to Orlando, isn't it?"

"Relatively speaking."

"But not close to South Africa?"

"Not really."

Alfredo watched me pour into my glass. A few of the peanuts that had so delighted him still bobbed around in the beer.

"Foam," he observed with almost scientific interest. "Do you like your beer with foam?"

"A little."

"Me, too. I always did like a little *espuma*. Most of the kids here don't, though. Know why? Because they like to drink a lot of it, and they like to drink it fast. They don't enjoy their beverages. They're all a bunch of drunks. A whole lot of *borrachos. Borracho borracho borracho.*" He giggled a little and took a long draw at his whiskey. He was leaning against the wall, his slim, aging frame slumping backwards in an ever more pronounced manner; at times when his muscles faltered only the wall prevented him from completely collapsing.

"Tell us about your *novia*," said Ernesto. "What was she like?"

"What's there to say?"

"*¿Qué sé yo?* How do I know? What do you remember about her? Or are you too drunk to remember anything?"

"The way she laughed. The way the corners of her mouth would wrinkle and her eyes would squint until they almost closed. When she laughed she would raise her head a bit toward the sky. I remember riding the trains with her. She loved to look at all the little kids, talk to them, give them candy, tell their mothers how nice and cute they were. I remember going with her to Luján, too, to see the basilica. We sat in the back row of pews together and she held my hand. She asked me if I ever prayed. I was honest with her and said no, and told her that I hoped that it didn't bother her. She said it didn't, and I could tell she was telling the truth. When we left the church and walked out into the sunshine of the plaza she said she'd prayed for me."

"That was really nice. You said that well, even in Spanish. I feel almost like I could've fallen in love with her." Ernesto did seem somewhat moved.

I had even been touched a bit by my own sentimentality. The beer more than likely helped, too.

"*Did* you love her?"

"Probably. Or I soon would have."

"What else? What more do you remember?"

"She liked tequila."

"Did she?" Ernesto seemed impressed. As a bartender, he probably didn't encounter too many women who drank tequila. Of course, not many women probably set foot in his dingy, testosterone-dominated bar, either. Unless they were on the job, so to speak.

"Yeah. Never got drunk on it, though. She didn't drink much. When we'd go out she'd have a Pronto because she liked the taste."

"Which color Pronto?" It was Juan's first comment in a while.

"The yellow kind."

"Horse piss! The blue's a lot better."

Ernesto came to my defense. "How would you know? Only girls drink Pronto, *pendejo*. What are you, some kind of *trolo*? Some fruit who drinks wine coolers? Let him go on with the story."

"She'd have her bottle of yellow Pronto, then later on she'd have a tequila. She especially liked the part with the lemon and salt. She really didn't drink much, though. I never did before, either."

"Yeah, you were a *traga*. You told me once. A big nerd. Always studying." Juan shook his head in joking disapproval.

"Let's have a tequila for Theresa, *negrita reina de la selva africana*," proposed Ernesto, fishing among the bottles stored behind the bar.

"She wasn't black. And she didn't live in the jungle, either."

"I know. Only *jodiendo*. Here, drink!"

He had set three shot glasses of cheap tequila on the countertop, along with a shaker of salt and a quartered lemon. In his hand he held a glass of his own. I drank and was suddenly awash in memories of packed dance clubs with buzzing tequila bars, of her deftly weaving her way through the surging crowd, sweet-talking the bartender into giving out two shots for the price of one, handing one to me, and both of us downing them simultaneously. Then we'd join the swarming crowd on the dance floor or find seats in the lounge upstairs and sit and talk while below us the electronic music pulsed and throbbed. The memory of it seemed especially poignant to me as I sat there on the barstool. I hoped I wouldn't cry under the combined weights of reminiscence and alcohol.

"I can't believe you used to be a *traga*," Juan interjected incredulously into my wandering thoughts. "You, a nerd. I bet you didn't do anything but study. Study study study. *Siempre estudiando.* Always studying. No time for cute little *negritas* back there in the *Estados Unidos.*"

"We corrupted him," declared Alfredo. He pointed at me. "We corrupted you! We'll get you Yankees yet! One exchange student at a time!"

"Then we'll get the Falklands back!" expounded Juan, triumphantly hoisting his wine bottle in the air.

"Who gives a *carajo* about the Falklands when we can have all of America?" Alfredo proclaimed.

"And the women, too!" Juan returned.

"We'll conquer you with Quilmes!" shouted Alfredo, half-jumping out of his seat. This time as he slumped back onto the stool, he missed the attempt to lean his back against the wall. He collapsed with a crash to the floor.

"Do you have Quilmes in Yankee-land?" inquired Juan, ignoring his fallen friend, who was slowly and shakily struggling to regain his feet.

"No. We've got Mexican beer, though."

"Swill. Mexican beer is dirty piss-water. Quilmes is gold."

"I don't know," I teased. "I hear Bolivian beer's even better than Quilmes."

"Nothing in Bolivia is better than what we have in Argentina," Juan spat.

"Not even the women?"

"The women? The women? They don't have women in Bolivia. Just a bunch of Indian swine. *Chanchas, son las mujeres.* Just a herd of pigs."

"What are they like in South Africa? Not just the women but in general, I mean." Ernesto seemed genuinely curious as he placed another liter of beer in front of me.

I cringed a little, but not as much as I would have had I been completely sober. This was the kind of question I'd become accustomed to receiving in my five months in the country, but a kind of question I'd never gotten used to answering. *What do you think of Argentina? What's a better country to live in, here or there? Why doesn't Michael Jordan run for president? What's the difference between Americans and Argentines? Everybody carries pistols in the States, right? It's violent there, isn't it? You eat Big Macs for breakfast, don't you?* And now, *What are South Africans like?* What was I to say? They were often only interested in generalizations that conformed to their version of reality, but I always wanted to be objective, to carefully answer the question in a way that approached the topic from every possible angle. Too often, though, the person who had asked had a short attention span and was only willing to listen to answers that reconfirmed his or her preconceived notions. I supposed, though, that many Americans would treat foreign visitors likewise.

Juan saved me the effort of searching for an appropriate response. "*Boludo,* they're just like us. South Africa's really similar to Argentina."

I had to smile. For some reason, I'd noticed, more than a few Argentines felt a strange kinship with South Africa, regardless of whether or not they actually knew anything about it. More than once I had been with her when someone asked us where we were from. The United States got mixed reactions, but upon hearing her response our inquisitor would invariably smile broadly and exclaim, "*¡Sudáfrica! ¡Que lindo!* South Africa! How nice!"

Juan continued his cultural discourse. "The country looks the same, the people look the same. At least, the ones that aren't black look like us. The ones that are black look like Bolivians. They do a lot of the same things there. They play rugby and soccer, they drink *mate* and play *truco* and eat lots of *asados*. They probably have even more barbecues than we do. The only things they have that we don't are lions. Lions and giraffes. *Johannesburgo* is just like Buenos Aires, too. There's probably even an *Obelisco* there."

I almost choked stifling my laughter. I couldn't tell if he was being serious or not. I let it go as standard drunk-talk.

"God, I hope not," Ernesto remarked about the Obelisk comment. "That *verga grande*! That dick of a monument is such a disgrace. Looks just like a big *pija*, a giant concrete cock sticking up in the middle of Avenida Nueve de Julio. They don't really have an Obelisk in South Africa, do they?" He turned to me for a second opinion.

"Not that I know of."

Juan was slightly offended. "Hell, who are you to say? You're just a Yankee exchange student who hangs out with a bunch of drunks instead of going to high school. You wouldn't know anything about South Africa, anyway, because they're more like us than they are like you."

"Even though they speak English ..."

"Even though they speak English."

"Even though I had a South African girlfriend ..."

"Even though you *thought* you had a South African girlfriend. We all know who *la negrita* really had eyes for." Juan raised his eyebrows seductively.

"*Do* they speak English?" Ernesto seemed puzzled. "I thought they spoke Portuguese."

"Some of them speak Arabic," offered Alfredo with slurred sagacity, trying to demonstrate that he hadn't spent his entire life on a barstool.

"That's why she should've been with one of us instead of you. There's a magical bond between our two countries." Juan nodded smugly as he said this.

I shook my head in pretend disbelief. "You're drunk."

"No, you're drunk."

"*I'm* not drunk," offered Alfredo to no one in particular, and belched loudly.

As my counterattacks tapered off, they grew bored with the subject of my legendary black girlfriend and delved off on a new line of boastful bravado. Their rantings meandered to the inevitable talk of soccer, politics, and a slew of national and global problems they felt qualified to solve at that particular moment. Excluding myself from their conversation, I became engaged in my own one-sided internal rambling.

Maybe I shouldn't have decided to get drunk, I thought. Perhaps I might remember her better sober. But do you want to remember her or forget her? I asked myself. I'll never forget her. So I might as well remember her all I can now and get it over with.

I recalled the train rides into Buenos Aires on my way to see her and the train rides home when the day was done. The trip took exactly one hour and fifty minutes in either direction between Mercedes and Liniers if everything ran smoothly, plus the five minutes or so in Moreno that gave me time to change trains and grab a couple of *empanadas* and a copy of *La Nación* at one of the little kiosks lining the platform. Yet the trip there and the trip back had two very distinct feelings to them. The approaching city grew and expanded in a jungle of life and activity, surrounding me as I neared her stop. And on the way home, leaving her and Buenos Aires behind, the capital and its suburbs slowly decayed into the lazily unconnected breeze-blown small cities and towns of the *pampas*.

I remembered riding the trains with her further into the city; talking with her on park benches while the pigeons noisily chattered along with us; sitting in cafés over midafternoon coffee and croissants; the Friday or Saturday night tequila ritual; aimlessly enjoyable outings in Buenos Aires and the surrounding areas; the *Madres de los desaparecidos* marching on Thursday afternoons in the Plaza de Mayo, calling for answers as to what had befallen their children, vanished during the Dirty War; the little tourist train that made its way north along the coast of the Río de la Plata, where if you looked out the window you'd see sailboats and behind them skyscrapers far off in the downtown distance; subway stations glowing with neon, abuzz with commotion and electricity; shopping along Calle Florida; the occasional movie on Lavalle; cold delicious ice cream cones beneath the enormous, gnarled old shade trees in Plaza San Martín.

The details of distinct, individual memories intermingled with the mental patterns of familiar places and haunts: monuments, parks, plazas, restaurants, and buildings we'd frequented together. All of our conversations were an indistinct blur in my mind; I could only remember the underlying patterns of what we'd always talked about. We would discuss our experiences as exchange students, comparing our new schools and host families, new friends and new homes, giving each other an outlet to vent frustrations that could not be expressed nearly as well to a Spanish speaker with no point of reference nor any reason for being sympathetic to our situations.

We always talked about our "other" homes, too, the mythical places across the sea that each of us held in the back of our mind beneath the immediate presence of the second home that was all around us. We tried as best we could to convey to each other the world we had left behind for a year, contrasting it in terms of our new environment. The idea of a snow-covered Christmas had enchanted her, as had the stories of deer season in late leafless November, of maple syrup in early spring, and fireworks on the Fourth of July. I became enthralled by the thought of bustling and at times tantalizingly dangerous Johannesburg, where she lived, and the sunny Cape, where she would be studying. Sometimes I dreamt of Table Mountain, picturing it as it peered over the precipice of Africa at the deep phantom of the ocean below, a huge majestic rock jutting out to the edge of the continent with Cape Town sprawling beneath it.

As I sat there in the bar, a semi-hallucinatory sleepiness suddenly pounced upon me. My thoughts grew less coherent and more abundant, spinning out in a loosely related string of free associations. I simultaneously felt happy thinking about her and sad that she was gone and content sitting there with a

cold beer at my disposal and peanuts close at hand and tired I'd been in Buenos
Aires all weekend long riding trains and subways and chatting it up with her
host family pretending to be calm and it felt comforting there in the dark
familiar run-down bar and look at these Argentines oh how macho they are talk
talk talk responses attitudes so predictable less individuality in this country (or
maybe I don't notice the underlying patterns that exist in our culture because
I'm right in the middle of it all the time back home) I can predict their behavior
and what they say almost perfectly by now does that mean I'm turning into one
of them? what am I now American, Argentine, American-Argentine, Argentine-
American, or just some kid from the States here on a kind of beer-soaked
learning vacation? am I sad or happy or am I merely just here? she's not here
she's gone and I'll probably never see her again but that's surprisingly okay
with me and I'm really calm five months in this laid-back carefree country have
done me good a year ago if this were happening I wouldn't be nearly so calm
about it (of course a year ago I'd never be seen with a beer in my hand, either)
but what the hell she was ready to get back and get on with things being an
exchange student is essentially a charade anyway you have to get on with your
life sometime or another the charade never bothered me though because I knew I
was at least learning Spanish and besides I shared the charade with her but now
she's gone and I'm alone in the charade sure there are others but not her but oh
well and really when I think about it I'm not really upset I don't feel like
punching any walls or setting out to overthrow—

"Are you okay? *¿Todo bien?*" Ernesto's polite inquiry interrupted my
wandering thoughts.

"Yeah. Fine. *Todo bien.*"

"You seem pretty *tranquilo* for just having seen your girlfriend off on a
plane." He was right. Rambling thoughts aside, I was actually accepting it fairly
well, so far; that kind of bothered me. But what could I do? The day was
coming. And she was ready to go home.

"How many beers have I had?"

"Four liters. And one shot of tequila to the memory of your *novia.*"

I ordered another Quilmes.

"So what are you going to do now that she's gone?" The other two, squabbling between each other about the extent of Madonna's sex appeal, were not paying attention to Ernesto's show of concern.

"Good question," I said. And left it at that.

Ernesto uncapped the liter bottle and poured some into my glass. A few surviving peanuts jostled and swirled in the foamy amber surf. Then the bartender returned to Juan and Alfredo, whose conversation had suddenly jackknifed its way to the inevitable topic of Diego Maradona, cocaine addict and Argentine original, undoubtedly – in the nation's collective opinion, at least – the best *fútbol* player to ever strut the face of the earth and the idol of every Argentine child to ever knock around a soccer ball.

I drifted more deeply into my own thoughts. Daydreams mingled with memories and the soothing comfort of slowly sipped beer with its slight taste of salt and peanut oil. I sipped some more and soon realized that I had stopped thinking about her and felt that was for the best, even if I hadn't been bitter before. Maybe I would wake up the next day and her memory would be erased completely. As though she'd never gotten on the airplane, as though she'd never even been there, as though I hadn't been in the bar getting drunk alternately thinking about her and trying not to think about her. Maybe I'd wake up without even the slightest trace of a hangover.

Distant and removed from the other three, I absorbed myself in the argumentative cadence of their voices. The discussion had assumed a life of its own, an extended series of free associations and loosely related topics that steamrolled forward without a moment of silence. The beer was undoubtedly taking effect now, and I became extremely content to sit there quietly as around me they continued to carry on.

I was drunk. Drunk, not thinking of her – not thinking of anything at all, really – and glad of it. The only thing that occupied my existence was Argentina. Argentina, land of the flat never-ending *pampas* and home of the *gaucho*. Birthplace of the tango, country of Maradona and *machismo* and red wine and red meat and Buenos Aires, the city that couldn't decide if it wanted to be European or Latin American or the southern hemisphere's version of New York. Buenos Aires, home of *el Obelicso*, the concrete cock looming above Avenida Nueve de Julio. Buenos Aires, capital city of Argentina, the country where the Spanish first set up camp, the British built the railroads, and the Italians came to live. Argentina, my temporary home, recently robbed of the presence of South African royalty, of *la negrita Theresa, reina de la selva africana*. I was in Argentina, sitting in a bar with two drunks and a bartender and a bunch of empty bottles. I was an exchange student who never went to school, and these were my friends.

The unintelligible sounds of their far-off conversation carried me through the night.

jagged fragments
of jaded lives

She would always feign wonder at the world.
"Look! Palm trees!" she said in Florida.
The way she'd said, "Look! Buildings!" in Toronto.
I hated that. I finally told her so, more or less:
"Tell those palm trees to go fuck themselves."

Drinking whiskey and making her mad.
Either way I won, you see. At least the way I saw it.

The bathroom stall reads like a pornographic oracle:
"Loose chicks suck dicks."
I wish I could think of something to add.
But all I can do is sit with my pants around my ankles. Taking a shit
and working on my pocket flask.

The maniacal state legislator sits with his legs crossed awkwardly.

"You've got one more minute."

He's only given me four minutes, so far.

"I gotta go."

He approaches the man at the door.

"Can you get me a car?"

He comes back to me. His eyes twinkle crazily.

"Oh, one more thing."

He tells me something inscrutable and meaningless.

"Interesting, huh?"

Pats me on the leg. Then leaves for good.

Moving stuff out of her apartment. Because it seemed like things had started out way too fast.

But how can you back off from something like that. Without backing off all the way, I mean.

"You've been drinking."

He would love me to deny it. So he could deliver a lecture.

"Yeah. Yeah, I have."

But I don't have enough of a conscience for denial.

"You want some? It's good shit."

I don't have much of a conscience at all.

Kevin's girl was doing shots and furiously smoking cigarettes inside the bar. She greeted me with a sloppy hug and bloodshot eyes. Kevin stayed where he was, fixed silently across from her in the booth.

"What's up with her?" I asked Fred when I got to his booth.

"She found out she's pregnant. Takin' it a hell of a lot better than he

is."

A fridge full of forties.

"Come on, man. They've got a fridge full of forties. Come on, man,
it'll be great. It'll all be good."

I doubted things could get any worse. But that was then.

Lament of the night cops reporter.

The intermittent murmurings of the scanner puncture his night. And
twice every shift, toward the beginning and toward the end, he calls the
departments to check up on things.

— *"one hundred people surrounding the house"* —

— *"bulging eyeballs"* —

— *"throwing rocks and sticks"* —

"Man, is it dead tonight."

— *"white male, no shirt, intoxicated"* —

— *"outside the office building"* —

"Haven't heard a peep for hours."

— *"chasing cleaning ladies"* —

"Nothing going on except the finals of 'American Idol.' And even
that's nothing to write home about."

— *"possible fatal"* —

"Nothing happening."

"Nothing going on."

— *"says she wants her slippers back"* —

"Not a thing."

— *"Keep your eyes on that parking lot"* —

— *"We've spotted the alligator!"* —

— *"red pickup truck"* —

"Nothing happening right now. But I'll tell you a story, Pete."

— *"It's a big one!"* —

— *"Hispanic female"* —

— *"wrapped around a telephone pole"* —

"It's so uneventful I'm about to take a nap."

— *"possibly armed"* —

"Nothing doing. Knock on wood."

— *"shots fired"* —

"Nothing going on except my broken heart. But you don't wanna hear about that. Do you?"

Driven to drink because it's too sunny outside.

At least, that was how he justified things to himself.

As if he needed an excuse.

She goes down on me as we lie on the dormitory floor.

"Do you have a condom?"

My head spins. The blackness of the room swirls around me.

"Yeah ... "

"Let's do it."

I grasp the sparse carpet. The swirling slows.

"But," she continues, "I've never done it before ... "

It's hard to say who's more drunk.

"Save it for someone who matters, then."

And with that I pass out.

The things you remember about Ohio.

Walking across a chilly autumn parking lot with the first gray smears of dawn overhead, trying to see through your hangover, and then eating greasy food at the Wal-Mart cafeteria and the eggs taste a little like the liquor from the night before.

"That last bit's just between you and me. Off the record."

"I understand."

Of course I understand. If only he knew why.

The most profoundly stupid thing I'd heard in a long time:

"I hate you because there's nothing about you to hate."

Or just the most profound.

At work. I listen to Erica and I despise her, that neurotic workaholic edge in her voice when she's on the phone. No life. The type of person who goes home at night and has nothing to do but anxiously await the start of the next work day. It's obvious it's all she's got in the world. I know I have no right to, I know it's none of my business, but I despise her all the same.

"What's she got to look forward to?" I ask Bill at the bar.

I answer my own question:

"Nothing."

Then we order more drinks.

"He wanted to get in my pants."

"Did you let him?"

"No way. He was cute, though."

Drunk, crazy guy to not-so-drunk, sane guy:

"What exactly is the matter with you, anyway?"

They were friends. But there was the possibility for more. There was definitely friction between them. They'd kiss every couple of weeks. Then she would stop and make excuses revolving around her need for post-boyfriend freedom. Together at the bar one night. He was gone, far gone. On whiskey and beer and Bloody Marys. She was whining, telling stories about "boys" she'd met and made out with lately, saying how boring they were. They'd always call her the next day, though she didn't feel like calling back. And she never did.

He looked down at his drink. Looked up at her. And opened his mouth.

"Shut the fuck up," he said.

Then he didn't budge. He waited, unspeaking, until she finally left. Some twenty long and silent minutes later.

Twenty beer cans line the rock outcropping. The lights in the valley below twinkle slowly to life.

"It looks so peaceful," she says, sitting beside me on the ledge.

"Yeah," I agree.

I hate the people to whom those lights belong.

If only I would've gone to Montana instead.

Things would be different then.

Right?

"But this is the last time."

Hating her for loving him. Hating himself for hating her so much – so much that he would allow her to drive him to her apartment, where he proceeded to imagine other women while he writhed inside her naked flesh.

two happenings

in argentina

I was in a commuter train once on my way into Buenos Aires. We'd made a stop at one of the numerous suburban subdivisions of the capital's outskirts. Some people outside and some people inside changed places, the doors pneumatically *whooshed* closed, and the train should have continued on its way. But it didn't.

Some of the train personnel had jumped onto the platform and were pursuing a small boy. The boy was frantically scrambling beneath the metal turnstile that separated the world of the train station from the world outside. He was barefoot and dirty and dressed in castoff clothes, and had apparently not paid for his ride. The train personnel ran him down and wrestled his squirming form into their many arms. The boy hit and clawed and snarled at the men, with more force and ferocity than might be expected from a malnourished being of his size. One of the men, cursing a bleeding arm, slapped the boy across the face. The boy hit back; the action, in turn, was answered with another sharp blow from another uniformed train man.

Upon seeing what was happening on the platform outside, the car full of passengers in which I was traveling suddenly burst to life. Men and women who had been half-dozing or listlessly staring at magazines and newspapers were on their feet and shouting. *"¿Por qué le pegan al niño? ¿Por qué le pegan al niño?"* Why are you hitting the boy? demanded the people who, in the manner typical of strangers on a crowded commuter train, had just a moment ago been making a concerted effort to not speak to one another. Yet now they were united by the cause of the boy outside who was pitted impossibly against the red and yellow uniforms of the train.

Several men delivered kicks and punches to the doors and windows of the train car, but the Plexiglas would not give and they were forced to watch helplessly as the boy was controlled and subdued. Then the train slowly pulled away from the platform. The passengers remained on their feet a few moments more, although they could no longer see what was transpiring. Then they begrudgingly sat down and were silent once again, angry at authority and pondering the fate of the boy on the platform.

That happened in a train. Another time I was walking down a city street when I saw a little dog get hit by a car. The tire crushed the dog's hind legs. The dog screamed and yelped, dragging itself onto the sidewalk and under the cover of a nearby hedge. It continued to whimper and cry, reaching back to lick its wounds in a futile yet instinctive response to the trauma. Some of the people who had witnessed the occurrence laughed and pointed at the little dog and its plight. Many of the ones who laughed were uniformed school children on their way home for lunch. Nobody stopped to tend to the dog or comfort its distress. Some of the children kept laughing, though, as they continued down the road.

i am a west main

oddamn the buses. Goddamn University Bus Service.

I never ride the buses. They're too damn slow, nothing more than hulking 1960s General Motors diesel-fueled dinosaurs that lurch and lumber and regurgitate passengers and belch smoke and bleed transmission fluid onto the asphalt all over campus. Big, aging beasts that won't quite die yet don't have a hope for any sort of rejuvenation, either.

No, I don't ride the buses. But I do drive them. Forty hours a week, more when there's open time or charters to be filled. That might seem hypocritical, making money off of something you don't believe in, something you don't even think is all that safe. I guess it doesn't make sense. But sometimes nothing here at the university makes sense. Especially after you've been driving a goddamn bus all day and then you try to shift your mind to history or economics. It's damn near impossible. The diesel fumes don't help any with the conversion, either.

So it's Friday afternoon and I'm driving my bus now and just my luck the thing has no heat and outside the snow is falling on the suburban Ohio landscape, slow and white and pretty, and I'm only half paying attention to the bus route because I like to watch the fat flakes of snow as they fall to the ground and cling to the trees and light poles outside. The snow has livened up a normally mundane task; I still haven't reached the bored-as-hell-and-ready-to-go-home, zombified stupor stage, which I normally would have arrived at about two hours ago. It's almost as though I'm driving an entirely different route.

Besides due to the snow, I'm also distracted because I'm trying to listen to what one sorority chick is telling another at the back of the bus. It's weird how using one sense can rob attention from a second sense. Like right now, I almost missed a stop. And I didn't slow down very quickly before I let that guy in the wheelchair get all the way across the road, either; I just missed nicking him, in fact, and now he's thrusting a well-deserved finger at me as I drive past. And yet I'm still paying attention to the road with both eyes, too, even though I'm admiring the snow. I'm just also listening to the sorority chick whine and moan about what seems to her to be a woeful and burdensome existence. Which must be what's distracting me, although I never thought you drove a bus with your ears.

I can tell she's a sorority chick because she keeps talking about all the other sisters and the house and whose turn it's been to do the dishes but how it's *her* who's had to do them all because *some* people don't pull their weight and how gross the dishes were on Wednesday, you wouldn't believe all the absolutely gut-wrenching stuff she had to scrape off, caked-on spaghetti and mangled meatballs and *oooohhh* it grossed her out just thinking about it, and not only does she have to deal with nonsense like that from people who don't pull their weight, but on top of that she is just so stressed out lately, if only people would do what they're supposed to then maybe things wouldn't be getting to her this much.

"Honest!" she says. Her voice is kind of grating and nasal. Now I'm sure she's a sorority chick. She sounds like one up and down. She's the kind of obnoxious chick who was a cheerleader in high school and who joined a sorority in college because she wasn't cut out for the intensity of college cheerleading but she still wanted to be surrounded by a gaggle of other airheaded chicks with whom she could gab on a regular basis. She sounds like she's got a megaphone caught in her throat and pom poms clogging up her sinuses.

"Like I don't have enough things to worry about as it is without putting up with other people's crap!" she says. "I mean, school is enough to drive me crazy these days! I told them at the chapter that I just can't take on any more projects and keep a passing average in my classes, too. And just try telling the professors they're piling the work on too heavy! I mean, I've been getting C's on papers. I never got C's in high school! If you ask me, these professors are expecting too much. They set their standards way too high. They must think we've got no life or something, like we've got nothing to do but study. We're only college students, for God's sake!"

It's really a one-sided conversation. The other sorority chick just mumbles an occasional "mmm hmmm" and lets the loud dissatisfied one keep being loud and dissatisfied. She speaks nonstop, something like an auctioneer but with far less important things to say. I wish she would at least take an extended pause to breathe or shove a sock in her mouth or something. I've had a headache the whole day, and she's making it worse with all her yapping. It's hard to concentrate on the snow. I try, but each flake I watch hit the ground makes my head throb even harder, like a tiny fluffy hand grenade that floats for an eternity before landing. And there are a lot of snowflakes. So you can imagine how my head feels. I just wish the sorority chick would can it for a while.

But she doesn't. She keeps gabbing. And besides all that, she says, she is so tired she doesn't know if she'll be able to shop without absolutely falling asleep on her feet. She had to get up at 9:00 this morning. Nine o'clock! She felt like a corpse then, dragging herself out of bed and she doesn't feel much better now, seven hours later. I wish I could tell her that I've been up since 5:00 and all I've had to eat is the extra packet of sugar that I swallowed straight instead of putting in my coffee when I started work at five-thirty.

She's starting to piss me off with her whining. She's the only passenger I can hear. And it's not like everyone else on the bus is all silent and sedated, either. They're chatting in normal tones, but I can still pick out her distinct, nasal whine above all the rest of the voices. That would be a cardinal sin in my first grade class; Mrs. Graves always said she should never ever be able to hear one voice above all the others. That would be in flagrant violation of the sacred six-inch indoor voices rule.

The sorority chick never would have made it in Mrs. Graves's first grade class. She's using about her hundred-yard voice right now, I figure. So as I am driving my bus and watching the snow I am also thinking of first grade and Mrs. Graves and beginning to almost hate this annoying sorority chick, though I guess hate is a pretty strong word. Too strong, probably. You're not supposed to hate your passengers if you're a bus driver. The bus service wouldn't like that very much.

Not that they put it that bluntly in the in the paste-a-smile-on-your-face indoctrination segment of training that they call "Basic Passenger Relations." They just drill it into our heads that we're always to be "respectfully cheerful to all passengers," which is kind of difficult to do if you hate someone, I guess. But I suppose if someone is that prone to hatred, a decree by University Bus Service isn't going to do much to deter their feelings. So I must not be a hateful person because I am still nice to my passengers. I can just get kind of irritated after a while. This job will do that to you.

Plus, I think too much. And driving a bus gives you more time to think than is probably healthy for a person. After about the first month – normally a nightmare of wide turns, tires bouncing off curbs, and closing the doors on people while they're only halfway out of the bus – the job gets pretty easy and all the tasks become second nature. So then you've got plenty of time to think and daydream, though the passengers probably wouldn't be too happy if they knew their safety wasn't always the foremost thing on your mind.

I like to eavesdrop on people, too, so being a bus driver is a really good job for me. Or it's a really bad one; depends on how you look at things. If I didn't eavesdrop I wouldn't be so mad as often because I would never hear all the passengers who grumble and groan, complaining that they're late or the bus is slow or saying how old the damn things are and how absolutely tacky the decor is inside, the seats are like something straight off "The Brady Bunch," aren't they, and why doesn't the college get some new ones, for God's sake, tuition is high enough, you'd figure some of the money would filter down to these shitty buses someday.

But no matter how much they've been pissing and moaning, I always act bright and chipper to the passengers. "Have a nice day!" I say, even if they go out the front door instead of the rear door like they're supposed to and in the process get in the way of someone who's trying to get on the bus, causing a big pileup and slowdown as the two opposing bodies try to maneuver themselves past each other at the same time. "Have a nice day!" I always say anyway as the perpetrator finally wriggles his or her way out. "Have a nice day!" I'll call out, just as chipper but a little more sincerely, to the people who actually read the signs and exit through the back door.

And, "Hi!" I'll say with mock cheerfulness to the person who's now getting on the bus, and, "Hi!" I'll say to the next, and the next, sometimes tossing in a "Good morning!" if I'm driving early or a "Good evening!" if it's late or an old-fashioned, "Hello!" now and then for variety.

I swear it makes me feel like some sort of trained monkey. Especially when they don't answer or acknowledge me or anything, which is almost always. Especially in the morning, when they all look brain dead or comatose or something like that. I swear, it seems like the average college student's body refuses to function before noon. They stumble up the stairs of the bus practically snoring, with their eyes still sealed shut. But you would think they would have the energy to say something back to me, at the very least. Just mumble something – they wouldn't even have to open their eyes. Even if they tell me to stick my good morning up my ass or to go to hell or something. Anything to acknowledge the fact that I acknowledged them. But they don't say anything, and sometimes I feel like a damn automated talking monkey with a commercial driver's license.

I meet a Campus Circle going the other direction and I automatically think, *I am a West Main, I am a West Main.* It's a refrain of sorts that I chant sometimes. I drive a different route almost every day of the week and it's easy to get them confused. I'll get caught up for a moment not knowing if I should turn or keep going so whenever I think of it I just chant *I am a West Main* and that way I keep in mind when to turn and when not to. I am a West Main. I am not a Campus Circle. Not today, anyway.

Campus Circle sucks. It only takes twenty minutes to do a whole lap of the university, passing by all the dorms and the student center and the major academic buildings. So that's three laps every hour, which gets boring as hell after a while. It's so boring that a few of us have this contest going on to see who can drive the quickest lap of Campus Circle. So far the record stands at just under eleven minutes, which will be tough to break. But I'm trying. At night's really the only time when you stand a chance of breaking the record, when there's fewer passengers and fewer cars on campus. But during the day you can still give your Campus Circle driving some sort of purpose, since you can study the terrain, practice the best way to take each curve at the maximum speed possible, and figure which stop signs are tucked away in remote enough corners of campus so that you can go right through them without the university cops being around to see. Anything goes in the Great Campus Circle Race, which I must say has lent the route a hint of excitement that it never had before.

A snowy day like today is especially nice on Campus Circle, because if there's one route in dire need of an occasional change in scenery it's that one. But when it snows Campus Circle gets even more crowded than it usually is. Normally you're lucky if you can find a seat. And the truth is that most of the people who ride the bus don't even really need to be riding it in the first place. The buses are slow and the campus is small. You can usually walk to wherever you're going quicker than the bus will get you there. And walking builds character. But do people walk? No. They wait and wait and wait for the bus to come and then go only two or three stops down the line. And when the bus gets more crowded the people get more irritable. They get on and bitch and complain about anything and everything: bus-related, school-related, you name it. On Campus Circle they crowd like cattle and chew their cud and moo about how hard school is. How they never got less than an A in high school they moo moo

moo and complain that they have to crowd together and make room and maybe touch someone else, be it ever so briefly as the other person slips past when getting off.

For the most part, the people who ride West Main don't complain as much as your run-of-the-mill Campus Circle cattle. First of all, West Main is less crowded, so there's a smaller irritation factor to begin with. And lots of the people who ride it actually need the bus. It's not as though they're just too damn lazy to walk to class. West Main is really one of the bus service's few true examples of public transportation per se, as it actually lets people who don't own cars get where they need to go around town. People going to work, older continuing-education students from in town, and students who live off campus but who don't own cars are the main riders on West Main. Not only do most of the West Main riders not own cars; I'd bet many of them couldn't afford one.

West Main passes through the city's version of the projects. The city's not all that huge, though, so neither are the projects. But they're big enough. Big enough that you get a sense of monotonous sameness from seeing all the bland gray apartment buildings that look exactly like each other. Little kids play with broken bottles and old tires along the side of the road. I always drive slower just in case one of them doesn't look and darts out into the street in front of me. The roads themselves are neglected and kind of remind me of Swiss cheese, they're so covered in potholes. "Serenity Meadows Community Housing Development," the city calls the projects. People who don't live there call them "Serenity Ghettoes." The faces of the people who live there are a different mix of colors than the all-white faces you tend to see downtown.

The only people who don't actually need West Main to carry on with their daily lives are people like the sorority chick and her friend who use it to go out to the shopping center in Strasburg. Right now I can hear Miss Bitch whining about how she chipped a nail and now she'll have to repaint them all because she's out of that color, and how about that economics test, it was so absolutely *hard* wasn't it, who was to think that the professor would actually figure they would have had time to read the book, all she looked at were the notes, but she looked at them for two whole hours and she hopes there's money in her account when she goes to the ATM because her dad said he would put more in but the last time he said that, it was *three whole days* before he put any in so she couldn't buy that dress she'd wanted, and don't even ask her about her parents because lately they did nothing but get on her nerves. They just didn't understand what it was like to be young and independent and have problems of your own, honest to God they didn't.

What a rigorous life she must lead, I think to myself. Then I ignore her and try to focus on the route. *I am a West Main. I am a West Main.*

West Main's not a bad route to drive, really. Especially if you have to drive it for eight hours. Eight hours may not seem like all that much time, but it is when you're stuck sitting in the same seat for that whole duration. At least with West Main you actually go somewhere, instead of making the same goddamn loop every twenty minutes ad infinitum. A little change of scenery goes a long way when you're driving a bus and don't even have a radio and you're stuck in the same seat; watching the snow offers profound entertainment value, indeed. Stuck in the same broken, defective seat, in my case today. I can't adjust this one. My knees are jerked unnaturally upward, so they're halfway to my chest. And the vinyl seat cover is ripped up the middle. The gash is patched together with duct tape, but someone did a bad job patching it and the foam padding is spilling out nonetheless. Our buses are shit, vintage 1960s S-H-I-T. Especially the ones without heat. Like this one. And while they do suck, it still gets on my nerves when the passengers gripe about them. The only people who have a right to gripe, I think, are people who have to drive them for six or eight hours at a time.

It may seem like I complain a lot. The truth is that it's really easy to do. The passengers do it all the time, and it's easy for me to complain when I'm around them so much. Bad attitudes breed more bad attitudes. Complaining is just as contagious as the flu that I'll inevitably get from someone before winter's over. They toss their dirty Kleenexes on the floor and I have to pick them all up when I'm done driving. When they're bored they breathe on the windows and draw pictures in the fog and then wipe the whole mess away with their dirty flu-infested hands.

I'm shivering and cold as hell and wishing the bus had heat but in a way I also feel comforted that the sorority chicks have to sit here in the cold, too. It'll do them good to feel uncomfortable for once in their lives. But I feel bad for the other people's sake because they probably keep the heat turned way down low at their homes in Serenity Meadows, if they even turn on the heat at all.

"My God, can you believe that? I mean I have *never* been so offended in my life. Honestly."

I have been successfully ignoring the sorority chick for a bit, but that is all down the tubes now. She's still droning on, and now I can't help but hear it.

"There is no way she will ever be president. She can't even run the social committee without totally flipping out whenever she actually has to do something that even *resembles* work. Really! And there's no way she'll ever get him, either. No matter how much of a slut she tries to be. And she's getting pretty fat if you haven't noticed. No way will he even so much as bum a cigarette from her. No way *at all*."

As I listen to her I try to guess what she looks like. I must have seen her when she got on. But how was I to know I'd want the information for future reference? Anyway, I was probably too busy saying "Hi!", too busy pretending to be cheerful to really notice. But I could tilt the rearview mirror down a little and get a good view of her now, because it sounds like she's sitting in an aisle seat somewhere in the back. I could tilt the mirror, but I want to guess. She's probably blond, wearing high-end mall-store clothes and a black wool coat with faux fur around the neck, carrying one of those shoulder bags with the embroidered sorority letters. "Shag bags," they call them, for when they go to the frat houses to shack up with their studly boyfriends. And I bet her lips are painted some eye-grabbing color – they probably match the nail she chipped – and she's probably got this permanently sassy look on her face that she perfected after studying the pictures in some fashion magazine.

So I imagine what I think she looks like and as I do this I am still driving and watching the snow and listening to her jabber, too, and hating – no, *despising*; bus drivers don't hate people, remember? – this chick because she has money and she thinks she's all the shit in the world with a mountain of rose petals to boot, and she probably thinks I'm nothing. I mean, she probably *would* think I'm nothing if she were to even think about me at all in the first place. Bus drivers don't really occupy lofty positions on people's personal prestige meters, even student bus drivers for whom driving is only half of their existence and who – knock on wood – won't have to do it for thirty more years. Most of the time when people get on and I say hello or good morning or whatever to them they look at me as though I might throw off my seat belt and leap up and bite them or something. As though on top of that I have rabies, to boot. Or like I'm dressed in some weird-ass clothing, some loopy gothic vampire suit or a full-fledged drag queen getup. Sometimes they're really taken by surprise and weirded out when I say hi to them, and you'd swear I was a drag queen with fangs who's convulsing and foaming at the mouth, all the while gnashing my jaws at them in an attempt to get at their jugular. Or something like that.

We're going through the projects now, and the regulars who always get off here are getting off once again. The manic depressive who delights in droning on in a steady monotone about what a burden it is to be manic depressive is the first off. "Thanks, see you later," he says in a drooping voice that is not unlike how that blue donkey from Winnie the Pooh sounds when he sags and sighs his way through Christopher Robin's magical fairyland.

There's all kinds of people who ride West Main. Another guy who I've never seen sober always tells me the same story about how his father used to own a small newspaper in Missouri back in the days of moveable type and how as a kid the guy would hang around the office and the reporters would occasionally buy him a Coke at the drugstore soda fountain next door. I guess he drinks a lot more than Coke nowadays. He always staggers on and off of the bus, never able to plant one foot squarely in front of the other. I was stopped this one time letting people on through the front door but there was no one who was exiting, but all of a sudden the drunkard started yelling at me from the rear of the bus to open the back door, *open the back door, goddammit!*

So I opened it, not knowing what was wrong, hoping I hadn't squashed some helpless Serenity Meadows kid with my back tire or something. But that wasn't it at all; the drunk bastard just ambled down the stairwell and stuck his head outside and barfed. I could hear the stream of vomit whoosh out of his mouth from all the way up front. It was real loud and chunky, and after he was done puking he still stood there with his head out the back door, gagging and clearing his throat for a few seconds. And then he just climbed back up the stairs and went back to his seat and sat there like nothing out of the ordinary ever happened.

Some of the regulars don't say anything – nothing coherent, anyway – especially the ones who have disabilities or who have nervous ticks and are occasionally shaken by spasms or lapse into fits. Like, there's this old woman whose skin is kind of red and peeling and charred-looking. She has this pass with "No Expiration Date" stamped on it, and I tried to throw her off the first time she ever got onto one of my buses, because as far as I knew the longest any of our passes was good for was a month. I told her it wasn't a valid pass and that she had to pay a dollar, and she started moaning and carrying on and basically going a little nuts.

"Lifetime pass," she wheezed. Her voice was all raspy and sandpapery. "Got in an accident ten years ago … university … bastards … owe me $80,000, plus medical … all I get … lifetime pass. The bastards …"

Her voice trailed off at the end, and she almost choked on a wet, phlegmy cough that reminded me of the violent noises that garbage disposals make.

She was getting pretty pissed, and she was really freaking me out, too. And the pass did look authentic, albeit a bit rumpled and dirty. So I let her stay on. But later, when she had gotten off and there was no one left on the bus, I called dispatch and asked what the deal was.

"Was this an elderly woman, kind of hunched over?" the supervisor asked in a knowing sort of way.

"That's affirmative," I answered.

"Yes, that pass is good forever," he said.

I was never able to find out anything else. And so the disfigured lifetime pass woman is on today, too, but she'll be getting off at the next stop. She rides my bus all the time now. I don't think she holds any bitter feelings towards me, although I can't be sure because she's never spoken another word to me again. I haven't asked to see her pass since then, either.

There's also a lady on today who I've never seen before who's got her four-year-old son and his five-year-old cousin with her. The cousin's parents are in Germany, she tells me. The father's in the Army and the mother, who's German, is in the psyche ward. She tells me this very nonchalantly. Her nephew can speak German, which explains why he probably sounds a little weird to me, she says. I haven't heard him say anything, so I don't have any idea what he sounds like, but I don't tell her this. Her own kid is jabbering away, though: a bunch of baby talk-like gobbledygook that doesn't make sense at all.

"Shuddup!" the mother says, and smacks her boy. It's a sharp, echoing smack that makes me wince. "Yew don't know German! Quit pretendin' yew know German. Just 'cuz he knows German doesn't mean yew know German.

"He thinks he knows German," she says to me, as though I hadn't noticed the exchange.

The last of the project-dwellers who gets off is the man with the patched yellow rubber raincoat and the cowboy boots into which he always tucks the legs of his dirty and grease-smeared khakis. He wears an enormous cowboy hat that covers his eyes and behind him he drags a plastic garbage bag that is always filled to the bursting point. He staggers off the bus, taking every step in turn, with a healthy pause at each one. The garbage bag bumps along after him, like some sort of faithful plastic pet.

The sorority chicks are the last ones on now. I don't look back, but I just know. I'm surprised they even stoop to riding with the other people. I'm surprised Daddy didn't buy the loud one a car when she went off to college. Most of my dislike is directed at the loud one. I don't know why. The quiet one who just says "mmm hmmm" is probably just as uppity, but she doesn't get to me like the whiny one does.

"I'm *so* glad it's Friday," the whiny sorority chick sighs. "I have waited sooooooo long for this weekend. I just need to relax so bad. You would not believe."

Friday. I lose track of time and days. My existence is measured with laps of Campus Circles and West Mains, of East Mains and Stadium Shuttles. Days mean nothing to me. But it is Friday and I'm off in another hour but I picked up a charter tonight, three extra hours of driving someone to the airport, some high-paid university stiff going to a conference or else some kid with money flying home for the weekend.

I'll come back from my charter pretty late tonight and the sorority chicks will be long since finished with their shopping. They'll have gone for a cappuccino or something like that to ward off the chill from the cold day and the cold bus. They'll probably also have taken long naps and hot showers. They'll be rested and ready to go out and I'll be dead tired, too exhausted to do anything except sleep, too broke to do anything really even if I weren't exhausted. It's a shame, too, because there's this girl from my English class and I'm interested, and what's more she seems to be interested, too. She told me to call her sometime, but I'm always too damn tired. Or too damn broke. Or both.

I study a lot, too. So much that I think I overload my brain sometimes, given all the thinking I do on my bus routes and all the sleeping that I should do but I *don't* do. But I can't skimp on work, and I try not to skimp on school since I'm paying for the shit, so instead I cut out sleep which makes me prone to rambling semi-coherent thoughts and eventually turns me into a real cranky son of a bitch after about two weeks of getting only four hours of sleep a night.

So now we're in the parking lot of the shopping center and I'm sure the sorority chicks are going to get off now and go spend their parents' money. And sure enough, the stop request bell dings and I pull up to the next stop for them. I figure they'll probably go out the rear door since they're way in the back, but instead they walk all the way up the aisle to the front of the bus.

"Have a nice day."

I really don't feel like saying it. I've already said it too many times today. But I say it anyway. I was actually going to purposefully refrain from saying it. I had decided that a while back, convinced myself that I didn't really give a rat's ass if they have a nice day or not, especially the loud one. So why bother asking? But I forgot that that's what I had decided. So, "Have a nice day," I say. Bad habits die hard, I guess.

One of them, brown-haired and kind of plump, is already off the bus and in the parking lot. But the other, blond and slender with a bag slung over her shoulder, turns, smiles, and addresses me as she begins to descend the stairwell.

"Thanks. You, too," she says.

I know it's her, *the* sorority chick, and not the one who has been quiet because I recognize the high-pitched, sort of screechy voice. And then she is off and I am watching her walk toward the department store. She has a nice shapely bottom, and I follow its pleasant, animated movements with my eyes as she walks. Then, for the briefest of moments, she turns and waves to me. She has a nice smile, the corners of her mouth curving in a pleasantly sassy way. Her lipstick is a bright shade of red that stands out prominently against the white snow that is falling outside.

I guess hate *is* a pretty strong word. Too strong, probably.

Though this doesn't stop me from chuckling to myself when she slips on a patch of ice and smears her shapely bottom all over the parking lot.

always in trains

The city: Buenos Aires. The *barrio*: Once. The Plaza: Miserere.

Hand in hand, we slowly climb the subway station steps and pause a moment at the top to behold the plaza. Blandly gray, trash-littered, graffiti-coated, it nevertheless assumes a certain beauty in the waning late-afternoon sunlight of this mid-spring Friday. The plaza is crammed with people – some sitting idly, unhurried, unconcerned; others rushing purposefully about in every direction. Children entertain themselves by climbing on the benches and monuments, while pigeons feast on stale popcorn that lies strewn about the ground.

In the street, buses make their slow, methodical rounds about the perimeter of the plaza, bearing numbers like badges. **52, 168, 201**. The numbers are emblazoned across the tops of the buses in big bold block type, meaningless to some people yet all-important to those who care. To each person who clambers aboard a bus and fishes for change in his or her pocket, there is a number that signifies a direction, a route through the urban labyrinth, an area of the capital, a certain neighborhood and, at the end of it all, a home and a family – along with warmth, love, and belonging.

The numbers on the buses tell a story in themselves. We do not worry about the numbers, though, for it is always in trains that we make our way back home.

We continue from the top of the subway steps and proceed toward the station. Someone stands on the corner, cooking candied peanuts in a metal tub. The aroma follows our course, salty-sweet and sticky-smelling. The contents of kiosks spill out onto the sidewalks, along with brightly colored placards that shout ¡OFERTA! in an attempt to lure passersby. The newsstand owner has his offerings prominently displayed, clothespinned to wire racks for momentary perusal: city maps to keep the traveler from getting lost, something to read to keep him from getting lonely.

Also all around us are T-shirts, soccer jerseys, tennis shoes, jewelry, boxer shorts. All manner of cheap *cosas piratas*, laid meticulously on blankets and crying out for attention.

Ignoring this mini-bazaar, we proceed up the steps and into the station. Inside it is hot and steamy, much warmer and more difficult to breathe than in the plaza outside. The floor is teeming with people, each one with a direction, a goal, a mission in mind. We are accosted by a myriad of faces and ages, clothing that marks particular occupations and walks of life. Construction workers, caked in cement dust; suit-clad businessmen, leather satchels at their sides; cleaning ladies with mops, brooms, and dustpans clutched under their arms; policemen; a grim-faced soldier toting a machine gun at the ready; a nun on a bicycle; a priest listening to a Walkman and glancing nervously about, his eyes darting from to and fro; three Mormon missionaries, Americans, looking conspicuously pure with their well-trimmed blond hair and engraved plastic name tags; a skinny kid wearing soccer cleats and an oversized Maradona T-shirt; two big men in dirtied rugby uniforms, their legs bulging like tree trunks and sweat glistening on their laughing faces; a dozen Boy Scouts, each one shouldering a pack bigger than he is, solemnly filing behind their scout master; scores of students balancing textbooks and school supplies.

The people are darting in every direction, swirling and circulating like a living vortex. Our clasped hands are pulled apart several times in the crowd, and each time we feel instinctively for each other's fingers at our sides.

Food stalls occupy the edges of the station center, their stark white counter tops adorned with colorful spills and stains. The sizzle of spattering grease, the clatter of pots, plates, and pans, the intermingling smells of baking and frying, and the hurried shouts of orders being placed all puncture the general commotion of the station. The offerings at one stall are basically similar to those at the rest – all of them variations on the same theme, yet each one slightly different, as well, no two grease-stands offering exactly identical combinations of fats, starches, and proteins.

PANCHO, SUPER PANCHO, CHORIPÁN, PEBETE, COMBINACIÓN Nº 2, HAMBURGUESA, PAPAS FRITAS, TORTILLA, MUZZARELLA, NAPOLETANA, TORTAS, FACTURAS POR LA DOCENA, CAFE C/ LECHE Y 2 MEDIALUNAS, GASEOSA, COCA EN LATA, QUILMES, PORRON, TRES-CUARTOS, LITRO, EMPANADAS (POLLO, CARNE, JAMÓN Y QUESO, FRITO, AL HORNO), COCA-COLA BIEN FRIA, MOSTAZA, MAYONESA, MILANESA COMPLETA, CHIMICHURRI – the words litter the countertops and menu boards and are hurled through the air from customer to counter boy, to cook and back. The food slides across the counter, money changes hands in a flurry, and the hungry traveler sets upon his quick meal with the purposeful air of someone who has a train to catch, someone dining out of necessity rather than for pleasure.

We make our way past the food stalls to the ticket booths and machines, from which snake haphazard lines of impatient travelers. A little boy, his face covered in a lifetime's worth of grime and dirt, pushes the buttons on the machine for us, then humbly passes us our change and tickets. One pitiful palm remains extended, the boy hoping that some of the change might be his. Next to the machine an elderly couple sleeps on a pile of cardboard. Dressed in rags and with their arms clutched tightly around each other, they will not be boarding a train today.

On the journey from the ticket booths to the gates we are once again enveloped in the raw vitality of the station. It is a writhing mass of bodies, waves of movement that swell and crest and wrap around corners, up and down hallways and stairways like the undulating tentacles of some great beast. A general sense of chaos pervades the atmosphere – yet it is a beautiful, restrained, systematic chaos.

More than of our own wills we are instead pulled, drawn toward the gates by the currents of activity around us. Fighting for space, we press through the turnstiles. A man coming from a recently arrived train, ticketless and hoping not to get caught, vaults the turnstiles and hits the ground on the other side running. A policeman dashes off in short-lived, futile pursuit, but the subject is quickly lost among the throbbing life of the station floor.

Four platforms lie ahead of us, reaching westward like the fingers of an outstretched hand. Above them hangs the sun, a large round globe of late-afternoon light slowly descending from the heavens.

Two trains are waiting. One, about to leave, is bursting with passengers. We board the second train. It is still relatively empty and we easily find seats. We wait, holding hands in the dim artificial glow of the fluorescent lights overhead. Alongside us we can see the other train, jam-packed far beyond capacity. People hang out of doorways, arms dangle out of windows in an attempt to catch some hint of a breeze, faces press tightly against the window-glass. The train's whistle sounds, beckoning to the final stragglers desperately running down the platform. Then the train begins to pull out, slowly at first. We stare outside as the now-moving faces pressed against the glass stare back at us. The train gradually gains speed and it is soon rattling into the distance.

Our own train quickly begins to fill with people, and the world of cheap food moves inside with them. Vendors begin their persistent journeys from one end of the train to the other, their way becoming increasingly clogged with the passage of time and the entrance of more passengers.

"BE-BII-DAS ... HE-LAAA-DO ... DOS TABLETAS DE CHOCOLATE CON ALMENDRA Y MANÍÍÍ ... PANCHO ... BOM-BOO-NES,

UN PESO LA BOLSITA ... CARAMELOS ... " the vendors cry in their distinctly clipped voices, appealing to those hungry passengers who hadn't time to eat anything back in the station.

The space around us is completely packed now, congested with bodies sitting and standing and balancing packages and bags. The train begins to move, and several people shove their way into the car moments before the doors snap shut with a pneumatic *whoosh*. For a minute or two the train noisily rattles and surges, building speed until it is running smoothly. We pass through the train yards and abandoned warehouses, where the rusted skeletons of old engines lie in rest. The board fences that surround the yards are warped and rotten, the small patches of grass completely overtaken by weeds.

Soon we have passed the train yards and are surrounded by the city. Shortly a new breed of vendors begins to make its way through the train, selling all manner of gadgets, housewares, and other assorted goods – everything from alarm clocks to underwear, batteries to butterfly knives. They offer imitation Tupperware, wallets with *"increíble!"* zip-up pockets, combination knives/corkscrews/bottle openers extraordinaire, purses, socks, radios, and every other sort of product imaginable.

"¡SEÑORAS Y SEÑORES, SU ATENCIÓN POR FAVOR!" they chant. Thus begins a demonstration and explanation of the product, its qualities, its features, the thousands of uses toward which it can be put. And, of course, the super-low price of the day is always emphasized: *"DOS POR UN PESO ... UN PESITO ... SOLAMENTE UNA MONEDA ... LLEVÁ TRES POR EL PRECIO DE UNO ... SOLAMENTE PARA HOY ... "*

Their routine is always the same, as though scripted: the salesman stands framed in the entryway of the train car, like a preacher addressing his congregation, and delivers his pitch. Then he deftly weaves his way through the congested mass of bodies, handing out items or placing them on the knees of indifferent passengers. He reaches the end of the car and, before making the return trip, allows each potential customer a moment to contemplate the true ingenuity and affordability of the product. Then the vendor returns, either to retrieve his wares or to collect payment, impassively professional when an item is handed back unexamined.

There are also beggars and charity cases, the sick or injured or out-of-work pleading for assistance, announcing their hardships aloud and then making the rounds with their hands extended.

A pregnant woman, wearing no shoes and accompanied by three half-naked toddlers, pleads for money to buy her children milk. A little girl distributes hand-scrawled slips of paper which read, **POR FAVOR AYUDÁME YO TENGO SEIS HERMANITOS Y NO TENGO PAPÁ Y MI MAMÁ TRABAJA PERO NO NOS ALCANZA PARA COMER GRACIAS**. A young boy passes out pocket calendars bearing pictures of St. Christopher, patron saint of travelers, and begs for a few cents in return. The most sympathetic of souls – of whom there are few – hand back the calendar along with a coin. Also making the rounds is a deaf man, who offers for sale a concise sign-language dictionary, which no one ever seems to have a use for.

Other than the clatter of wheels on rails and the monologues of vendors and beggars, the train is eerily noiseless. Strangers sit or stand next to one another in silence, staring fixedly out of windows, at the seat in front of them, or at the pages of a book or magazine. Occasionally a baby utters a short whimper, but it is quickly shushed by its mother. The two of us speak in hushed tones, but our voices nevertheless echo loudly in the relative absence of any other sounds; the English words draw a few brief glances of puzzlement, but nothing more. At the far end of the compartment, two drunks pass a can of Brahma back and forth, cackling harshly as beer sloshes onto their clothes. Nobody pays them any attention.

The stops of the train fall into a pattern, one which we have experienced countless times before. **CABALLITO** ... **FLORES** ... **FLORESTA** ... The stations passing the window assume a repetitive, almost comforting familiarity. Each subsequent station is similar to the last – ticket booths and turnstiles and concrete platforms, hot dog stands and boxy little kiosks.

VA. LURO ... **LINIERS** ... **CIUDADELA** ... The areas we pass through along the tracks are similar, as well. One segment of the suburban jungle dissolves into the next in a rapid cycle of butcher shops and book stores, gift shops and kiosks, arcades, electronics and hardware stores, *perfumerías* and *panaderías* and bars and pool halls. And of streets crowded with cars, *remises*, and buses, groups of kids on corners smoking cigarettes, old men on dilapidated benches talking or drinking *mate* or playing *truco*, families seated outside on the sidewalk in plastic chairs watching television – an endless world of neon and plastic and paper, of people and buildings and traffic.

R. MEJÍA ... **HAEDO** ... **MORÓN** ... announce the blue signs with white letters that stand like sentinels at each station. Each stop is accompanied by the shrill clanging of warning bells, the whistle of the train, the surging and rocking of the cars as the engine reduces velocity. Then follows a flurry of commotion in between the brief opening and closing of the doors, and then another interval of erratic jolts and jars as the train again builds speed.

The grip of our clasped hands becomes tighter now, our words more hurried. According to the timetable, the next stop lies thirty-three minutes from Once. It's been nearly forty now – the train's running late – but nevertheless we know our time together is short. Then suddenly we are at the stop and there is but time for a momentary kiss before she is off and waving at me through the window and then she melts into the swirling crowd on the platform. When we say goodbye, it seems, it is always in trains.

Alone now, with no one to talk to, I become one of the blank faces. I sit silently, staring out the window at nothing in particular. **ITUZAINGÓ** ... **SAN A. DE PADUA** ... **MERLO** ... **PASO DEL REY** ... Like the previous stops, they all blur together in a sea of similarity.

Then we are in Moreno and I am suddenly on my feet, rushing along with many others to board the final diesel train of the day to the more western destinations. Tiring, thirsty, I hand a peso to a vendor as he ambles past in the opposite direction. Fishing into the Styrofoam cooler strapped around his neck, his leathery hand emerges with a straw and a can of grapefruit soda. A mumbled two-way *"gracias"* follows, and then he is on his way and I am boarding the train just as it is about to leave.

Unlike the hard plastic seats of the electric train, the seats on this train are of padded nylon, the majority of them torn in at least half a dozen places. I nod hello to the man who takes the seat across from mine and politely inquire where he's headed and where he's been. He responds with a thorough description of San Telmo and a concise history of the tango, including his opinion regarding the genre's best artists (he's particularly fond of Carlos Gardel). He is still talking when we arrive at his stop. As he heads for the door he calls back to me to come and visit him sometime – maybe we can go to San Telmo together. It does not seem to matter that I do not know his name or address, nor he mine. Then he is gone and the train is in motion once again.

After the man has left, I rise from my seat and move to the closest exit. Its door is open, affording a view of the passing scenery, and I seat myself on the top step. From here I am at the very periphery of the outside world. The leaving behind of Moreno has brought a slight change in scenery. We are still surrounded by city, but now in places the urban continuity is broken up a bit by larger open spaces and more frequent glimpses of grass and trees.

GRAL. RODRÍGUEZ, reads the sign in front of me, identifying the final stop which is truly contiguous with Buenos Aires. As we pull away I see the seven familiar blue and white concrete benches that sit on the far side of the road, benches on which I have never sat, but which I know almost intimately by sight. As I sit in the doorway and watch General Rodríguez drift past, I note the slow transformations taking place all along Route 7. Many businesses are closing, their metal overhead doors grating shut and banging harshly against the ground. Other establishments are just preparing to open – *parrilla* owners mound glowing coals into their solid, outdoor brick grills, waiters at small cafés fill the sidewalks with tables and chairs.

We leave Rodríguez behind, and with it the final vestiges of the capital's urban world. I crane my neck around the door frame. A pulsing red semi-circular strip, quivering on the horizon, is all that remains of the sun. Then it is gone and the world is bathed in the sudden half-shadow of dusk. Everything seems to magically, instantaneously slow down just a bit. The stops come with even less frequency than before. The autos that move alongside the tracks become a little older, have more trouble matching the pace of the train. Conversation on the train, already scarce, becomes nothing more than a subdued murmur. A lone vendor advertises his wares, near the head of the train and out of view from where I am seated. *"ALL-FAAA-JOO-RES ... "* he calls. The word creeps down the aisle. It echoes long, slowly, and slightly mournfully.

Outside it is getting darker now. The highway has diverged in another direction, and in places the little road that runs parallel to the tracks is no longer paved. One world is slowly decaying into another, man-made constructions being overtaken by natural design. The sultry city-heat has given way to the fresh, breeze-blown warmth of dusk in the country. Now there are even fewer houses and buildings. Instead, fleeting glimpses of trees and sheep, horses and bridges and streams flash before my eyes. Dogs romp in the tall grass beside the tracks and shirtless, barefoot children kick soccer balls about in the dirt. The dust stirred up by the occasional pickup truck or mounted horse plays in the fast-fading traces of light which still linger behind the sun.

By the time we reach Luján, the details of the basilica's distant spires are barely distinguishable in the final dying embers of daylight.

Now there remain only *pueblos*, small towns with narrow dirt streets. **JÁUREGUI ... OLIVERA ... GOWLAND.** The stations appear all but deserted, and only one or two people get off at each. Far off in the distance I catch an occasional glimpse of the highway, but for the most part we are completely separated from any trace of civilization. Before me stretch miles and miles of fertile *pampas*, covered in dense blankets of wheat, corn, and soybeans. The stalks of wheat, and the seas of grass in which roam cows, horses, pigs, and sheep, swing peacefully back and forth in the gentle breeze of day's end. There are orderly lines of *ombú* trees, stretching almost to infinity, left in key locations as windbreaks and shelter for the animals. Now and then a stream trickles across the landscape.

LA ALICIA, RESTAURANTE EN EL CAMPO, declares a large wooden sign planted squarely in the middle of a field. The restaurant itself is nowhere to be found.

The echo of the train's whistle is lonelier here in the country. With no buildings to absorb the sound, it carries across the *pampa* like the ghostly lament of a lone animal. As I behold the vast unpopulated countryside and listen to the whistle, I am filled with a feeling of melancholy solitude. The precise sensation is difficult to pinpoint. Not sadness, exactly, but similar in a way – a strange sense of exhausted calm that lingers inside of me and seems to hint at sensations to come.

Then Mercedes, the end of the line. I know it is approaching before I see it, but in a moment it is there and all around me the warning bells at the railroad crossings are clanging one final time. The city passes me by quickly at first – the low, squat, dusty-white houses on the outskirts of town last but an instant – then more slowly as I spy the silos of the grain plant; slower still moves the train as we pass through the more well-to-do residential area. We are almost at a crawl when the cathedral's steeple, ten blocks off in the downtown distance, creeps into view, peeking above the rooftops. Then the train stops with a jarring finality and we move no more.

I remain seated in the doorway for a moment, dazed by the sudden cessation of movement, movement which has been my companion for more than two hours. Then, prodded from behind, I wearily rise from my stoop and hop down onto the platform. All around me, the final passengers on the final diesel train of the day are also slowly exiting the cars. They wheel their bicycles down the steps, hand parcels through the windows to awaiting family members, collect their bags, bundles, and children.

From the platform, I crunch across the gravel that lays scattered about the other, vacant set of tracks. Glancing to the west where the train does not go, I glimpse the remains of the day, the muted half-glow of the since-vanished sun. Around me, many passengers toss their tickets to the ground. I do the same as I pass through the empty station building with its locked café and shuttered ticket window.

The instant I exit the station I suddenly feel very empty inside. It is as if I miss the train, as though part of me let go of my hand and got off at a stop thirty-three minutes from the capital, as though the rest of me sits unoccupied and motionless on the tracks back at the station.

Feeling thus emptied, I begin the five-block walk to my house. Shuffling quietly, pensively homeward, passing in and out of the lengthening shadows which are about to give way to night, I can still hear the faint clanging of bells and the rattle of wheels, sense a phantom commotion in the air about me, feel bodies brushing against mine on the empty street.

As I trace my solitary course homeward I know that, when years from now I look back and picture myself in Argentina, it will always be in trains.

presence

The old man is a recurring sight in the city. He assumes distinct forms – sometimes tall, sometimes short; round and chubby, or splinter-thin; different hair, bald at times; dressed as often in a suit as in blue jeans and a fading shirt. But he is always old, and he is always alone. Sometimes I see him emerging from a corner kiosk, brown paper bag in hand. He walks with a head-hung shuffle, back bent and distant eyes drooping in fathomless reflection. His is the vacant form dining singly at a table for four at 6 p.m., before most people have even left work, much less considered dinner. The ubiquitous bottle of wine sits in front of him, his only companion. Sometimes he appears in cafés. He arrives early and stays late. The half-sleeping waiters cluster, wait, check their watches and hope for him to hurry. But he doesn't. He takes his time. He sips his wine slowly in between long slices of thought and memory. Often he orders another bottle, and the waiters grudgingly oblige. Though they are tired, they know that an old man like this needs a pleasant, nonjudgmental café to sit in, for solitary wine in an uglier place would do him even more harm. I seem to see these old men – this old man – with greater frequency now. Or, quite possibly, I just notice him more. I am beginning to fear – irrationally, I'm sure – that one day it will be me in his place, life suspended. Me with the bottle of wine my only companion and the night a perpetual state of mind.

intersection

S o anyway, I'm sitting in my car at this intersection in Florida this one time. I've got the window rolled down. This bearded bum starts to stagger across the street. It's a wide street, like four lanes on either side. He gets halfway across and pauses on the median. Then he's walking in front of my car. He sees the license plate and stops. He looks at me. He starts to come toward me.

"Ohio!" he says. "Ohio!"

He's standing right next to me now, looking down at me where I'm sitting in my car seat.

"Where you from in Ohio?" he asks.

"Hartville," I tell him. "You know where that is?"

"Course I know where Hartville is!" he says. "Used to pick vegetables there – lettuce, radishes, celery."

He pauses for a second.

"Hey," he says, "can I have one of your cigarettes?"

"Sure," I say, and fish one out of my shirt pocket for him.

He looks into the distance at something, contemplates life for a second, then looks at me again. He points.

"You watch yourself down here," he says, as though conveying great and pressing advice. "You watch yourself."

"Yeah, I know," I say. "Tampa sure isn't Ohio."

About then the light changes from red to green and around us cars start to move. The bum still has like three lanes to cross to get to the other side of the street.

"But I mean, you *watch* yourself," he says.

"Yeah," I say. "Better be careful, man. Those cars are moving."

"Fuck them cars!" he says.

Then he shakes my hand and continues to stagger across the street. Cars have to brake for him.

Some of them honk. Some don't bother.

empanadas and expatriates

I became certain of my wife's affair with her tango teacher when I found the birth-control medication in her purse. That also happened to be the last day I would ever see her – at least, as my wife – as well as the day on which I finally came close to getting the empanadas right.

I arrived home that afternoon from downtown Buenos Aires with a throbbing headache. I'd just gotten off the rush-hour subway, where I had endured the usual jostles, shoves, and sweaty press of commuter bodies. On top of that, I'd been aggressively prodded to accept Jesus by a pair of pious-looking old ladies and to please give a donation by a dozen different destitutes smelling of booze, and I could swear that I felt the man in the three-piece suit grope ever so fleetingly for my wallet when he bumped into me on his way off the subway.

I hadn't eaten anything all day, and my stomach was an empty gulf, its vastness intensified by the flak-like pounding of my temples. I didn't feel like doing much of anything except filling my stomach and going to bed. But I had to get dressed for the evening reception at the Guyanese embassy that I was to cover as part of my reporting job at the Buenos Aires *Tribune*. In addition, I was forced to argue with my wife about whether or not she would be accompanying me. Not that I personally cared much one way or the other. But I had no choice except to serve as mediator between the two bickering, neurotic halves which insisted upon waging all-out bipolar debate regarding this matter – and all other matters, as well – within my wife's brain.

Despite the feverish semi-lunacy that had been creeping into her personality for the past four months that we had lived in Argentina, my wife remained ravishing. Even as she stood there bickering with herself like a four-year-old with no attention span, I found myself admiring her eyes as they squinted in anger, the way her mouth wrinkled up in a sexy pout, the determined sassiness that emerged as she firmly planted her hand on her hip.

"Why should I go? It'll be a filthy pit, just like the last embassy," she intoned jerkily to both me and to herself. "Remember that fat diplomat who smelled like fried eggs and who spoke that weird language nobody understood? Nah, it'll be fine, you'll see. It will be lovely. Not every embassy party can be flawless. But it's Guyana! It's so Third World! Hell, what else have I got to do? Maybe I could head downtown to the mall."

Finally having convinced herself to attend, she half-sulked and half-galloped to the shower and left me alone with my headache.

I innocently opened her leather handbag in search of an aspirin. Instead, I found myself clutching one of those round, plastic, day-by-day dispensers filled with the proverbial pill. This in and of itself might not have been anything to arouse suspicion, except for the fact that it had been almost a year since my vasectomy and, as far as I knew, I was still consistently shooting blanks, so to speak.

My wife was beautiful and wouldn't hesitate to let you know, verbally or otherwise. In graduate school in Northeast Ohio, where I met her, I'd been impressed by her straightforwardness and seduced by her body. I, in turn, wooed her with some not-too-shabby love poetry that was, if I must be frank, my only noteworthy literary attempt during my grad-school days, aside from the articles I wrote for the college paper and at my ongoing job for the *Reliance Record*. I was a journalist by training and profession, though, so my *non*fiction output, at least, should have been decent. But I yearned to really be a *writer*, to live in a cabin nestled among the mountains, chopping my own firewood and crafting existential masterpieces that cast sublime light on the universal human experience, not articles about the abnormally high quantities of deer that were getting mangled to bits by tractor-trailers on Route 225.

Although I must say that I certainly didn't mind my job and would have been content staying there with the deer for quite some time. Besides, the short stories I wrote or attempted to write either ended up in the wastebasket or were mailed back to me along with some literary magazine's stark prefab rejection letter. The stories seemed to all resolve themselves, if you can call it a resolution, with the protagonist committing suicide. It was an inevitable consequence in my short fiction, although the methods varied greatly from story to story. I had done wrist-slashing, plunges off bridges, crossbow shootings, and a quite admirable self-electrocution involving a toaster oven and a full bathtub. It was a bit of a liability to appear in one of my stories. Insurance companies, I'm sure, would think twice before selling one of my characters a policy.

But my wife, I suspect, was not content there in Ohio. I'm sure that in her version of a perfect world she would have chosen to marry someone a little further up the social ladder, instead of a humble journalist, especially a general assignment reporter for the *Reliance Record*. But I suppose she was, at the time, unable to locate any independently wealthy real estate magnates who could also write a passable line of mediocre love poetry. So she settled on me, instead.

We continued to live in Reliance for a couple of years after getting married. I quickly finished grad school and kept working at the paper. She took her time finishing her own master's degree, and then took her time beginning her job search. She was looking for just the right opportunity, she said. In reality, I'm sure, she probably *was* looking, but more than likely the potential opportunities she wanted were in Boston or New York. She was from out East and had come to the Midwest, I suspect (Although I never asked her; she had a determined air about her that made logic and explanations seem of secondary importance.), on some sort of romantic whim, a desire to get her master's in public relations in an "authentic" setting amidst "real" people. Maybe she thought fresh air would help her put an exciting new spin on things at whatever prominent PR firm for which she was destined. It must have been something of that nature, because she never seemed to be overly enamored by the thought of remaining in the Buckeye State forever.

I was putting out feelers, too, so to speak, although I was looking to more southern climes. The urge to travel had been subtly gnawing at me recently, and I began to investigate English-language papers in Central and South America. This search was fueled, in part, by my explicit desire *not* to go to New York or Boston, where I strongly suspected we would soon be headed if my wife had her way. I directed my efforts at Argentina, where I had spent a semester studying abroad as an undergraduate.

It had been the only international experience of my life, but my Spanish was passable when I arrived and got much better as the weeks went on. I traveled a bit and learned to like the country very much, although I really didn't have anything to compare it to aside from the United States.

I didn't have any experience in international journalism – not even editing wire reports – but I sent a résumé to the Buenos Aires *Tribune* nonetheless. I kept my search quiet, though. I felt a little sheepish, in a way, about the whole thing. I should have done my traveling before graduating with my bachelor's, I thought, or before going to grad school, or at least before getting married.

But if I were to go to a big city I would much rather have had it be in another country. The foreign lands of the American East Coast held no allure for me whatsoever. And the growth of our two-person family was not something I had to worry about, either. My wife had persuaded me to put a nix on the possibility of children about a year into the marriage. I'm kind of foggy on the argument she used, now – something about having kids being incompatible with leading the fast-paced lifestyle for which we were destined. I'm not sure why I swallowed the line. At the time, after all, I was still working at a job where I often experienced long spells where it seemed I wrote more often about animals – be they mad cows, diseased rats, prize-winning dogs or bass, or deer both dead and alive – than I did people, much less people of the "fast-paced" sort. Often the most fast-paced people I covered in a given week were the members of the Women's Downtown Quilting Society, who were known to become a bit raucous if one of them brought along a flask to their Saturday night meetings.

The threat of becoming entwined in a wild and glamorous lifestyle seemed far from impending. However, I was neither strongly opposed to nor in favor of having children, so I probably agreed to her proposition of the vasectomy for much the same reason I had decided to ask her to marry me in the first place: Why not? And she was probably naked when she brought up the topic, which tended to gravitate the resolutions to those types of discussions toward her point of view.

A move was seeming more imminent all the time. She was reading the *New York Times* on a daily basis. She had given up on the *Record* altogether. She didn't even give it a cursory check to see if I had written any stories each day, which I invariably had. It is, after all, not a very abundantly staffed paper. So it was much to my relief when one day in May a letter arrived for me bearing an Argentine postmark. I read the letter several times. It seemed like an exciting opportunity: general assignment reporter for the Buenos Aires *Tribune*, "covering political, economic, sporting, and social events for the Argentine capital and the metropolitan area." But overall the letter was very vague in tone. It offered no specifics about pay or housing, nor when I was to begin should I accept the job. "Please contact us as soon as possible," was all the letter said, and provided a phone number.

"I've been offered a job in Argentina," I said matter-of-factly to my wife as I stood before the stove preparing dinner that evening. I tried to keep my tone as casual as possible.

I continued to chop carrots. I had contemplated all afternoon how to put a positive spin on the matter. *I've been offered a job*, I said. Not, *I kept sending my résumé to the Buenos Aires* Tribune *and made follow-up calls ad infinitum and harassed them until they gave me a shot at a low-level position that was vacated when one of their reporters came down with a disabling case of gonorrhea* (I found this last bit out later, in an unsolicited lecture delivered by a coworker regarding in which night clubs to find the "clean girls."). No. *I had been offered a job*. It made me sound like a much sought-after commodity on the international journalism market.

"Oh, really?" she said. There was actually a hint of interest in her voice. "In Argentina?"

"Buenos Aires," I added. Had to slip that in. "You know, Evita Perón, tango, late nights on busy streets, cafés. The Paris of South America, they call it."

Again, I tried to maintain an air of nonchalance while rattling off the list of attractions the city boasted. It was a precarious balance to strike. I tossed these attractions at her as though I had really lived it up when I was there. But I also strived *not* to sound as though I were trying to lure her – which, of course, I was.

But I had been so strapped for cash when I was there – as I would be, now, truth be told – and I was so busy studying that I hadn't lived anything close to a stylish and exorbitantly carefree existence. Nor would I have really wanted to; I was perfectly content – happier, even – hanging out in the working-class suburbs and the little bars and lunch counters that jammed the areas around the train stations.

That's just the way I was. If we were to end up in Boston I would have probably hung around the docks talking to sailors and fish vendors, or in New York staked out a bench in Central Park and passed my spare time reading secondhand, moth-eaten novels and tossing stale popcorn at the pigeons.

"Hmmmm ..." she said and actually put down the *Times* altogether. "You were there before, weren't you? Do you have any pictures?"

I abandoned the dinner preparations, leaving partially chopped carrots scattered across the counter like deer carcasses on Route 225. I eagerly went in search of my copy of *Buenos Aires: A Portrait of Beauty*, a weighty coffee-table tome full of glossy pictures and flowery prose. I did not show her my own photos, most of which were of trains or subways or construction workers having barbecues in the middle of their work sites or priests drinking wine in seedy bars next to prostitutes and transvestites or shoeless, shirtless kids playing soccer in back alleys with balls made of old underwear wrapped in duct tape – the kind of quirky details that had really interested me about the city.

"How beautiful ..." she said, purring over the book, a slight smile on her face and the gears turning almost audibly in her head. She had stopped at a picture of Plaza San Martín. The sun formed a lattice pattern on the ground as it shone through the thick branches of the plaza's stately trees. The photographer had skillfully captured a scene that did not show any homeless people snoozing away on park benches or dog turds ripening about the plaza.

She did not relinquish the book until almost midnight. By then the matter was settled.

•   •   •

The neighborhood welcome wagon at our apartment in Buenos Aires consisted of a butcher and a baker and the deaf landlady, all of whom shared the second floor with us.

"*Buenas tardes*," said the butcher, thrusting a bag of sausages and beef ribs at my wife when she opened the door. She recoiled at the plastic bag's bloody contents. I reached out and accepted the present.

"Why, thank you very much," I said in Spanish, and I meant it.

The meat in Argentina is first-rate (providing the butcher who handles it has thoroughly washed his hands and practiced other hepatitis-deterring behaviors). I considered it quite a privilege to have a butcher for a neighbor. Likewise for the baker, who presented his own offering – a sack crammed with that day's *galleta*, crusty rolls each the size of a person's fist – to my wife. She had less trouble accepting the bread, although she still cast a wary eye on the baker, who was covered in a fine dusting of dirt and flour, and whose lack of teeth made the possibility that he could eat his own *galleta* questionable.

Despite the present, the butcher also invited us over for dinner that evening. I graciously accepted. Then the deaf landlady, virtually shrieking, asked if we would not come over to her apartment to have some tea in the meanwhile and settle the details of the lease, since it was rare that she had the chance to speak with people from abroad, yes this would be a lovely opportunity indeed, perhaps she could even get a little help with her *inglés*, as she'd like to go to America to visit her second cousin someday.

"Tea" turned out to be *maté*, the shredded-up leaves of a plant that looks like tea and grows like tea but whose dried leaves have a stronger, earthier flavor and aroma. "*MAH-tay*," the landlady intoned, molasses-slow and doubly loud for my wife's benefit. "*Vamos a tomar un poco de MAH-tay.* We are going to drink some MAH-tay." She looked pleased with herself for speaking slowly so that my wife, despite the fact she knew no Spanish, might still come to realize through some mystical linguistic osmosis that we would be having a spot of *maté* there in the landlady's kitchen.

The landlady invited us to sit at her battered, thoroughly broken-in table. A sheet of Plexiglas covered the table top; beneath it were faded and cornerless photos of Jesus, the Virgin Mary, various saints, and the Argentine World Cup team. The air in the kitchen was a musty mixture of fish, olive oil, and incense. The blinds were drawn to keep the kitchen dark and as cool as possible – it was January, the peak of summer, and intensely steamy outside. The deaf landlady clattered around in the drawers, slowly withdrawing the *maté* items. Her movements were slow and creaky as she put a kettle of water to boil on the stove and plunked the wooden *maté* cup and its accompanying filtered silver straw before us on the table.

"It looks like a bong or some kind of pipe," hissed my wife, examining the *maté* cup. "What kind of place is this?"

The landlady continued to shout at us about nothing in particular. She told us everything she knew about her second cousin in America who worked in some sort of restaurant, although she wasn't certain which kind, although she suspected there couldn't be that many types of restaurants in America, after all, American food is all basically the same anyway, right?

She scooped the dried, chopped-up *maté* leaves into the drinking vessel. A small cloud of green dust billowed out of the cup with each successive scoopful of *maté*. My wife watched, puzzled and bewildered.

"That really looks like something you could get high off of," she said, frowning at the finely chopped, dusty, dirty-looking green leaves. The *maté* comes mixed with little bits of the plant's stem that give the dried infusion some weight. The strange leaves, coupled with the ornate drinking vessel, lend the ritual an aspect more peculiar than simple high tea.

The landlady plunked a platter laden with stale biscuits and tomato jam before us. "Eat, eat!" she urged us. I dug in, as did the landlady. My wife passed.

The kettle whistled on the stove. The landlady shuffled over to retrieve it, and poured me the first round of *maté*. I drank the steaming liquid through the silver straw. It was hot, but it tasted good and brought back memories. I drained the vessel and returned it to the landlady.

Now it was my wife's turn. The vessel, refilled with water, was passed to her and she took a tentative sip.

"That tastes worse than armpit sweat!" she spat, screwing up her face into a contorted mass of distaste. "And it's hot! I scalded my lips on the metal straw!"

The landlady cackled with glee. "She doesn't like it! The *gringa* has never had *maté* before! Tastes pretty good, doesn't it?"

I laughed with the old woman. My wife glared at me. She passed the next time her turn to drink arose.

After that initial episode, I believe, the eventual outcome of our Argentine foray was inevitable. Since I had yet to show her any of the city, my wife may have still been enchanted with the idea of living in Buenos Aires, but she was instantly and unequivocally less than enchanted with the idea of sharing the city with Argentines.

And the neighbors among whom we lived were true Argentines. They were very amiable and often dropped by the apartment for a little visit that ended up lasting two hours and culminated in an invitation to dinner for the two of us, much to my wife's chagrin.

"These people need to learn to mind their own business!" she shouted defiantly as I hung up the telephone one evening. "I am *not* going to go to that man's apartment downstairs again for dinner. He eats like a swine! Did you see him shovel those beef kidneys down his gullet last time? And his wife was even worse! She drank two entire bottles of wine!"

Thus, I was forced to go unaccompanied to dinner with the neighbors, telling the first of many such lies that placed my wife at home in bed, feeling ill. The ever-thoughtful hosts sent their regrets, along with a sack of grilled intestines and udder, leftovers should she regain her appetite anytime soon.

The neighborhood in which we lived was far from trendy. It was a twenty-minute subway ride downtown, far from any part of the city that might be remotely considered the stomping ground of movers and shakers. As it turned out, we actually lived in the cheap garment district. The area was renowned for illegal immigrants. There were probably as many Paraguayans and Bolivians living around us as Argentines, I learned, but they lived and toiled in basement sweat shops and only ventured out under the cover of night.

My wife seemed amazed by the common-ness of the people among whom we lived. She had undoubtedly expected to be immersed in a wealthy expatriate crowd, a Parisian-style jet-setting bunch with little to do but invent problems and diversions to occupy their time and attention. I don't doubt that she came fully expecting a country club awaiting her, complete with a golf course, spa, riding stables, and little boys in miniature tuxedos to fetch her drinks.

Such a culture did existed in Buenos Aires, in the guise of import magnates and ambassadors, international bankers and computer company executives. They were the primary consumers of the English-language press. But I was there only to write about these people as a meagerly paid reporter for the Buenos Aires *Tribune*, not to live their lifestyle as a card-carrying member of the expatriate aristocracy.

In my spare time, I showed my wife around the city. The places I would just as soon have skipped were those in which she wanted to linger – elegant multistory shopping malls, galleries, jewelry stores, cineplexes, sports bars, anywhere that offered even a superficial resemblance to life in big-city America and the chance to run into English-speaking tourists. She wanted nothing to do with train stations and street vendors and even the cozy little bars that littered the area around our apartment. They were dirty and unhealthy, she claimed. They had bad atmospheres about them that bred disease and contamination and wickedness.

She'd make it a point to steer me to the typical tourist hangouts whenever we were downtown. We'd never miss the Casa Rosada, stylish Calle Florida, or the tourist-trap areas of La Boca, an old Italian quarter that actually had retained much of its charm (though, unfortunately, not in the places my wife wanted to see and be seen). On Sunday afternoons she dragged me out window-shopping for hours around the trendy Recoleta area, home to twin tourist meccas: Hard Rock Cafe and the grave of Evita Perón. There she would invariably point at tourists, engaging in the same guessing game every time.

"There's one. That has to be an American!" she'd shout with glee.

"No, he's Canadian."

"How do you know?"

"I just know. I heard him say something."

"But he speaks English, then! Let's go see him!"

And we would inevitably end up talking to some hapless businessman who had wanted nothing more than to go drink a beer with a familiar label on it and eat a plate of nachos or some other morsel of universal sports-bar cuisine in an attempt to ward off the feeling of culture shock.

"Oh, we just love B.A.," my wife would croon for the benefit of her captive. "It's so beautiful to stroll up and down the streets in the afternoon. And the parks! I was just at the embassy the other day with my friend and I told her, 'You know, I don't think there's any other place in the world where I would be as happy.' And the subway! It's wonderful! You can get almost anywhere! You simply must try it. It's a real cultural experience, especially around rush hour!"

She actually had gone to the embassy one day while I was at work. I came home to find her furious. They had not let her in because she had not taken her passport, nor did she have any appointment, nor any specific business to attend to there. She had imagined the embassy as some sort of social club instead of the enormous, walled bureaucratic compound that it is. Much to her chagrin, one cannot simply pop by the U.S. embassy in Buenos Aires to sip cocktails, nibble crepes, and reminisce about the home front.

I grew to know and like Buenos Aires all over again, and she drifted steadily apart from me as she realized, I think, that she could never like the place. My job would not – at this early stage in my career, nor probably ever – gain us access to the socialite expatriate utopia that she had envisioned. My Spanish got increasingly better, while she refused to learn a single word. At first I tried to at least get her to order her own meals in restaurants. If she did not attempt to place her own order, I said, she shouldn't get to eat. But she made it very clear that she would starve to death, then, thank you very much.

Despite her apparent lack of interest in learning Spanish, I suspect she really did want to learn but found the task daunting. I could tell that she was frustrated at being, or so she felt, a clearly superior individual surrounded by an inferior culture. It was a culture in which not only was she incapable of calling the shots, but one in which she could not even order a glass of water.

One day she informed me that she would be taking a tango class. I offered to go with her. After all, I mused, surely she'd need a partner, and I had always wanted to learn the dance.

"Oh no," she said. "These are one-on-one tango classes. Ralph only offers private, individualized instruction."

Ralph. At least she could have found an Argentine instructor, I suggested. Somebody who might teach the dance with an authenticity that foreigners couldn't quite attain. And more cheaply, too, as Ralph's services, as she quoted them, were not exactly on the frugal side.

"No, no – outsiders are better teachers of the tango," she asserted. "They truly study things. They look at tango objectively. Art must be scrutinized with the eye of an outside observer. Argentines take the tango for granted. It's very typical of them to be surrounded by such great possibilities, yet to settle for such squalor."

I was a bit perplexed by Ralph's sudden entry onto the scene, but I did not press the matter. At least she was pursuing a hobby other than complaining about the filthiness of the city's pigeons and bemoaning the fact that they all seemed to congregate on our building's front stoop, and basically whining about how Buenos Aires was such a dirty city in general. I had long since given up reminding her that almost all big cities are far from spotless, not least of all the cities on her beloved American East Coast.

She was getting increasingly dissatisfied with Buenos Aires, with Argentina, and with life in general. I was occasionally assigned to cover a cocktail party at some foreign embassy, the debut of the latest Hollywood movie to hit South America, or an official visit by a deputy U.S. secretary of state. She often came along with me. Such events kept her stable, but hers was a very precarious stability, at best. When not with me on assignment or downtown prowling through the malls and galleries, she was prone to sit in the living room watching American sitcoms, all the while ranting about what a terrible, despicable country we were living in.

As she sat she would often sip *maté*, a taste which she had strangely acquired. It was the only thing Argentine whose constant presence she could tolerate, although she could only stand it with several heaping teaspoons of sugar per cupful. That is how I found her as I arrived that day with my headache – sipping her *maté*, her blank gaze fixed upon an episode of "Gilligan's Island."

I cleared my throat and asked if she would be coming to the party at the Guyanese embassy with me. Instantly, she leapt to her feet and hurled her *maté* to the ground. The cup hit the floor and tumbled onto its side, splattering damp and steaming olive-green *maté* grounds all over the carpet. She approached me, stopping only when we were face to face.

The Guyanese embassy had to be a shithole, she hissed fervently. After all, wasn't an embassy a reflection of the finest a country had to offer? And what was there in Guyana? She didn't know, herself, never having been there, but it certainly couldn't be very grand. She suspected it was all swamps and jungles and pygmies and tropical diseases and twelve-pound cockroaches that spread vile tropical diseases that made Ebola look like a mild case of hemorrhoids.

And then, building on the theme of nations she didn't really understand but couldn't stand anyway, she launched into her what-I-despise-about-Argentina routine. All they ate was meat, she bemoaned, and disgustingly charred and blackened meat at that – all that fire and woodsmoke from those big grills just absolutely ruined all traces of tenderness and taste, there wasn't a vegetable in sight, all the men made catcalls at her and tried to pinch her in the ass, the taxis smelled funny, the subways smelled funnier, too many people lacked the initiative to go out and get a job and thus ended up begging coins on street corners from people who worked hard to earn everything they had, for God's sake, and the water tasted like corroded batteries, they all thought they were right all the time, they thought they knew English but really spoke it as well as preschoolers with cleft palates and all they could say half-decently were the few snippets they had managed to retain from subtitled American movies and thus went around saying "Run, Forrest, run!" and "I'll be back" *a la* Arnold Schwarzenegger. They had this big concept of the U.S., she said, just because some of them had been to Miami – as far as they were concerned the unofficial capital of both the U.S. and Latin America – and spoke the same language as the people in Miami did and they figured they'd seen the U.S. through and through. Hell, she said, they practically believe Mickey Mouse is sitting in the White House. And they measure distances from Orlando. Oh, Ohio? That's close to Epcot, right? And they all seemed to think they had America figured out really good and they liked to tell us how to run our country and it made no sense whatsoever and perverts that they were they couldn't see this Lewinsky thing ("Lingweeski," they all said, not without a sense of awe and admiration toward the American president) for the grave political matter that it was, they just felt kind of proud of Clinton for getting his knob polished in the Oval Office and at the same time they felt vindicated because they, the Argentines, weren't the only ones who had oversexed and unqualified horny maniacs running their country. Things at home were better, more civilized, just plain *right*. Argentina was backward, filthy, and in general a lousy place to be stuck.

And Guyana, she was convinced, had to be even worse.

But I could tell that, in the quasi-schizophrenic demeanor that permeated all her actions lately, she was excited. She wanted nothing whatsoever to do with the party at the Guyanese embassy, yet simultaneously was dying to go. An embassy party was an embassy party, even if it didn't promise to be the most stunning gala in expatriate-land. So she went off to shower and get ready for the cocktail party. But one thing was certain, I could tell from the distant purposefulness in her gaze: she would arrive intent upon getting very, very drunk, an increasingly frequent pastime for her those days.

And apparently she had decided to toss another element into the volatile cocktail that was her life. The certainty of what had been a lurking – but ignored, or perhaps denied, by me – likelihood hit me then. As I stared at the bottle of birth-control pills, I realized that my wife was quite possibly on the verge of waltzing out of my life in the arms of her tango instructor. It had to be him. And even if it weren't him, it was obviously *somebody*. It made sense, I concluded. After all, of late it hadn't been me too frequently – and the pills would not have been there on account of me, anyway.

I put the container back in her purse and began to get ready for that evening's party, not sure how I would bring up the subject, not even sure if I would broach it at all. I hadn't managed to procure any aspirin yet, either, and the subway still lurched and clattered away against the inside of my head.

·   ·   ·

As soon as we entered the embassy's social room , my wife dodged the platters of hors-d' oeuvres that were making the rounds and headed straight for the bar. I watched as the bartender poured her a tall drink, no ice, then reluctantly took her glass back and filled it completely to the brim at her nagging insistence.

My wife ignored me the entire evening. She divided her time between the bar and people whom she had never met but who she seemed convinced wanted to hear all about what was on her mind at the moment. I chatted with the *Tribune's* wine critic, who was downing gin and tonics like ice water. I asked him if he shouldn't perhaps be sampling some of the Argentine wine that was available. After all, I pointed out, he *was* the wine critic.

"Nah. Argentine wine isn't as great as they think it is," he scoffed dismissively. "Truth be told, this is a dead-end job. The real wine writing is done in France, Italy, California, maybe Chile if you're talking South America. Hell, even New Zealand is more prestigious than Argentina in the world of wine. Here, they think anything that costs more than a dollar and doesn't come out of a box is fine stuff, indeed. Argentine wine tastes like over-inflated nationalism. Trying to tell them it's no good is like trying to tell them the Falklands belong to Britain."

He took an enormous gulp of his gin and tonic. Fat droplets spattered his cheeks; he indiscreetly swiped at these with the sleeve of his shirt. Examining the glass and finding it empty, he plunked it onto the tray of a passing waiter and ordered another. He did not ask in Spanish; instead, he spoke in gin-laced English – loudly and slowly, as though this would overcome any linguistic barriers should the waiter not have been considerate enough to study English in anticipation of the wine critic's arrival at this particular party. Then the wine critic turned back to me.

"I'll just try a little tad of the wine later when I'm good and loosened up. And maybe ask some other people what they think about it, too," he said. "Why don't you go try some? You seem cultured enough. Have a glass or two and tell me what you think."

Then he staggered off before the waiter had returned with his drink.

I don't recall what finally brought me face-to-face with my wife. Given her drunken wanderings around the room, an eventual run-in between us was probably inevitable. She did not see me as she approached and lost half her drink – wine, now – when we collided. She stared into my eyes, not recognizing me at first. Then her face became angry and she jabbed me with her finger.

"I've been thinking," she said with slurred, meticulous sagacity. "Thinking about this place ... this country. About this city. Especially about its monuments. And its people. I've been thinking ... and you know what I've concluded?"

I looked at her without saying anything. Streaks of red wine trailed out of the corners of her mouth like rivulets of blood.

"The city and the people have something in common: They're both fakes!" she hissed at me, forcefully but still restrained. She wasn't yelling; she was whispering very pointedly, all the while maintaining her composure, a peculiar talent of hers.

"This whole city is a fake! The people try to be who they aren't. They think they're cultured Europeans, but they're all just South American fakers. This city is a fraud! They say it's just like Paris, my how lovely, my how original, such a grand city for strolling and absorbing its architectural genius. Well, they stole all their monuments! The racetrack, the congress building, the train stations, that Big-Ben clock, the theater. They're all copies straight from Europe! Except for that Obelisk," she said, naming a tall, slender, pointed monument situated in the middle of Avenida Nueve de Julio.

"That Obelisk is a direct rip-off of the Washington Monument. But it's still a copy. They're all copies and they'll never be great works of anything as long as they're in this miserable city! They're all frauds! Examples of South America trying to be what it isn't, what it never will be."

Her voice was rising now, despite her obvious efforts to maintain it at the scathing whisper with which she had started. The glass seemed too much weight for her to bear; her arm was shaking spasmodically, showering the floor with wine.

"And about that Obelisk," she continued. " The Argentines, they're right in what they say! For once they're not bullshitting. For once they're right about one thing! You know what it looks like? It's a giant penis! It's nothing but a big granite cock! It's the ugliest monument I've ever seen, and our version in the States is just as ugly. One giant deformed gray phallus right in the middle of downtown!"

She was staring straight at me. Her eyes were wide open and bloodshot. She smelled like a winery fermentation tank.

"This place is ugly and it's dirty and I should have never come here! It's one big penis of a city! I'm leaving!" she hissed matter-of-factly. And she turned away from me.

Stammering, I offered to accompany her, but she refused. She'd brave the smelly cab by herself, thank you very much. She left the embassy without her coat and with a bottle of wine under her arm. I was fairly sure that would be the last time I would ever see her; but in reality, I *would* see her again, though by then she would not be my wife.

My wife had walked right out of my life and into the arms of a tango instructor named Ralph. As I watched her leave I was reminded of a time when we were both together at the train station and I had convinced her to chance the contamination she so dreaded and have a snack with me at one of the lunch counters. I had eaten there before; the man who ran the place made the best empanadas, little half-moon pies filled with meat and cheese and other goodies. We sat down at the counter and I ordered us empanadas and beer.

"You know," I said appreciatively to him as he handed me my change, "these are very good empanadas."

He nodded with conviction, as though I had verified what he had already held as the unshakable truth. "Thank you. The empanada is a thing of great beauty. Tell me these are not the best empanadas you have ever eaten."

"They are. They really are."

"You're just saying that ..."

"No, really. These empanadas don't belong in a train station. They're far better than the ones they sell in the fancy places downtown."

He told me that he agreed, that his dream was to someday open an empanada store. I ordered another empanada – cheese and onion, my favorite – and asked for the recipe.

"Are you kidding? You probably have money. You'll open your own store."

By now my wife was getting impatient. She had made a halfhearted attempt to nibble on her ham and cheese empanada and had decided it was not worth eating. It had been the sixth or seventh variety she had tried since coming to Argentina, none of which had seemed to suit her. She always looked at the empanadas with a mix of disdain and fear, as though they had been rolled around out on the street before being served to her, or as though there were a chance that cockroaches and fruit flies might come barraging out one of the little pies should her teeth penetrate too deeply. I saw the empanada vendor glancing dubiously her way as she likewise kept her distance from this latest specimen. She, in turn, glared at me.

I did not think about my wife and took a long gulp of beer. "I've tried to cook them at home," I told the man across the counter, "but I haven't had much luck. I tried and tried and tried, and finally got them to come out using the ready-made crusts. But making the dough from scratch was a problem."

He considered this for a moment. "You're probably trying too hard. Not thinking like an Argentine. You Yankees are all too analytical. You have to not care. Don't even think about the possibility that they might not turn out. And don't worry about them being perfect when they do come out. Just cook them. Drink some wine, turn on the radio, make them like you don't care, put them in the oven, and drink some more wine for good measure. It never fails."

At the apartment that night after the embassy party, I was greeted by silence. My wife was gone. Her dresser drawers were dangling open, and clothes lay strewn about the floor like detritus after a storm.

The bottle of wine with which she had left the Guyanese embassy was sitting on the kitchen table. I turned on the radio and poured myself a glass. The wine was very good. I'd have to recommend it to the wine critic, I thought.

A sudden notion seized me, and I had soon fished out my recipe for empanadas.

Make them like you don't care, he had said. And I didn't care. I poured myself another glass of wine and fished in the cupboards for the flour. I began to brown some ground beef on the stove. Meanwhile, I mixed the flour with water, salt, and eggs and kneaded the whole mixture on the counter.

When the dough was pleasantly malleable but still firm, I began to rip off small pieces and flatten them out into little circles with a rolling pin. My wife had watched me perform these actions before. She would position herself behind me, leaning against the kitchen door frame, *maté* or alcohol – sometimes both – in hand. She would cluck her tongue incessantly, almost gleefully, it seemed. It always felt as though she were trying to cast failure upon me with her presence.

I had another glass of wine. It tasted even better than it had before. I really would have to recommend it to the wine critic. I examined the label. It was even of Argentine origin. He would be surprised. Or, perhaps more likely, he would accuse me of having poor taste in wine.

The meat was cooked, so I spooned a little bit onto each one of the dough circles. Then I gently folded each of the empanadas in half, turned up their sides like miniature pie crusts, and crimped the outside edges with a fork.

Two dozen unbaked half-moons paraded across the counter. I drained the wine bottle and put the empanadas in the oven. Then I went off in search of more wine. I retrieved a bottle from the hall closet, uncorked it, and poured myself another glass. And I waited.

As I drank the wine I thought about my wife. I imagined her dancing a tango with Ralph beneath the Obelisk. Argentines did often joke that the monument looked like an enormous concrete phallus looming over downtown

Buenos Aires. And based upon her comments from that evening, my wife had finally come around to their way of thinking on at least that count.

I pictured her being swept and spun about by Ralph, who in my mind bore a strong resemblance to Harrison Ford. They glided sensually around the perimeter of the Obelisk. My wife lifted her head back with delight, exposing the nape of her neck, which rippled with occasional peals of pleasureful laughter. And in between the laughter she let loose with gleeful-sounding barrages against Argentina and everything Argentine. The insults floated on the air like poison-tipped feathers. The two of them swirled and spun, performing all the difficult steps of the tango with expert precision and uncanny, almost instinctual coordination. Their movements were unified, comfortable, coupled.

But I found myself undisturbed by this bizarre figment of my imagination. I let it continue to unfold in my mind. I watched her dancing, laughing, and complaining beneath the Obelisk as it thrust upward into the nighttime sky.

Then the oven timer buzzed, wrenching me from my thoughts. I went to retrieve the empanada-laden baking sheets from the oven. The empanadas were flaky and golden-brown, with spicy meat-vapors steaming from within them. My mouth began to water, and I reached for one.

They were the best empanadas I had ever attempted. Not quite perfect, but pretty damn close.

hanging by a thread

L et's say you've been afflicted with major depression for the last ten years and you're finally coming to grips with that fact. Your life thus far has been something akin to being gay and being closeted, as much from others as from yourself. You're subconsciously aware that there's something fundamental – something about the way you look at the world versus the way society says you should look at the world, the way most people *do* look at the world – that troubles you. But you've always written it off as a personality flaw or a construct of your imagination or bored ingratitude at having a run-of-the-mill, middle-class life, free from significant hardships. A life millions of people the world over, you tell yourself, would be profoundly grateful to be able to live.

•   •   •

"I see. Yes. That's all very *interesting*, and you may be *getting* at something there," the psychologist said. He had this disconcerting tendency to accentuate semi-random words, as though delivering a lecture to a four-year-old. "But you seem to be *missing* something very *fundamental*: anger. Wouldn't you say that you're a very *angry* person?"

"Well, I don't know that I'd classify it as 'anger.' And it's not just one thing or emotion," I said. "It's more subtle and more pervasive than that."

"But you said yourself that sometimes you *hate* yourself. Wouldn't you call that *anger*?"

"In a way. But that's not what I mean …"

The frustration was mounting inside me. I'd done everything the pamphlets said. Accepting you were depressed was the biggest hurdle, they assured. Not nearly enough people even took the first step. The literature made it sound like a walk in the park after that. And the problem was, once I accepted it, it was impossible to hide behind all the false pretenses I'd created over the years. The incapacitating sadness was engulfing me.

"I think, perhaps, that you don't just hate *yourself*. I'd venture a guess that you hate *everything*. I think you have very serious anger-management issues."

I was deflating like an inner-tube being sat upon by a brontosaurus. He saw me as just another angst-prone twentysomething kid whose girlfriend broke up with him or who was bummed out because all his friends were getting married.

"I see a very *angry* person sitting in front of me. I see someone who's pissed off at the *world*," he said. "I wish I could take a *picture* of your *face*. You look like those boxers do when they scowl at each other when they line up for weigh-ins. *That's* the kind of look you have on your face."

He seemed genuinely pleased with himself. He bridged his fingers and looked through his spectacles at me, gazing down his prominent nose.

"Well, we seem to have run out of *time* for this week," he said. "So why don't we just pick up here next week?"

"But …" I stammered. "I … I … I really think there might be something chemically wrong with me. Some sort of imbalance. Look at the background history I filled out. There's been at least one suicide in my family, a history of mental illness, a history of drug and alcohol abuse …"

The obvious pieces that had taken me so long to fit together came spilling out of my mouth in a desperate torrent.

"You've hung in *this* long. Another week or two won't hurt anything," he said, obviously convicted to the roll-up-your-sleeves-and-delve-to-the-bottom-of-your-Freudian-complexes school of thought.

"Can't I at least get a psychiatric referral?"

"Do you want to be taking a *pill* for the rest of your *life*?"

"If that's what I have to do, then, yes."

"You know, you're not just going to be able to take a *pill* and make everything *better* overnight."

"But I've tried therapy by itself, and it was just a superficial solution. I realize that therapy is *part* of the solution," I pleaded. "I know that ..."

•   •   •

Not being gay, I've never had the experience of telling the people I love that I long to be with other men. That I will never be able to provide my parents with biological grandchildren. I've never had to see the reactions of my poker buddies who delight in telling tit jokes or my friends at work who are constantly trying to fix me up with women they know.

But a friend of mine who is gay told me about how he agonized for more than a year about how to tell his mother. He'd met the man he wanted to spend the rest of his life with and he wanted her to accept this and understand this. On more than one occasion he came close, only to bring up some inane subject or another ("How's yoga class, Mom?") at the last minute. And when she would ask about single life in the big city, he'd give some non-response or another: "Well, you know, it has its ups and downs."

When he finally did tell her, it was on the spur of the moment. He was visiting for the weekend and they were watching an Adam Sandler movie on television. Maybe it was the penis jokes, he said. Whatever it was, something spilled the crucial final drops into his already swelling reservoir of deniability.

He turned to his mother and said, "Listen, Ma, I'm gay."

How else, in the end, do you really say such a thing?

Her response came so quickly, he told me, that it was apparent she'd long expected the topic to arise. First, she dropped her bowl of popcorn onto the dog's tail. Then she shrieked.

"No! No! That can *not* be. You're wrong. No, no, Michael. You don't know what you're saying."

"But Mom …"

She got up and left the room. From the kitchen, she continued the litany. "No. No. Listen to yourself. No."

And that was it. No amount of prodding had yet been able to convince her to consider the topic again.

"I should've been upset with her," he told me later. "And I was, somewhat. But more so, I was mad at myself. I somehow hadn't managed to impart the importance of this to her. The failure was mine."

And that's pretty much how I felt as I emerged from the clinic, the universe swirling around me, the gravity of my failure combining with the already enormous burden of my existence.

My hopes toppled down upon me, entombing me beneath their weight. For a decade, I hadn't known – or hadn't admitted – that I was standing in the shadow of the Leaning Tower of Pisa. And now that I'd finally worked up the nerve to look skyward, here it came, tumbling down to crush me like a prune.

•   •   •

When put into words, it sounds melodramatic: *the already enormous burden of my existence.* Emotions are hard enough to describe, let alone emotions as particular and distinct as those that accompany major depression. Words are insufficient to capture the feelings; even more insufficient than they are to describe, say, love or hate. Those, after all, are universal emotions. Everyone at least has some idea of what you're talking about. Trying to tell someone who's not depressed about what it's like is like being blind and trying to convey to the sighted how you perceive the world.

The literature says it as truthfully as it can be said: in clinical terms. But while accurate, these descriptions fall far short of what it's like to be inside the vortex.

Crying spells. Lengthy periods of sadness or feeling "blue." Difficulty sleeping or sleeping too much. Lack of energy. Changes in appetite. Worry. Anxiety. Indifference or feelings of futility. Irritability. Questioning one's self-worth. Lack of concentration. Indecisiveness. Inability to experience pleasure. Withdrawal. Recurring thoughts of death. Contemplation of suicide.

When you're depressed, every moment seems absolutely futile and full of an awesome, impending feeling of finality. And what's worse is this finality repeats itself. Day. After day. After day.

City streets in the dark, with the lights on inside the houses. Twenty-four-hour diners. Cigarette butts mounding out of ashtrays. The sludgy remnants of whiskey sours. Cornfields by moonlight. Buses idling against bruised November skies. People standing hand-in-hand beneath a theater's marquee. An old man hobbling through a department store all by himself. Lighthouses. Empty swing sets. Children playing baseball. Snow-covered sidewalks illuminated by street lamps. The fragile rustle of fallen leaves beneath your feet. Train tracks disappearing into the distance. Families ice-skating on a frozen pond at dusk.

You feel like you're not a part of anything in the world, like you don't belong, like you'll never belong no matter how much you strive. But conversely, the whole world seems imbued by a profoundly human sadness that touches you, pierces you to the core.

There's this poem by Pablo Neruda where the narrator keeps saying how he's tired of being a man. Tired of existing, essentially. It's called "Walking Around," and that's really all the narrator does. Kind of ambles aimlessly from place to place, questioning the worth of his existence.

At the end, he's talking about passing through all these places: offices, shops and, finally, patios. And in the patios there's clothing hung: "underwear, towels and shirts that cry/slow, dirty tears."

I don't know whether or not Neruda's actually talking about depression. But once you realize you've got it – or it's got you – you tend to see depression everywhere. Things you were unexplainably drawn to before suddenly seem to possess this eye-popping sense of clarity. *Of course! That's what they're talking about!* you think. Though you know that you're probably just projecting.

For me it was Modest Mouse songs, Raymond Carver stories and Ansel Adams photographs. These, among other things both artistic and ordinary, became emblematic of my infinite loneliness.

•   •   •

"Want to hear about a new cocktail I invented?" I asked.

"Probably not ..." my girlfriend replied. Her voice was as full of fear as mine was of scorn and self-loathing.

"It's called the 'Dead End.' The ingredients are a bottle of vodka, ninety-six cold and sinus caplets and a handful of muscle relaxants. Directions: Go out to the woods on a cold night, find a knee-deep puddle of water, remove all clothing, sit down in the water, mix, drink – and die."

"Oh God. Oh God. Just *stop*. Please just stop! Stop doing this to me! Stop doing this to yourself!" Tears drowned her end of the telephone. "I think you should go to the emergency room."

"No. I can't do that."

"Well you need to do something. I can't take this."

I was pushing her away. It was what I most wanted; yet, at the same time, it was what I feared the most. Here was this human being who was willing to let herself be subjected to long-distance torment for the sake of me getting better. But the closer we grew, the more I'd always treated her as I treated myself: with derision and distaste and self-destructive circular logic.

"You don't understand," I said.

"Well I'm trying to. But you won't let me."

"Because you don't care."

I couldn't handle the idea of someone caring about me. After all, I couldn't even fathom caring about myself.

"I do care," she said. "I care about you very much. I don't like to see you hurting."

"Then why don't you help me? Why are you so far away?"

Again, the tears.

"You're the one who moved," she sobbed. "You're the one."

I'd left her behind two months before, moved from Florida to Massachusetts. Things were going no better for me up north when at last I had a moment of clarity. How many times had I moved before, fled one place for another in the hopes that things would be better there, certain that location and circumstances were the sources of my discontent? (Ten, at least.) I was convinced that things would change in the new place, that things would be different, that I would feel more comfortable, feel more a part of the world. But I finally realized that my very existence was the fundamental thing that troubled me. And move as I might, it always seemed to come along for the ride.

And this time, the luggage seemed an even bigger burden than before.

•   •   •

When you get down to it, I guess support groups are really about getting you to support yourself – while providing this atmosphere that exudes comfort and makes getting better a group effort, as much as is possible with personal recovery. After all, you alone must define your destiny; that's a pretty simple concept that takes a lot of getting used to when you really think about it.

Shortly after I got rebuked by the psychologist, I mustered the energy to attend a session of a local support group. It was held on a Wednesday night in a basement conference room in the local hospital. It was for people with all sorts of mood disorders, mainly depression and manic-depression and anxiety attacks.

We shared our burdens beneath the fluorescent lights while we sipped lukewarm coffee from paper cups. We started off by introducing ourselves. Then we shared our diagnosis, if we had one. Then we said how our week had gone.

I hadn't been diagnosed yet. But I told them how I felt. And the rest of the men and women in the circle nodded their heads. And they understood.

"My week ... has been ..." sputtered one man in coveralls. "Oh man, it's been awful."

And he sobbed.

Another woman had been at her job for a month. She hadn't held a job that long in five years.

One man just got visitation rights to see his infant son.

After the introductions, it was pretty much an open forum.

One woman refused to speak. Physically could not speak, though it appeared by the agonized expression on her face that she was struggling with herself so as to be able to do so.

We talked about regrets. We talked about recovery. People discussed the medications they were taking, the medications they had taken, the medications they'd heard were worth taking. They discussed doctors.

I mentioned the psychologist.

"Oh my God – you went to him?" one woman said. "Man, I feel sorry for you. He's a prick."

One woman recommended a doctor, a family practitioner.

"She's not a psychiatrist," she said. "But any medical doctor can diagnose you and prescribe medicine. And she has personal experience with these things, which counts for a lot."

It made me feel strong – and at the same time, secure and protected – to sit and talk to these people. These depressed people and manic-depressive people and chronically anxious people. There people like me.

Afterwards, we went to a diner and ate sandwiches and drank coffee and smoked cigarettes. And relished the idea that we were among friends who understood that they would never really understand us – and that that notion was okay with all concerned.

·   ·   ·

The doctor was about forty. She was motherly without being unprofessional. Concerned.

"I understand what this is like," she said. "You've done the right thing in seeking help."

And this time, I believed that. I really believed it.

·   ·   ·

After that visit with the doctor, I started taking a pill each day. I hadn't been quite sure what to expect. I half imagined losing my personality entirely, getting something akin to a lobotomy in a bottle. But instead, I just felt … *regulated*. Calmer. I slept more normally. I didn't ignore my hunger pangs. I felt capable of happiness. I was sad once in a while, of course – but my emotions drifted back to middle ground in due time.

I was beginning to feel okay – with myself, with the world, with myself as it fit into the world. For better and worse, I felt *okay* – for the first time in a decade.

·   ·   ·

"Things will be different, now," I told my girlfriend. "They *are* different now."

"I've … I've heard that too many times," she said. "I was just hanging in there until I was sure you wouldn't kill yourself."

"But please …" I begged.

"No, I can't," she said. "I don't think I can ever get over the things you said to me."

"But *try*," I said. "Please."

"No," she said. "It wouldn't be fair to either of us. My heart's broken. It's going to take a really, really long time to fix it."

"I'm sorry," I said. "So sorry."

"Goodbye," she said. "Goodbye."

I didn't blame her. And I *did* feel sad – for a long, long time. But I didn't plunge into an abyss with no foreseeable end. That was a positive, if bittersweet, change.

•   •   •

I told the support group about the breakup the next Wednesday. They responded with stories of their own.

One man lost a wife. Another lost two wives. Another cancelled his wedding on the night before it took place. One woman lost custody of her kids. Another woman's husband started beating her because she "wouldn't snap out of her funk," as he said by way of justification.

More than a few took to drinking or drugs or both, which led to their own problems, chemical, legal and heartbreak-wise.

•   •   •

As effective as it is in many respects, there was a fundamental dilemma to taking a pill to "correct" the way I thought. The medicine achieves an internal equilibrium – but the symbols, the world, remain the same. The tendency to get sad at everything is gone. But being sad, disconcerted, outcast – that's the only sensory experience it seemed I'd ever known.

It was like being transported to another country, where people still do the things people do back home – eat, sleep, work, go out, fall in love, have families, entertain themselves – but in a manner that's every bit as foreign as it is familiar.

•   •   •

"I have a date," I told the support group. "This Friday. It's a girl I know from work."

We always ended each session with a positive thought, something we were feeling good about or looking forward to. I told them how I had been self-confident enough to pick up on her flirtation and ask her out to dinner outright. Usually I'd say something stupidly blunt ("So is this a date?") as we sat there having drinks or eating dinner, unsure of myself as I was. But this was definitely a date. And I was looking forward to it.

All around the circle, my friends smiled at me and wished me well.

•   •   •

"Didn't you want any wine?" she asks. We have just sat down to dinner.

"Well, that would be nice," I say. "But I can't. I'm taking this medicine ... It makes me get drunk really fast."

"Oh?" she says. She doesn't ask what kind of medicine. But the kindness in her eyes lets me know that it's okay if I tell her. And okay if I don't.

"Yeah ... I actually ..." I say, debating whether or not to tell. "I was depressed. Major depression. For something like ten years."

"Oh ..." she says.

"So I have to admit, I was a little scared even asking you out. This is my first date since I started trying to get help."

"Did you still have a girlfriend then?"

"I did. In Florida. But I haven't seen her again since I left. We're still friends," I say, "though it's a little delicate right now. Understandably so. That's why I was nervous about starting to date again … I mean, I'm not a bad person, I don't think. But things got out of hand there at the end. I said things and did things that I never would've thought I was capable of saying and doing. Mean, mean things. And I'm really, really sorry about them."

My candor surprises me. I half expect her face to sour or even expect her to get up and walk out. For a moment, the old fear grips me again. That I can't get anything right. That I will never belong. That I am destined to be alone even from myself.

But she stays put. She sips her wine and smiles a reassuring smile at me.

"So what's it like?" she asks. "Getting better, I mean?"

"It's … different," I say. "Hard, sometimes."

Things spill from my brain and out of my mouth. How I still sometimes crave gray skies and a six-pack in the morning. How it feels weird to just sit down and read a book on a Saturday afternoon and feel … ordinary. Wonderfully, dreadfully *ordinary*.

"I miss the sadness sometimes," I say, fighting the urge to cry. "I miss everything."

Missing the sadness is like the phantom limbs amputees say they feel. But they've got proof – sensations floating in the thin air where an actual arm or leg used to be. What do I have but memories of memories?

She reaches across the table and clutches my hands in hers.

"It's okay," she says, looking at me with her soft green eyes. "You'll be okay. You *are* okay."

And my hands return her squeeze and I smile, warily but optimistically.

And I believe her.

tres maneras de mentir

"*H*ay tres maneras de mentir. There are three ways to tell a lie," the man in the all-night café told me with a pensive crease upon his face. "You can tell it badly, you can tell it well, and you can tell it in such a manner that it was never a lie at all, that it is crafted so profoundly and so skillfully that it becomes the instant and undeniable truth."

That's what he said to me as he sat smoking thoughtfully, one hand wrapped around his dainty espresso cup and several empty whiskey glasses scattered on the table in front of him.

To this day I'm still not sure if I believe him. I'm not even certain that he existed in the first place.

the woman i'm seeing

The woman I'm seeing has this son. She doesn't try to hide the fact that I stay the night. It kind of bothers me. But she's good in bed (ravenous, at times, like at any minute the opportunity to have sex will go away forever, evaporate).

In the morning, she walks around in her underwear. Right in front of the kid. I can't do that.

The kid, in the morning he narrates his bowel movements. First he'll run all around the apartment, then do circles in the kitchen, then run back to his bedroom, then run into the bathroom, all the while saying, "The pressure's too much! The flood gates are gonna burst! It'll be a catastrophe!"

Then the bathroom door slams. But the narration continues:

"Here it comes, ladies and gentlemen, the one you've been waiting for!"

I try not to smile.

"I'm so sorry," she says.

"Don't be," I reply, making it sound as though putting up with this is a grand concession on my part.

Truth be told, I like him a lot better than I like her.

without even a hangover

to call my own

Maybe if I were more of an asshole, the girls I really want to date wouldn't want me so much for a close friend. And since it would be really hard for me to be *too* much of an asshole, maybe the asshole-me would still be nice enough that the girls I really want to date would want to hook up. You know, instead of just being friends.

But it never works out that way.

So I'd gone back to my old college town for the weekend to have some beers and see some friends. It seemed like I hadn't set foot in Ohio for years, even though it had only been five months since I graduated and moved on to the soulless, superficially sunny state of Florida. But I guess five months can be a lot in a college town when you consider that eight semesters comprise the entire universe of a typical college experience – eight gigantic, endlessly brief semesters that each bring an added dose of change and romance and friendship and drama and subject matter and syllabi and broadened horizons and new drink specials downtown.

I lost track of the beers that Friday night on that October weekend when I went back to school for the first time. Thirteen, I think. Actually, eleven beers and two whiskey sours. I think. First I went to see Mark Ritchie at the Golden Quail where he bartended. The first beer was on him, the second on the guy at the end of the bar who'd asked me if I might move down some so my cigarette smoke wouldn't get in his face. (After the guy had left, Mark apologetically told me he's something of an anal-retentive dickhead. But hey, he bought me a beer. He can't be that bad.) Then Mark accidentally – or maybe not – mixed two whiskey sours instead of two amaretto sours. Never one to decline an opportunity to help out, I happily disposed of the mistakes.

Then I left the Quail and drank a beer with my buddy Bob while he did his laundry. Next, two beers at the Hayloft with Lisa and her boyfriend. They complained about the state of affairs at the student newspaper. Same old shit as always, Lisa said – which made me miss the place even more. Then it was over to Mark's apartment. He was just off work. His girlfriend was over and so was our friend Raquel. All three of them were starting out their last year of school.

Raquel hooked up a lot, but never with me. But it wasn't for a lack of trying on my part. When I say "trying," I don't mean overt, shameless flirting and ogling. The fact she was a good friend kept me from lusting too much over her body. But when I put the whole package together in my head – brains and bubbly personality, plus an unspoken, in-the-background appreciation for her butt and bust – she always seemed like great girlfriend material.

And I can't really pull off overt and shameless flirting unless I'm really drunk and talking to a girl who I either don't know or don't have any kind of respect for – or both. So really, when I say "trying," I really just mean wishful thinking. But very *forceful* wishful thinking.

We went to a party that was supposed to be cool. But it was full of rich kids dressed to a '70s theme none of us had been informed of. They were all listening to rap music and drinking Zima and keg beer. Raquel was interested in hooking up with the host of the party, a guy she'd obsessed over, on and off, for years. But the host had already downed a bottle of gin by the time we got there. He was more interested in telling us how drunk he was – he started at four that afternoon, man! – than in talking to Raquel and appraising her outfit and appreciating the fact that it took her a whole hour to get dressed.

We each drank a beer and laughed at the shirtless, fortysomething neighbor who was drinking vodka out of a coffee mug and staggering back and forth between his apartment and the college party. He stumbled twice for every successful step he took. Then I went to the bathroom, intentionally pissed on the toilet seat and stole a Zima from the refrigerator. And we went back into town and drank beers at the Zenith.

On the ride to town, Raquel drove and smoked three furious cigarettes and said what a lousy party it was. And how men were complete assholes, total wastes of time.

The closest I ever got to hooking up with Raquel was once at this bar downtown when we were both drunk and sitting at the same table. She was to my left, holding my hand under the table, and this girl to my right was also holding my hand. The girl to my right pulled my head toward her and kissed me. So there went any chances with Raquel that night. I ended up going home with the other girl. We both passed out on her bed, still wearing our shoes.

I teased Raquel as we drank our beers at the Zenith after we left the '70s party. I usually tease her; it's the closest thing to flirting that I can bring myself to accomplish. She's fully aware of her charm and is capable of flirting far more overtly than I am. She's capable of flirting with me, even, though she would deny she's flirting. That's the problem. We've got some sort of mismatched wavelengths going on or something. Failure to interpret each other's signals correctly. Or maybe we're still not entirely sure what signals we really want to send. Or maybe we're not comfortable with the signals we know we *should* send. Or maybe I'm just hopelessly, misguidedly obsessive.

So we were at the Zenith, passing a cigarette back and forth and her fingertips brushed against mine. She smiled kind of slyly and told me that I hadn't better *dare* try to hold her hand. So I started to tease her.

"Remember that time at the Cornerstone Cafe when you were drunk and you were holding my hand?" I asked.

"I wasn't holding *your* hand. You were holding *my* hand," she rebutted. "And then you went home with that other girl."

I had to take a big gulp of beer while I dissected the statement. I *had* reached for her hand. I'll admit, I was probably doing more holding than she was. But she wasn't *not* holding. She hadn't pulled her hand away. And I wasn't overpowering her hand. Which means she was squeezing back.

I dissected that. Then I belatedly realized that what she had said just then and the way she had said it – "I wasn't holding *your* hand." – hurt my feelings. The accumulated weight of the delayed realization made it sting even more.

Another perplexing realization hit me about the time I finished swallowing the mouthful of beer: She had brought up the other girl. Which meant ... or maybe it didn't ... or maybe it did. Too late, anyway, as I'd finished my gulp of beer and it was time for a response.

"Whatever ..." was all I could manage. *Way to go.* All I could do then was take another drink.

And I did actually ask her out once. We had a conference over coffee after I'd all *but* asked her out, kind of said asking-her-out type things in a teasing, sarcastic way. Though we both knew what I was talking about. We both knew I was completely serious. So she said we should go have some coffee and talk. We drank coffee and smoked cigarettes and talked and I feigned disinterest in whether she'd want to go out with me or not, an *it's-really-not-that-big-of-a-deal-just-thought-it-might-be-worth-thinking-about* kind of facade. And she pretty much told me that I was too good of a friend for her to want to date. I was *too nice* to date. Some bullshit like that.

And then she bemoaned her inability to find someone who she wanted to commit to and who wanted to commit to her and who wasn't, like, an absolute asshole.

I smoked another cigarette and tried to maintain the facade.

At the Zenith, Mark and his girlfriend were talking to some people they knew and Raquel and I had a corner of the bar to ourselves.

"You know," I said, "in a way I was scared to come back this weekend. In case I'd run into Jill. Even though she moved back to Michigan."

Or at least she *said* she had. As far as Jill was concerned, I would never again be able to tell what was true with any degree of certainty. Which is why I didn't really think about the matter that much.

"Do you guys still talk?" Raquel asked.

"Hell, no. I never want to see her again. Ever."

"So you guys are done, then?"

"Hell, yes. She's insane. Absolutely insane and completely mentally unstable. And I don't just say that out of spite. She was truly the most messed-up person I have ever known."

And that was no exaggeration. Not by a long shot.

"What did she do?" she asked.

"Oh, you don't want to hear about it," I said. But I knew she did want to hear about it.

I really wanted Raquel's attention and her pity (and her body) more than I wanted to dwell on my own troubles. I don't really have hang-ups. Or, if I do, I'd like to think they're still firmly embedded in my subconscious.

"Of course I want to hear about it. What did she do?"

So I told her. The telling took several minutes, a cigarette and half a beer. When I was through with the story, Raquel's face had softened and her eyes were wide. I'll admit, it's a good story to tell; not the best to have lived through, though. I'd rather not get into it now. Suffice it to say that it involves general neurosis, distrust, halfheartedly slit wrists, threats of more effective suicide attempts, a feigned pregnancy, an abortion that never happened, and subsequent stalking stretching from Ohio to Florida – none of the aforementioned things on my part.

"I am so sorry. I'm so sorry you had to go through all that." She shook her head slowly back and forth, bewildered.

"Well, apparently I deserved it. I must've."

I didn't really think I deserved it, though. No one deserved to be put through that shit. And I think I can objectively say that I'm really *not* a bad guy. I especially don't go around doing things to people that I know will hurt their feelings and damage their psyches. So, no, I did *not* deserve to have exactly that done to me.

"No you did *not* deserve it!" Raquel seconded what I already thought but wouldn't admit to her because I wanted her pity. "And you know that. *Especially* you didn't deserve it. You're nothing but nice to people. And you never could have seen that coming. I mean, I knew she had some issues. But I thought it was just mild insecurity like all girls have."

"So did I. Now I'm kind of scared of girls." Which wasn't true. Not exactly. I really wanted to get laid at that point in my life. *Needed* to get laid, to disprove to myself that the last girl to ever find me desirable would also be the most deceitful and mentally unstable girl I'd ever known.

"Maybe I'm destined to only be involved with crazy chicks."

"You liked me before you liked her," she said. I was surprised she would even mention that. "And I'm not crazy."

But you didn't like me back – what I should have said but didn't. Instead I just shrugged and drained my beer.

"It really pisses me off," I said. At least, it pisses me off when I think about it. Infuriates me, even. But I usually don't think about it. Maybe that will become impossible, even counterproductive, as time goes on. Or maybe not.

"It makes me feel as though I wasted my entire senior year," I said. "Part of me just wishes I could do it over again." Though I knew that such a wish was rather lame and childish and melodramatic and even a bit sad, logic could not obstruct the false nostalgia that had overtaken me.

"I'm *so* sorry," Raquel said. And I couldn't help but remember that she would occasionally seem jealous of the fact Jill was dating me.

We changed the subject then. It wasn't a very smooth subject change. But it was so necessary that smoothness or lack thereof didn't matter. We ordered more beers, so that helped.

And soon the bartender was yelling at everybody to go the hell home, that they were closed.

We stood for a few moments on the sidewalk next to her car. Mark and his girlfriend had already gone back to Mark's apartment. The nighttime October air was cold and clear. The wind off the river nipped along the avenue. We clutched our arms to ourselves and walked in place to keep warm. I looked at her. She looked at me. We paced a moment more.

When Raquel and I hugged, we both held on a little longer than we should have.

But if she were ever pressed on the matter, I'm sure she'd laugh and be indignant and blame it all on me, just like that night she held my hand under the table at the Cornerstone Cafe.

Then I stumbled down the street to Mark's apartment. He and his girlfriend were watching TV. I had one more beer – drink number thirteen, I guess, though I don't remember for sure – and we ate some potato chips. Then I went to sleep in what he calls his "guest chambers," really just a walk-in closet with a musty mattress on the floor. The closet smelled of old socks, stale beer, and unrequited love.

I woke up early and put on my shoes and quietly left the apartment. I didn't have a hangover. It was bright and crisp outside, just the kind of autumn weather I'd hoped to encounter. It was still in the 90s every day in Florida, which added to the superficial sense of seediness and debauchery that seemed to hang about the state. Autumn to me always seemed a genuine kind of season. Seas of strip malls, Disney World, and rainstorms the temperature of bath water are *not* my idea of genuine.

Autumn always makes me nostalgic, melancholy in a hopeful kind of way. New possibilities emerging from the ashes of the spent summer. Something like that. And while a remote, logical corner of my brain was questioning the worth of wanting to re-live things that weren't all that healthy or great or profound to begin with, the absence of a hangover inclined me to be even more wistful and nostalgic as I walked the downtown Saturday streets of the small Ohio town where I used to go to college.

No hangover. No homework. Just an endless day with nothing to do but smoke cigarettes and try to forget the curves of her body and the too-long embrace that didn't last nearly long enough. I almost convinced myself that it really *was* better for me to not be an asshole and us to just be friends. Almost.

Meanwhile, the rustle of brittle leaves nearly brought me to tears.

years ago

Kids these days, the old man says and shakes his head in mock disgust. He's not as bitter about these things as his wife is. He can still smile as he says it and still happily go about his life for the rest of the day without worrying himself about the degeneration of Argentine culture and civilization. But when he does think about it, it gets him worked up nonetheless. Back in Spain it was never this way, he says. Back in Spain there was no time for screwing around. Back in Spain you had to work to stay alive. Early to bed, early to rise it was in Spain. From the time you were old enough to scatter grain for the chickens. And you kept working as you kept growing. If you were a boy you went to the fields or you went to the factory or you went to sea. And if you were a girl you went to someone's house for *servicio domestico*. And if you were a girl but better in the fields than with a broom, you went to the fields, by God. His sister, he says, had arms like a man's and a face as sun-browned as leather after years of work. In Spain, to go to school was an honor and if you went to school it was your duty to the ones who had to stay at home to do your best and study hard. But not these days. Not in this country. Now the kids sleep all day. They stay out late and can't get up in the morning. They go to the bars, they go to the *discotecas* and use up all their energy and are like corpses in the morning. And if they drag themselves to school, they sleep through class.

Eyelids made of concrete. And how they drink! Beer and beer and more beer, always down on the corner or in the cantina with a bottle of Quilmes. Nothing better than water, the old man says. Nothing like a cold, clear glass of pure *agua*. And back in Spain, when they didn't drink water, they drank wine. The best wine in the world, flavored with the Spanish earth. None of this joke-of-a-wine that the Argentines think is as good as liquid gold. And if you did stay up too late at the café and didn't go to bed until the rooster was beginning to stir, that was your own problem. You just had to rise with the rooster nonetheless. Kids these days don't even know what a rooster is. They don't even know the chicken on their plates was alive and clucking not too long ago. If, that is, they even eat chicken. These days it's hard to tell what they'll eat. Pizzas and *hamburguesas* and *papas fritas*, sweets and cookies. They don't want stew, they don't like garbanzos, they won't touch paella, squid and tripe are slimy and gross. In Spain, he says, we ate what we were served and considered ourselves lucky. None of this I want a snack or I don't like squash. In Spain you were in heaven if you had a pinch of sugar to sweeten your coffee in the morning and a stale rind of bread to dunk in it. Things were different then, he says. Things were very different, indeed.

youth, eternal

On Saturday nights we sat by the river's edge among the mangroves, feeling as though we were bound to live forever. We dangled our feet in the water, felt the river tug warmly and gently at our curled toes, and listened to the quiet hum of nighttime life in the shadows surrounding us. As we sipped beer from the thick brown bottles brought from the capital by barge every other week, we could pick out the sound of Pedro plucking his guitar outside his shack that lay downstream, around the next bend. The happy plucking sounds floated upstream, against the current, to reach us where we sat reclining on the bank. From the other direction we heard the stealthy limp of the three-legged black cat who lay in the mangrove-filtered sunlight at river's edge by day, but who by night stalked rats in the high thick weeds whose tops dipped down into the river in a sort of bowing penance. The sounds of the cat as it limped were all but inaudible. You had to know he was there stalking rats to be able to detect the off-kilter unevenness of his stealthy cat-steps. More omnipresent were the sounds and smells of frying plantains and front-stoop conversation that drifted toward us from the cluster of houses that stood in the shadows fifty yards behind where we sat at the river's edge. The plantains hissed and spat and sizzled in frying pans. Their salty-sweet, greasy smell honed in on us. It escaped the houses through open kitchen windows, meandered through the mangroves and found its way to the place where we sat beside the river dangling our feet. The conversation followed right behind the smell of the plantains, though it drifted in one big haze of sound from which it was difficult to separate any single word or phrase. Only when someone got excited or shouted above the general murmur did a distinct word or phrase puncture the air. Otherwise, the sound of the Saturday night front-stoop conversations was a happy hum that swirled around us like the warm water of the gentle river swirled around our legs as we sat there on the bank feeling as though we were bound to live forever.

shits happen

There's nothing quite like the smell of a young professional who's shit his pants. Nor is there anything quite like the gait of a young professional awkwardly yet craftily (as is possible, anyway) stiff-legging his way into an office building, lest the shat pants be discovered by his co-workers – or, for that matter, by people who have no idea who he is but who would never forget him once he became ingrained in their brains as That Guy Who Shit His Pants on the Way to Work.

Yes, before you ask, I was that man-boy. It was me with the disquieting, smooshy lumps in my underpants, with the warm, sticky, liquefied drizzle dripping its way down the inside of my left pant leg.

But don't act like you haven't been there before. Or really, really close, anyway.

Like inevitable and instant love, the need to go number two often hits you when you least expect it – and when it's least convenient. And no matter his or her resolve, no one is immune to its clutches.

•   •   •

66The morning had started off like most others did at that point in my early professional life: with a pot of coffee, four or five cigarettes and the creeping dread that it was going to be another mind-numbing, senseless day at the newspaper office (The memories of college were still too fresh for me to have forgotten that there exists anything but the mind-numbing toils of a 9-to-5 day at the office.). As I drove across the bay I smoked a couple more cigarettes. When I took the primary puff on the third, I had an instant gut feeling that I'd made a mistake. There were turds afoot, suited up in feathers and war paint, dancing around their ceremonial turd-fires, stirring their cauldron of turds' brew, whooping and chanting and banging on bongo drums in a clearing somewhere north of my rectum and south of my stomach.

I was, of course, in the midst of traversing a lengthy bridge when this realization hit me. Between the crest of the bridge and the shore, I went through every stage of impending gastrointestinal doom: The chills. The shakes. The sphincter-clenching. The false relief. The rocking and rolling. The gripping of the steering wheel. The chilly shakes. The near catastrophic convulsions. The renewed false relief.

Wracked as I was by this immediate need to relieve myself, I was struck by how relatively pleasant it feels to have the not-so-immediate need to relieve oneself, struck by the difference between the instant thermonuclear ticking time-bomb crap and the slow, steady, release-at-will crap, the one for which you can methodically reserve a crossword puzzle or the sports page.

Standing up to leave my car when I reached work was a mistake. However, I don't know of any way to exit my car other than by assuming an upright position, so I was left with no choice. To make matters worse (of course), there hadn't been any spaces available on the first floor of the parking garage. Or the second. Or the third. I was relieved to find, at least, that there wasn't anyone else waiting for the elevator, so I needn't take the stairs.

There was this Cheech and Chong movie where Cheech scooted his way through a clandestine marijuana processing plant, in desperate search of the bathroom. "Stay together cheeks, stay together cheeks," he urged his butt. I must have looked something like Cheech as I slinked toward the office. But the movie doesn't capture the interior landscape of a person thus stricken. A feeling of need, of helplessness looms immediate and huge on the horizon. It is a very bipolar experience. The proper, socialized, *human* side of the individual is in full bloom, occupied with only one thought: finding a toilet and putting this shit in its rightful place. But the animal instinct is also at work. *Just let go. Just let go. It'll be all better in a second. It can all be over if you want it to,* the urge tickles gently. *You know you want to just let go.*

I was halfway to the office building when I began to congratulate myself for my fortitude. *See,* I told the Beast within me, *I can make it. I didn't have to stop at McDonald's. And I* don't *have to resort to shitting myself. I can* make *it.*

But the Beast roared in response. A volcano erupted in my colon, spewing hot lava. An earthquake trembled through my intestines. A semi-digested tidal wave burbled throughout my insides. I felt like I was going to explode. And – whether out of pure need or out of panic, I'll never know – I just let go.

A moment of utter relief was followed by an eternity of warm and sticky embarrassment and the dumbfounding realization that I *had shit myself within sight of the office.* I tried to renege on my decision to just let go, tried to cut the flow off at the source, but once given permission to relax the sphincter is a stubborn creature, indeed. My pants continued to fill. The coffee must have hastened things along, because the consistency was anything but consistent. It was clumpy and lumpy and wet. And it smelled immediately.

When I reached the building there was a crowd in front of the elevator. *They have to know. They have to know. They* have *to,* I winced to myself, feeling even worse than you feel in those dreams where you stroll into class naked, in part because this wasn't a dream, but also in part because nakedness somehow seems more natural – and certainly less hidden, less illicit – than taking a crap via the unconventional in-the-pants method. Oh, I would've given anything to just be naked at that moment! Naked and gloriously *clean*! So I had no choice but to take the stairs to the second floor, which made containing the noxious spill all the more difficult. The absurdity of it, I lamented as I straddled each stair with the utmost of grace and caution, the absolute improbability of a healthy twenty-three-year-old male dropping a load in his drawers. And the *stench*.

It's not that shat dress pants smell fundamentally different than a baby who's shit himself. But the smell of ripe turds is synonymous with babydom, along with puke and drool and burps and crying and cooing. The smell of ripe turds is not synonymous with a twenty-three-year-old male wearing a shirt and tie.

By the time I reached the toilet, there was hardly any need to drop my drawers anymore, as the load had already been thoroughly dropped.

But now my overburdened underpants had to be removed. If I tried to take off my pants and shoes, I was certain I would spill the contents of my underwear onto them. So I pulled out my pocketknife and undertook emergency surgery on the elastic band of my underwear. With four gentle, precise cuts, the underwear was free and I was holding the precarious package by the severed ends of the elastic bands. I stood up partway, turned, and let the semi-shapeless turds tumble into the toilet. *Plop plop plop*, they splashed into the water. Then I sat back down, wrapped the ruined briefs in an obscene amount of toilet paper, and commenced to clean myself.

When I was certain I was alone in the bathroom, I crept out of the stall and buried the package in the garbage can, beneath a mound of used paper towels. Then I scrubbed my hands for a full minute.

But then an interesting feeling hit me. One of relief, yes. But also one of accomplishment. All in all, I had handled the situation rather well. There were no visible stains anywhere on my clothing. And no one who didn't get too close would be the wiser. I was scot-free – and liberated of the constraints of my underwear. I was, all in all, pretty proud. I smiled triumphantly to myself as I strode into the office.

The rest of the day was, as usual, mind-numbing. But compared with the adventure and intrigue of the morning, it seemed downright disappointing and depressing.

.   .   .

"That," my girlfriend at the time said, her mouth faltering just short of the plump cheeseburger she'd plucked off her plate, "is *gross*."

I'm not even sure how the topic of conversation had arisen, especially at that particular moment. I'm sure I hadn't said, "You know, sweetheart, there's this story about shitting myself that I'd really like to share with you." I'm sure it was much more organic and tangential than that. But I suppose I needn't have brought it up at all. The more comfortable you are with someone, I guess, the more you tend to forget that tactlessness and intimacy don't have to go hand-in-hand.

"Well, maybe," I said. "But that's not the point."

"What's the point, then? It seems like a pointless story, if you ask me. Pointless and disgusting. Pretty much like all your stories, come to think of it."

She wasn't mad, though. Just befuddled. And, at least a couple minutes before, she had also been hungry. She considered the burger, which, in light of my story, seemed to have devolved before her eyes into a charred hunk of greasy flesh nestled between two buttock-like pieces of bread.

"It's your diet, you know," she said.

"What about my diet?"

"That's just it. You don't eat. You smoke too many cigarettes and drink too much coffee and Diet Pepsi. It's no wonder that when you finally have to go there's no holding it back."

"But you're talking about the particulars here. My whole point in telling the story wasn't to focus on all the gory details. There's something about the essence of the experience that's significant."

"Well, you certainly didn't do a very good job of avoiding the gory details as you recounted that episode in blow-by-blow fashion. As I ate my appetizer, I might add."

"How was that guacamole, anyway?"

"Don't ask." She smirked at me. "You're gross. It's a good thing I like you."

Her hunger won out over the potential revulsion factor that my story might have possessed, so we proceeded to eat our cheeseburgers. Sometimes a vacation makes events that transpired *back home* more unreal, more distant, more discussable. But all in all, it *was* a strange topic for me to have brought up on vacation. At dinner, no less.

But still, I had to add: "You know how your shoe smells after you've stepped in a pile of dog crap? How that annoying ripeness lingers for hours, even after you've scraped the majority of it off your shoe? Well, for the rest of the day, my pants were like that shoe. There was just this aura about me."

"Okay, time out!" she cried. "I'm going to stop listening here pretty soon. I think it's just encouraging you."

I don't know if anybody noticed my aura that morning at work. I had only been at the job a couple months, but I'd already acquired the reputation of office eccentric, given as I was to mumbling to myself and fashioning hats out of the newspaper. So people pretty much steered clear of me, anyway.

After we'd finished our food, I couldn't help but raise a few philosophical points that I'd contemplated off and on, ever since that incident.

"We utter the word perpetually. 'Bullshit.' 'Would you look at this shit?' 'He has shit for brains.' 'I shit you not,'" I said. "It's almost as though the actual act and ensuing substance is a greater taboo than the vulgarity that represents it. Why? Everyone does it. It's even more universal a deed than sex. We talk enough about food – the taste, the texture, the price, the place, the preparation, how it goes down. So why don't we talk about how it comes out?"

I was a little too full of beer and my own ideas to pause for a moment and acknowledge how remarkable it was that she was still sitting there at the table with me, much less allowing me to continue to pursue that particular line of conversation.

"That may be so," she said. "But you're evading the central issue here: You're not just discussing your bowel movements; you're an adult who's discussing a bowel movement that wound up squishing around inside his underwear instead of going straight into the toilet where bowel movements belong."

"But that brings up a pivotal point," I said. "What's right is in the eye of the beholder. Just because you and everyone else conforms doesn't mean I have to."

"Oh, please. Postmodern pooping," she said. "I just think there's some things that are beyond the pale. You take dumps in the toilet; that's just the way you do it. No one will consider you any less of an individual because you do that. It's just *right*. And you know that. You're just glorifying the whole incident, I bet, because somewhere deep down inside you're ashamed of it."

My girlfriend, it might be noted, had a sticker affixed to the bottom of her toilet's lid. It portrayed a toilet with ferocious, wolf-like teeth, its mouth-lid snapped wide open, pursuing a handful of incongruous brown blobs. *Yum Yum! Eat 'em up!* read the sticker's caption, rendered in a colorful comic-book font. But this was the first time, in half a year of dating and all the bodily convulsions and contortions and closeness that accompany it, that we had discussed bowel movements.

"And by the way," she said, "You didn't think about going back home and taking a shower and getting fresh clothes?"

"Well, not really. That would've been an hour round trip."

"Oh my goodness..."

I could pee in front of her. She could pee in front of me. We'd talked about nearly everything else there was to talk about.

"How often do you go, anyway?"

"I don't know." I considered for a moment. "Once a week or so, maybe?"

"Once a week? Oh my God, Tom. That's not healthy."

"Oh? It's not?" I was puzzled. Not so much puzzled by the revelation that this wasn't healthy. Puzzled, instead, by why this obvious thing had not occurred to me before.

"How many times have you gone this week?" she asked.

"Um, none. So far, anyway."

"I've pooped every day we've been on this trip." *Poop*. She said *poop*, as though her bowel movements were somehow more dainty, less messy and raw and elemental than everyone else's. Like they were accessories she could do without. (Of course, I'm reading too much into a single comment. But somehow, her profession of regularity wounded my already fragile self-esteem, made me even more assured to myself that I was unworthy of her affection.)

"Have you thought about getting that checked out?" she said. "If you're not careful, you'll get colon spasms like I did when I was in college."

"Colon spasms? That sounds painful."

"They were. I felt completely stopped up, like my ass and intestines were made of concrete. I had to poop so bad – but I couldn't. I tried and tried and it just *hurt*. The doctor told me it was my diet. Lots of Taco Bell back then. And lots of coffee and cigarettes, like you. So you be careful, mister."

Colon spasms. The ailment hung in the air with a burdensome viciousness, like the words *guillotine* or *electrocution* might.

·   ·   ·

I learned something on that messy day at the office. Some *things*, really. For one, I realized that number two is, perhaps, the last great taboo. As I sat at work I was fully aware that, within the confines of our culture, I could not share my incident – or my relative competence at dealing with a messy situation – with my co-workers.

I also felt as though I'd gained entry into a veiled world of forbidden knowledge, which paradoxically had been in plain sight all along. I should say that this episode coincided with my transition from intern to full-fledged professional, and my accompanying realization that the professional world is not all that professional, that grown-ups often act anything but, that experience does not necessarily confer competence or maturity. You know the feeling; it's akin to seeing people who never gave a hoot about learning or school grow up to be teachers, and continue to not give a hoot, though they may pretend otherwise. I was finally beginning to see the little office games and politics and excuses and grudges for what they were: unprofessional and unnecessarily time-consuming, yet a fundamental part of work life.

And as I sat there that day, cloaked in my magic aura, I was both reassured and dumfounded by the fact that a young professional can find dealing with soiled pants to be the most challenging and rewarding part of his day. It made the whole idea of working for another thirty or forty years much less intimidating – and simultaneously much more frightening.

•   •   •

My girlfriend was more quiet than usual for the rest of the night. Her face bore a pensive look as we strolled the chilly streets of Boston. She hugged her arms to herself; I kept my hand at my side, expectantly, but she never reciprocated the gesture. Back at the hotel, she closed the bathroom door while she undressed, peed and brushed her teeth.

In bed, I grazed my hand across her forehead, through her hair, down her neck to her shirt. She clutched my fingers and set them onto the mattress.

"Not tonight," she said. "Please."

It was obvious that I'd gotten a little too close for comfort and she'd imposed a distance to compensate. She generally seemed to like my silliness. But perhaps, I was willing to admit, I had taken things too far. I tested the limits of her compassion and took advantage of her usual willingness to listen to whatever was on my mind.

When I was in college, there was an item of graffiti written (in what looked to be female penmanship) inside one the men's stalls in the library: *Guys – shit on your woman. She'll love it!*

•   •   •

Not long after that vacation, I had another accident. When I say another, I mean a second in a year's time. It's not like shitting my pants was a constant occurrence with me or anything. The first accident was in July. We started dating in October.

This accident occurred the following July. I'd just moved in with her. There had been other signs that things were moving too fast, but I didn't consider this until later.

This time I was out on assignment, working on some feature story or another, when the need hit – even more drastic than it had before. I'll spare the details this time around. But suffice it to say that there was no heroic rescue with a pocketknife. There was no consistency whatsoever. Just instant, omnipresent liquid shit. My pants were rendered totally soiled.

I called my boss and said, "I had a bit of an accident. I'm gonna have to go home and shower and change. I think I'll just make some calls from there this afternoon."

What else could I say, really? Thankfully, she didn't press me on the matter.

It was my girlfriend's day off. She came back from the gym to find me in shorts and an undershirt, typing away on her computer. A wad of clothing sat on her floor, enclosed in a triple layer of plastic bags.

I looked up at her. I tried to force a smile.

"I had an accident," I said.

What else could I say, really?

The look that settled upon her face wasn't one of shock, really. It was a patronizing mixed breed of disappointment, repulsion, and resignation. It was the look of someone who realizes something significant and knows this realization should have come somewhat earlier. Addressing me, she couldn't even form a complete sentence:

"Oh my God, Tom, oh my God…"

Under different circumstances, those same words could have taken the form of a gasped orgasmic utterance (OH MY GOD, TOM, *OH MY GOD*).

But in this case, of course, context meant everything.

muck of the north

Black men. Brown men. Field men. They work in the fields from early morn 'til late at night. They toil and pick in the strange dirt of the small town in the North. The dirt of the town is well known. The dirt is soft and black and wet and rich. *Muck*, they call it. It is like black gold. It spawns wealth in the form of green plants that the black men and brown men pick for the white men who own the fields. The muck does not come off the men's hands all the way. It leaves a black film that is like a skin of sorts. Like a scar.

The men rise at five and eat a bit and smoke and wait by their shacks for the trucks to come and take them to the fields. There they dig and pick and hoe, hunched and hot, for hours. Then it is time to eat. The sun is high and it is hard to breathe in the tough hot noon air. The men sit in the shade of the tarp that is strung from one of the trucks and eat and smoke and quench their thirst and doze for a while.

Then it is one and they start to pick once more. Their backs ache, their knees creak, their hands are gnarled. They did not think of such things for that brief time at lunch but now the pains are on their minds and they feel the aches once more and they wish for the day when the long rest will come and they will end their toil, when they will pick no more. But most are young yet, though they feel like old men. And the year is young, as well. It is but June and there is much work to be done yet up in the North 'til the men can head south in the fall, turn their vans and trucks to the south lands, to new states, to new fields to be worked.

Soon past lunch a storm brews. The clouds roil in the west, black like the muck. And blue, too. Black and blue clouds that will soon pounce on the muck fields. The dark sky will flash and roar and fling sheets of rain. The clouds build in the west and move to the men, slow but sure. The men work fast to pick as much as they can 'fore the rain comes, but it will be there soon. It will fall on them, drive them from the fields with its strength. They will flee to the trucks and then to their shacks. The rain will pelt their shacks and play *plink plank* on the tin roofs.

And then the rain is there and the men run to the trucks as it comes down hard. The clouds are dark, the air booms and burns, and the wind groans. The men are in the back of the trucks. Their breath is hot in the small space and they smell like wet muck.

The men are sad for the lost pay but their hearts are glad, too, for they go home and rest. They lie in the cots in their tin shacks and hear the rain as it plays on the roofs. The men smell of muck still, of earth and fields. They do not try to wash their hands of the muck once and for all. They know that it is there for good. Like a skin. Like a scar.

like the trains of argentina

Luis Marcelo was dying, he knew, although it wasn't the kind of death he would have preferred, it was not the distinguished sort of demise where he sprawled on his deathbed with a piercing look of final anguish on his face, clutching at his heart, waiting for the moment of epiphany and cloud-parting as the angels swooned and the family members who gathered around him wailed and moaned, their black-clad bodies shaken with every sob sputtered forth in the memory of Luis Marcelo, no, his death was a far less imminent one, more of a gradual decline toward oblivion and obscurity into which he could feel himself slipping, for instead of being confined to perpetual bed rest he was still walking and talking and going to the club, still rising in the morning and drinking his two cups of tea and eating a piece of dry toast with strawberry jam, still going to the tribunal every day after breakfast and hearing cases or writing decisions, still going home to lunch and the newspaper and his siesta of thirty-five minutes, still taking his post-nap walk, then returning to work where he often stayed late reading over court briefs, and Luis Marcelo still pounded on the table and made his wine glass dance at dinnertime when his wife was being difficult or when the meat was cold or the dessert the same they'd had the night before, and he still shook his fist at the radio commentators at night, still shouted himself hoarse at the soccer games on television, yes, he was still active but he was to retire in a month, step down from his seat as a district judge and make room for some bright young lawyer from Buenos Aires, but subconsciously Luis Marcelo wanted to die before that, to go before his death would cease to mean anything, to depart the earthly scene swiftly, completely, and conspicuously before he merely passed into the shadows and slowly faded from sight and mind until he was no longer anything but a suppressed memory that lingered just on the other side of the community's collective sense of reality, for he could already feel the long, slow disintegration taking root in his bones, as though one by one the cells of his body were succumbing to their age and imploding upon themselves, but not nearly fast enough to do any outwardly visible damage, although he was beginning to feel it, as it took less time to shout himself hoarse when soccer was on the television, as he cared less about the newspaper, as he grew more tired more quickly from yelling at the radio commentators and could often not stay awake long enough at night to hear the program to its completion, and his wife was ignoring him now when he pounded his fist on the tabletop and the wineglass danced a slow and lilting waltz instead of an energetic jig, and fewer people stopped to visit at his home or at the courthouse, and he often found himself sitting alone at the café, having to order a second coffee because there had been no one to pass the time with to keep him from finishing the first and at night when he lay down in his bed he could feel his strength escaping him and each eyelid felt as though it weighed several pounds, and every time he took a step during waking hours it seemed all the harder, so much so that his customary walk after his noontime siesta, once a lighthearted and energetic endeavor, was every day becoming more of a burdensome crusade as Luis Marcelo stubbornly persisted in walking the same distance and persistently failed in performing the act in the same easeful manner with which he had done it in times before, he walked now with shuffles not strides, but nonetheless he went on the daily walk past the industrial school, around the fenced perimeter of the national guard post, through the leafy center of the park, down the railroad tracks and past the train station from which trains still departed but from which there were not nearly as many trains as there had

been in his youth when you could ride all the way north to Bolivia or west to the
Andes in high style, in a private sleeping cabin with a soft bed and crisp sheets
adjacent to the dining car where they baked fresh bread every day and served
thick steaks and good wine but now the long-distance trains ran no longer,
replaced by buses and airplanes, and all you could do now was travel to the
capital and back in the rickety, graffiti-covered cars that the government had
bought secondhand from Spain, the cars with the broken windows and ripped
vinyl upholstery that smelled of urine and baby vomit, where you felt every rail
clatter through the seat and into your spine and a train ride nowadays was a
tiring and taxing thing, just as Luis Marcelo grew tired as he walked his daily
walk, feeling the difficulty of every shuffling step but most of all he felt a
sadness, a slowly spiraling melancholy that inched upon him, like a barely
moving but heavy and ever-present anchor dragging his soul closer and closer to
insignificance, not vanished yet, still hanging on like some of the old sleeping
cars that sat rusting in the tall grass at the rear of the train yard, the ones that no
one thought about now and that would eventually be gone forever from sight
and mind like the long-distance train itself, at one time not so long ago a shiny,
sparkling marvel, but now only a few dilapidated and unused cars, once
traveling toward the sunset through the pampas and beyond, its place now
occupied only by the secondhand commuter trains heading east to the throbbing
capital with its crowded streets and dirty port, and as he walked Luis Marcelo
could not help but feel like he himself was disintegrating, that he was dying a
slow and insignificant death like that of the trains of Argentina and every day,
although more often than not he did not admit nor even know that he did so, he
wished upon himself a different, more noble kind of death.

macgowan's run

On the late-afternoon train to Saint John, New Brunswick, MacGowan had absolutely no fear of death. He was not afraid of being suddenly shot or stabbed or kidnapped. He didn't worry that a gloved hand would snake around the back of his seat and press a chloroform-drenched rag to his face. He dozed freely, never considering the possibility that he might awake bound and gagged in a small, windowless room where mosquitoes buzzed lethargically in the humid air and a battered ceiling fan staggered its way about in drunken circles overhead.

He was certain that the train, which had chugged out of Moncton in the late afternoon, would arrive in Saint John intact and on time that evening. In MacGowan's mind there was no possibility that the cars would scream to a stop mid-route, the same look of sickening realization frozen on every passenger's face while they helplessly awaited the inevitable shouts of rebel troops who would soon be on board and fanning out, prodding with rifle butts, demanding valuables and identification from the passengers , their fatigues filthy and mismatched, their eyes narrow and bloodshot from lack of sleep and too much cane liquor, their movements twitching and jerky from the drugs coursing through their bloodstreams.

MacGowan looked out the window at the pre-Christmas snow falling on the New Brunswick countryside. The fat flakes peacefully nestled on pine boughs, farmsteads, and the granite headstones of the occasional 18th-century Loyalist graveyard. He imagined the faint roar of waves crashing on the craggy shores of the Bay of Fundy and listened to the muffled snores of the old woman with the translucent skin who dozed in the seat next to him.

He had nothing to fear. It had been that way the whole time in Canada, and also during the brief hours he had spent in the U.S. Safety was a strange, alien feeling for MacGowan after fourteen months of perpetual danger. Safety – he did not know if he would ever get used to it again.

· · ·

MacGowan didn't know why he hadn't gone home that Tuesday before Thanksgiving the previous month. He couldn't say for sure why he'd gotten off the plane in Albany, finally, after fourteen months of reporting on war in the South, only to board a Greyhound headed for Canada. Fourteen months of almost nonstop movement and activity and action, after which common sense would dictate a pause to rest and evaluate his physical and mental condition. But here he was, on the move again.

He had stepped off the plane in Albany with the full intention of retrieving his one and only bag, catching the bus, getting off at the corner newsstand where he used to buy the papers and his cigars, walking the three blocks to his apartment, climbing the steps for the first time in over a year, opening the door, and taking a shower. And then he would put on a pair of shorts and he would sleep, sleep for the rest of the day and all the night, too. And the next day, Wednesday, he would take the bus to Rochester and a cab to his mother's house where a few members of the family would already be trickling in for the big Thanksgiving dinner, bigger still this year in honor of MacGowan's presence.

But instead he went to Canada. Instead he kept traveling. He snatched his bag from the airport conveyor belt and headed instead to the Greyhound station. And he bought a ticket on the next bus north to Montreal. It had been an impulsive thing, the kind of uncalculated rashness that could have gotten him killed down South. If he would have done a similar thing down there, he probably would have died and whatever story he was chasing would have gone with him.

That's what happened when you didn't plan. Who cared if the rebels had firebombed five villages and raided a government ammo dump and there were surely some good pictures to be taken and good tales to be told? You didn't just flag down the next passing truck and shove a handful of pesos in the driver's face and tell him to drive, dammit, drive, without really knowing where you were going or what the hell you were getting yourself into. That was bound to get you dismembered or decapitated, disemboweled or shot full of lead, or merely bayoneted all over and left to bleed to death while the sun set and gleaming pairs of beastly eyes lurked in the undergrowth around you.

MacGowan had seen it happen to reporters much more experienced than himself; but he'd seen it happen early enough to keep from making the same kind of mistakes. Good tales didn't mean shit, he'd learned, if you weren't alive to tell them.

Maybe he had gone to Canada just because he *could* go, he thought as he gazed out the train window at the serene countryside; because for once in a seeming eternity he had no obligations and no gun sights tracking his every move, no reason to suspect that he might be about to die.

So he went to Canada and he kept moving, but he moved slowly and casually now. He lingered in Montreal a few days, then headed east by train. He would get off at the slightest whim, even if he had bought a ticket for a destination three hours further down the line. If something grabbed his attention – an intriguing old house within view of the station, a silo off in the distance, a winding stream that meandered through the fields a few miles back, or simply the town's name – he would grab his bag and hop off.

And as he watched the train continue on its way without him he could not help but laugh. At times he kept it to himself, but often the laughter escaped like gunshots, a loud but nervous kind of peal. He laughed at himself and at the world in general and wondered where he would spend the night and what he would do in this town in the middle of the Canadian nowhere, but his laugh also had an edge to it, as though he were surprised to be alive, amazed that he was even still capable – both physically and emotionally – of laughing at all.

It was a strange sort of feeling, to say the least.

MacGowan could even drink now. After his fourteen-month tropical deathwatch, he could sit at a bar and have a carefree beer or two or three. He didn't have to pick just the right table from a strategic standpoint, one that placed his back securely to the wall but still provided a viable escape route should he have to flee at a moment's notice.

Down South he rarely dared to drink in-country. Even the slightest falter in your concentration or response time was enough to do you in, he'd learned. He only tipped the bottle on rare and isolated weekends, when the death threats had far exceeded their usual numbers or when he simply could not take any more of the whole situation. So he would cross the border to relative safety, across the frontier to that neighboring, relatively peaceable country where a journalist stood only a favorable one in ten chance of being gutted in his sleep and where at the most, only three-quarters of all government and military officials were inherently corrupt.

MacGowan took full advantage of those infrequent sojourns. He remembered a seemingly endless weekend with one Swede buddy of his from a European wire service, a weekend of devalued currency and dirt-cheap beer, of bottle after empty bottle of aguardiente strewn about a cramped and dingy double-occupancy hotel room. It was on such weekends, during moments of drunken lucidity, that MacGowan questioned the motivation behind his very presence in the region: Was it due to a truly altruistic desire to foster understanding, or was it ego masquerading as altruism?

In Montreal, MacGowan sat safely at a bar next to a burly, thickly bearded French Canadian who made his living farming bison in Manitoba. The man was in town to see about a loan for expanding his ranch. The loan didn't go through, though, and someone ripped off his wallet in the subway. Hidden in his sock he had enough money for a bus ticket home and a night of thorough drunkenness.

"The bison is good animal. Hardy animal. It no need shelter, you no have to build a barn for it," the French Canadian intoned, his accent thick with heritage and sloshy with alcohol. "And it's good meat, good nutritious meat that make a man who eat bison a strong man. Bison build muscle."

MacGowan, beyond drunk, was not paying attention, but he did not betray this, and let the man continue.

"And it makes a good business. Cheap wheat from Saskatchewan, bison bought when babies and raised since then. Sixty bison and a man make a good living. No other job, I 'ave. Don't need one. Japanese love bison meat. You Americans, too." He smiled as he thought of his bison at home on the Manitoba prairie. Then he suddenly thrust his beer bottle at MacGowan.

"This is good beer. They make fine beer 'ere in Quebec. People in Quebec take pride in everything that belongs to Quebec. I know; I used to live 'ere. I worked in an abattoir up north."

MacGowan bought the bison rancher four rounds of fine Quebec beer, not because he was sorry about the man's lost wallet or elusive loan, but because he felt somehow indebted to the bearded fellow. In a way, MacGowan was overjoyed by the knowledge that the man would not end the evening by trying to shove a knife in his back or report his presence to the police.

And then in Quebec City one night, MacGowan sat on a park bench at the edge of the Plains of Abraham. It was long past dark. He huddled deep inside the heavy overcoat he'd had to buy in Montreal and downed half a dozen bottles of dark, strong Quebec beer in rapid succession. As soon as the warmth of the previous bottle started to subside and the winter chill crept in upon his consciousness, he uncapped the next bottle and began to drink.

It was thick and black and syrupy, good beer for a winter's evening. It was a local brew, one of the fine Quebec beers his friend from Manitoba so adored. He had lingered for a long time at the many bottles of local beer prominently displayed in the cooler in the corner grocery, directly above the imported American beers and several shelves above the other Canadian national brands brewed out-of-province. One premium line boasted colorful labels embossed with silver foil and depicting various scenes from local folklore, legends from Quebec city and the surrounding countryside.

MacGowan lifted one of the empty bottles up to the dim street lamp that illuminated the bench at which he sat on the Plains of Abraham. *Maudite*, the label said, "the damned one." The bottle bore a picture of a vicious devil and a flying canoe borne in the air, above the St. Lawrence river, by a blazing hellstorm. Drawing upon his mediocre knowledge of French, MacGowan pieced together from the label how, as a Quebec legend had it, some lumberjacks had once made a pact with Satan. Satan had flown the lumberjacks in their canoes, piloting the lead canoe himself, so that they could make it home for Christmas. The lumberjacks' town, some said, remained cursed to this day.

It reminded him of a similar story from the South, only a contemporary tale, a superstitious rumor that had been circulating still when MacGowan left. Villagers in a remote southeast region of the country claimed that the leader of one of the area's most feared and elusive rebel platoons was in league with Satan himself. When a town loyal to the government was raided and its inhabitants murdered, all the village buildings were burned to the ground, save the church. When belated help arrived to the ill-fated village, the church would be found filled with corpses, all of them shot through the heads and seated in the pews, reverently facing the altar.

There were rumors that a fate just as brutal awaited any government forces patrolling the zone. These went largely unconfirmed, though, because the government left that area almost completely untouched. But MacGowan had been with one of the rare government patrols in the area; this one was actually searching for the whereabouts of a previous group of soldiers that had simply disappeared.

When the patrol leader's back was turned, MacGowan ventured down a path that veered off into the forest at the edge of the clearing. The path dropped quickly down a steep embankment, through thick entanglements of scrub trees. MacGowan was staring down at the path, watching his footing, gingerly stepping over roots and trying to maintain traction on the side of the embankment.

Without warning, his head bumped into something. MacGowan stopped. For a split second there was nothing. MacGowan remained motionless, still looking downward at his feet. And then came another slight bump against his head. He stayed motionless, paralyzed, not wanting to look up. And then there was a third bump and a drop of something wet and slimy that slid down the nape of his neck.

MacGowan glanced upward to see a severed head swinging lazily toward him, the gaping hole where the neck once met the shoulders trailing foul-smelling drops of blood and pus. Its black hair was bunched together and bound with twine at the top of the skull, the already-decaying skin of the forehead stretched unnaturally upward with the twine-bound hair. This made the eyes appear leering and bulbous. They locked with MacGowan's own as the head arced its way back toward him. It was quickly losing the initial momentum it had gained when MacGowan first bumped into it, but it was still swinging. This time MacGowan ducked a little, breaking the spell of the eyes.

He continued down the trail, counting the heads as he went. Twenty-five there were, dangling down from the branches every twenty yards or so. The going was less steep, now, and MacGowan was nearing the bottom of the ravine. There was a clearing ahead and he heard the faint rush of a stream.

And then he was upon them. Still glancing upward for more dangling heads, he almost stumbled and fell right into the midst of the fatigue-clad bodies. They were laid out in neat, even piles, five stacks of five bodies each. All of them were headless and without digits on their hands, MacGowan saw immediately, except for one that sat on the ground facing him with its back propped up against the nearest pile. The foul breath of decay was in the air. MacGowan plugged his nose and lifted the tail of his shirt to cover his mouth as he bent down to examine the sole intact body. An eternal smile was plastered on the dead soldier's face, and out of his bulging mouth spilled fingers and fingers and more fingers, their protruding tips in various stages of rot, flies and maggots swarming and teeming on the decaying flesh.

·   ·   ·

MacGowan was reminded of that day in the jungle as he sat on the park bench at the edge of Quebec City's Plains of Abraham. The battlefield was dark and deserted. It was very cold out, at the most ten degrees, but with all the beer of the damned he'd drunk he did not notice. His head was spinning but he did not feel sick.

The wind whistled hollowly as it sailed across the snow-covered battlefield and dipped down into the valley of the St. Lawrence River. MacGowan left his emptied bottles on the ground and walked gingerly across the icy whiteness of the glazed-over fields. Around him were embankments and earthworks, fortifications and cannons. The stars blazed overhead, shining crisply in the black December sky. MacGowan reached the bluff at the edge of the battlefield. Far below him was a dark gulf of nothingness where the St. Lawrence lay, massive, unmoving, and ice-choked. The lights of Lévis twinkled on the opposite bank.

MacGowan did not feel any sense of despair or bewilderment as he pondered the demise of the French and British forces on the Plains of Abraham. Maybe it was due to the span of the centuries, the fact that the weapons they had used to kill each other were so distant from the automatic instruments of death MacGowan had seen. Whatever it was, those deaths in Quebec seemed somehow noble to him, somehow right in the historical scheme of things. But it must be time, he thought. It must have been the fact that he had only read about dead Frenchmen and Englishmen from a safe distance of several centuries, while he had seen dead rebels and government troops and priests and peasants and politicians in the South firsthand.

MacGowan was drunk, and pleasantly so, and these thoughts did not penetrate to his conscience as he stood there by himself on the Plains of Abraham above the St. Lawrence River. MacGowan stood somberly, quietly, pervaded only by a sense of utter emptiness. He did not feel the bite of the wind or the clawing of the subzero wind chill on his exposed face and hands.

That night he dreamed of bloody, endless campaigns outside the stone walls of Quebec City. A motley legion of corpses waged perpetual war on each other. Some were dressed in khakis and jungle camouflage; others were bedecked in leggings, tall leather boots, brightly colored coats, and black three-cornered hats. They rode in jeeps and tanks and on proud white cavalry steeds. Some brandished flintlocks while others bore grenade launchers and assault rifles. Some struck then hid behind the trees and embankments, struck and hid, while others marched rank upon rank, shoulder-to-shoulder, ever forward to their fate.

None of them had heads.

•   •   •

No nightmares had plagued MacGowan as he dozed through the late afternoon on the train to Saint John, New Brunswick. They were approaching the city, now, and around him passengers began to stir. The old woman with the translucent skin and bulging blue veins was awake in the seat next to him, and was once again telling him that he couldn't miss the reversing falls down the river a piece from Saint John harbor, that they were simply wonderful and he should also be sure to visit the brewery, Moosehead was famous even outside Canada, she'd heard, and my what a fine time he'd chosen to visit town, it was simply lovely around Christmas with the snow and decorations and lights downtown and the candles in the windows and all.

Christmas. Just over a week until Christmas, MacGowan thought. He had already missed Thanksgiving and at the rate his travels were progressing he wouldn't be home for Christmas, either. It didn't really bother him, though. He wasn't in any particular hurry.

The train pulled into the station and came to a gentle stop. He gathered his bag and left the train, exited the station, and slowly headed toward downtown. The bare room at the YMCA was a luxury suite next to many of the places he'd slept down South. He examined his face in the mirror. His tropical tan was only now beginning to fade. And his dark, dyed hair was showing blond at the roots now where it was growing out. The dye hadn't offered complete anonymity, but it had helped him to blend in somewhat in the South.

MacGowan left the YMCA and ambled down the streets of Saint John. The red stone pathways of the main square were meticulously laid out to resemble the design of the Union Jack. He stood in the middle of the flag where the bars intersected and observed a crowd of elegantly dressed townsfolk emerging from the Gala Theater across the street.

Saint John Youth Orchestra Christmas Spectacular Tonite, proclaimed the marquee above the theater entrance. MacGowan crunched down the path toward the street and stood directly across from the theater, out of which men and women bundled in scarves and heavy winter coats strolled arm in arm, smiling and chatting contentedly. Children scampered about, jumping up and down and exclaiming about the violins or the piano or the drums and how loud they'd been, how wonderful it would be to play in the band like the older boys and girls.

Bathed as they were in the glow of the marquee, the people seemed not quite real to MacGowan. They appeared angelic and apparitional. A he watched them beam and smile and laugh there in the white light while around them a gentle snow cascaded from the sky, MacGowan realized that there was very little chance that these men, women, and children would be murdered in their sleep that evening. To MacGowan, after living among people whose existence was tenacious, at best, to MacGowan, whose own life had hung in the balance for what felt like so long, such safe, happy people seemed almost immortal.

As he stood watching from the shadows, several of the townsfolk joined arms and began to sing Christmas carols. Their voices rang clearly, echoing through the stately trees of the Union Jack square.

Silent night, holy night
All is calm, all is bright
Round yon Virgin Mother and Child
Holy Infant so tender and mild
Sleep in heavenly peace
Sleep in heavenly peace

A time when he had heard singing in the South sprang immediately into MacGowan's mind, although it was an instance far from serene. Half a dozen rebels stood before a firing squad, their backs against a chipped and faded brick wall. They were naked from the waist up, their ragged shirts tied around their eyes as blindfolds. They were dirty and thin, the outlines of their ribcages jutting prominently through their skin.

The commander of the firing squad asked the rebels for any last words. There was a fleeting silence, and then one began to sing the unofficial hymn of the rebel army, a decades-old sonnet penned by an acclaimed poet from a time long past. One by one the other blindfolded soldiers joined in, their singing off-key but unified. And as they sang, the commander of the firing squad gave the order to shoot, one target at a time. Five successive batteries echoed in the vacant lot. The last rebel singing had been the first to start. He uttered the final word of the final line of the unofficial hymn of the rebel army. Then the shots punctured the air where his words had been. His blindfold reddened, he crumpled to the ground, and sang no more.

It was snowing harder now as MacGowan headed away from Saint John's main square and down a side street. The snowflakes darted about in the growing wind. They swirled and whipped along the ground, clinging together as they blew. Through the unfolding sheet of white, the neon sign of O'Leary's Irish Tavern beckoned to MacGowan from above. He slipped through the door behind an elderly man in a long wool coat and black bowler who he had seen emerge from the youth symphony performance. The man headed to the far end of the bar, where a few regulars stood chatting with the bartender. MacGowan remained near the entrance. He caught the bartender's attention and ordered a draft.

As he stood there at the bar, sipping his beer and listening to the Celtic flute music that floated softly from somewhere in the shadows behind the counter, MacGowan was aware of the fact that there would be no car bombings this evening in Saint John, New Brunswick. There would be no bricks through windows, no sporadic exchanges of gunfire, no protests in the streets, no military occupation, no curfew imposed under threat of imprisonment.

The men in the bar would have been shocked to know such thoughts had even flashed through MacGowan's mind, he realized.

But it was true. The townspeople would stroll home from the youth symphony to their warm, snug houses. Some might linger for a while in pubs or restaurants or coffee shops, but finally they would all go home and sleep the undisturbed and oblivious sleep of those who do not fear for their lives.

MacGowan drained his beer and threw some change on the counter for the bartender. He pulled on his coat and turned to leave, as he did so catching a glimpse of the old man with whom he had entered the bar. The silver-haired man was tipping a pint glass and exclaiming to the other men gathered at the end of the bar about the youth symphony concert.

What a fine performance it was, he beamed. Truly a joy. Quite a lot o' talent there was up on that stage. Beautiful music, all performed without a hitch. Such a fine, fine performance indeed.

MacGowan did not feel fine, he realized leaving the bar. The cluster of sleigh bells attached to the door jangled behind him as he went. The snow had picked up even more, and the air outside was now a quivering wall of white. He tucked his head as deeply as he could into his overcoat and began to walk. No, he did not feel fine at all.

Yet, while he certainly did not feel exaltation rushing through him now that he was rid of that place, he did not feel remorse, either. He did not feel guilt for only staying fourteen months when others were condemned to remain for a lifetime. MacGowan felt numb and utterly apart from the world. He did not feel a thing.

He wondered how long it would last.

dusty bottles, end of days

A n old Argentine man was slowly dying, and his son came to visit him every evening of every one of his final days. The old man, who had worked hard during his lifetime, had the money to pay for a personal nurse and had therefore chosen to end his life at home. So every evening his son returned to his childhood house to sit by his dying father's side.

"*Buenas noches, viejo*," the son would say, smiling cordially as he opened the bedroom door.

"*¡Hola, hijo mío!*" The old man would beam the response with more energy and excitement than should have been possible for one of his age and condition.

Then the son would be seated beside the bed and the two would chat as the room grew cool and the faltering late-day autumn light filtered through the window. The two spoke of the good things in life. For the old man had truly lived his life to the fullest, his son was now doing so in the robust manner of his father, and the pair shared an unspoken bond of being two of a kind. So they spoke of wine and food and women and travel and adventure. Of living. They laughed and smiled and each one was silently proud of his resemblance to the other.

When memories surfaced during the course of the conversation, it was in the same natural manner as any other topic might arise. They were not brought forth from an urgency to share as much mutual sentimentality as possible before the time came when no more nostalgia could be shared between the two. The memories were brought up as commonly as one would periodically bring up a memory during the course of any other discussion. The memories were discussed and relived as though they would be there for years to come to be relived in a similar manner, not with the fatalistic finality that one might expect of a dying man remembering certain things with his son for the last time.

The father was dying and his son knew it and the father was not ashamed of this. They both chose to ignore the fact and instead chose to make the best of their time, as anyone who loved life and living should see fit to do, they reasoned. And each one instinctively knew that this was what the other wanted. They had always understood one another that way. So they talked and were happy and enjoyed each other's company and neither one, truthfully, could have wished for anything more.

Toward the end of the visit the old man's dinner would be served and the son would go downstairs to the wine cellar and bring the old man some wine to accompany his meal. His father shouldn't have wine, the doctor had advised, but his son brought it to him just the same. The son could only hope that his own offspring would be as obliging under similar circumstances.

His father enjoyed wine and he enjoyed sharing wine with others just as much. He would always offer his son a glass and the son would sit and sip the wine and talk to his father as the old man finished eating. The old man had fine taste as far as wine was concerned and the wine he ordered the son to retrieve was always perfect for sharing and tasting and talking.

"You know," the son mused one evening as he sipped wine with his father, "the other day a freight train bound for Buenos Aires from Mendoza derailed a few kilometers west of here. Some of the cars were carrying very expensive wine that was bound for England. Very expensive. And very good, they say."

The old man raised his eyebrows with interest.

"A lot of people went to the wreck and managed to salvage some of the wine," the son continued. "They say there are several cases making their way around Mercedes. I'm going to try and get hold of a few bottles if I can."

"If you manage, I'd like to try some," said the old man with genuine enthusiasm. The idea of a find such as this interested him greatly, and this interest was made apparent in the smile on his face and the curious gleam in his eye.

The next day the son arrived bearing a gift, a bottle of dark red wine which until a few days before had been bound for London. He presented the wine to his father, who held the bottle delicately up to the light.

The son opened the wine and poured his father a glass. The old man meticulously sniffed the wine. He took a hesitant first taste, nodded to himself, then took a larger sip. He finished half of the bottle with dinner that evening.

When the son was about to part, the old man said, "How many more bottles did you manage to get hold of?"

"Two more," said the son.

"I don't suppose you would mind bringing them to me? I would like to drink it."

The son winced a bit at the thought of giving up such a rare wine obtained under such curious circumstances. He was very proud of himself for having been able to acquire it, and he'd been planning to save the other two bottles for the anniversary dinner he was going to prepare for his wife the coming week. Upon thinking this, though, he immediately felt ashamed of his petty selfishness and without thinking more about it brought his father the other two bottles the following day.

And for the next five days the old man drank of this wine for his dinner. Half a bottle an evening for each of five evenings. In these five nights he never offered his son a taste of the wine, which was markedly uncharacteristic of the old man and seemed almost alarming to his son. And while the son could have just as easily asked to be served or served himself, he never would have dreamed of doing so. He let this be, though, and thought no more of it.

On the sixth evening, when no more of the wine remained, the old man was about to die. He knew it and his son knew it. The imminence of death permeated the air. No dinner came that evening. There were just the two men, talking quietly to one another. The old man's force was rapidly leaving him, and his voice grew hoarser and more strained and his wrinkled eyelids sank until his eyes formed mere slits. The old man mustered his remaining energy and spoke his final words.

"Son ... " It was an almost inaudible whisper.

"Yes?" the man's son asked.

"That was terrible wine. I had heard as much from Padre Diego, but I wanted to see for myself. I often have found his wine advice less solid than his religious advice. But no, it wasn't worth the label they put on the bottle. Fit for the *ingleses* and no one else. It's a pity it never got to them."

The son was confused. "But *viejo*," he inquired, "then why did you try some of the wine the first night and then ask for the rest of it?"

"I couldn't stand the thought of you serving a wine like that to your wife on her anniversary."

The son did not reply. He was startled.

"You *are* planning to cook dinner for her next week, aren't you? It's your anniversary. You always cook for her on your anniversary." The father's eyes and voice were all but nonexistent by now.

The son only nodded. He was choking back tears.

"Well, it would have been terrible to give her wine like that on her anniversary. She's such a fine girl. And why did I not simply tell you it was awful? Well, better for me to have it, since I wasn't long for this world anyway."

The old man managed a nearly imperceptible chuckle.

"No use wasting good wine on an old bag like me. Good wine for the living ..."

These were the old man's final words, but he smiled as he uttered them. The son was silent as his father ceased breathing, exhaled emptily, and closed his eyes completely for the final time.

In the old man's last will and testament his son was left many things. Among them was the key for a small but well-stocked basement wine cellar with which the son was very familiar. And it was filled with good wines that he knew would be perfect for sharing.

They always had understood one another that way, father and son.

to whom it may concern

Miranda,

It was nice speaking to you yesterday. Thank you kindly for hearing out my eccentric gripes. The main e-mail string in question is attached. There was at least one other e-mail from Ms. Bryan (saying she would get back to me soon, which to her credit she did). And then, some time later, I received an e-mail from someone else at your recruiting company wishing to confirm that I knew that the job in question for Storeson Strategies was in Richmond, Virginia. (Of course I didn't!)

My main concern is, as I expressed to you yesterday, that there was absolutely no introduction, signature line, or description of the job in question in Ms. Bryan's communications. Their tone was impersonal and, lacking as they did any kind of explanation, somewhat demanding. When I did request more information, my inquiry was met with a bucket of jargon and nothing in the way of specifics. Her initial communication looked very reminiscent of spam, with misspellings, a massive number of message recipients, and a vague query for personal information. Essentially, it demanded – without so much as an introduction, a greeting, or an identification – that I send an updated copy of my resumé so that I could be considered for a current job opening at an unidentified firm.

However, to place blame solely on Ms. Bryan, I think, would most likely be unfair. Ms. Bryan could simply have been given a stack of potential candidates to contact and not known that these candidates didn't have the foggiest idea as to what she was referring. We are all of us, after all, just pawns in the machine of outsourced, soulless commerce that characterizes our contemporary economy, and to direct all of our frustration at (and perhaps to discipline) a single person would make only cosmetic difference, when in reality that person's behavior is no doubt at least partially dictated by the nefarious system itself, a system in which people are used while simultaneously being stripped of their humanity.

I realize that nowadays, outsourcing will happen. Companies will not conduct their own hiring searches. Companies may not, in fact, pay their own "employees" directly. Many companies will make maximum use of temporary labor to keep costs (and obligations and responsibilities) as low as possible. And those that do have "permanent" employees may not provide those employees anything in the way of benefits. It is a state of affairs where the outsourcing is outsourced and the employees are at best "resources," at worst numbers on paper. People are nothing if not expendable and replaceable in this system in which there is very little ultimate accountability, yet in which each actor is in a position to use someone else (or is striving to attain such a position).

Given all this, the least that representatives of recruiting firms such as yours can do is to make their identities and motives clear and their communications sincere and personable. (And the least that a firm such as yours can do is to provide a work environment in which such behavior seems the natural course of action, instead of something that must be forced and faked.) Otherwise, we have taken that final step toward complete social disintegration: Not only is the system of the outsourced workplace devoid of accountability and humanity, but so, too, is the act of simply communicating with our fellow human beings.

And although it would be unfair to single out one person to blame for the myriad shortcomings of the system we have all helped to create, we cannot throw up our arms and say, "It's beyond me! There's nothing I can do about the whole mess, so who cares?" We can rebel, in our own small way, by remembering that we are human and that those with whom we interact are human, as well.

In closing, I wish you a fine day and a splendid weekend. Thank you considerably for your kind time and attention. And please do keep me in mind for future positions which you feel might more closely match my qualifications.

best friends

Years later, when I thought back to those nights in the Ohio summertime when my parents would argue, I could never remember exactly what they had said to each other or where in the house they had entrenched themselves. But I could recall with piercing clarity where I had been, a boy trying not to listen but listening all the same: on the sandstone patio beneath the kitchen window, under the wooden picnic table, in a cobwebbed corner of the front porch, in the musty garage, on the creaky swing set out back, in the dew-dampened grass staring up at the stars. But more vividly than anything I remembered my dog, sitting attentively beside me, watching me and seeming to understand.

That dog was truly an amazing dog. Though lots of people think the same thing about their own dogs, I learned as I grew up and engaged others in conversation, just like they think about their parents and their brothers and sisters and their spouses in singular, standard-setting ways that they're unaware of most of the time.

There was an irrigation ditch across the country road from my family's house. On sweltering summer days, the dog would seek refuge in the ditch, wallowing in the muddy water. But the dog knew he wasn't supposed to be in the ditch. He also knew he wasn't supposed to cross the country road. If one of the family members caught him frolicking in the ditch, he or she would scold the dog and tell him to go home. But instead of crossing the road, the dog would follow the ditch through the culvert that cut underneath the road, follow the ditch as it curved toward the woods behind the house. Fifteen or twenty minutes later, the dog would emerge from the woods, having gone a mile out of his way so as to not be seen crossing the road.

On Fridays we ordered pizza. The dog would obediently watch us all eat, patiently awaiting the end of the meal. Then I would present the dog with the empty boxes and the waxed paper smeared with grease and cheese and topping remnants. The dog devoted the next hour to pushing the treats around the garage floor with his nose, lapping up every last bit.

That dog and I spent a lot of time together. We would romp through the woods, the dog waiting as I climbed trees and I waiting as the dog chased through the underbrush in pursuit of deer and rabbits. I would put the dog in his outside cage every morning before leaving for school. When he was still a puppy, the dog would obediently follow me to the cage and get inside. When the dog was older and we were sure he would not run away or get into trouble, I would put the dog in the cage and leave the door unlatched. When everyone came home at night the dog would be sitting on the porch or in the yard, but he would return to his cage and wait to be told that he could come out. I taught the dog tricks. I taught the dog to jump through a Hula Hoop, a trick the dog picked up after only fifteen minutes of instruction in the back yard.

That dog knew if someone was talking about him. If somebody said his name, or even if they said "dog," his ears would prick up and he would look intently in the direction of the voice. He had a large vocabulary. If someone told him to get his rug or his ball or his cow's hoof, he would march into the living room and pluck his rug or his ball or his cow's hoof from the copper pail where his toys were kept. The toys rested atop the back issues of *Food & Wine* that I used for making collages for school projects.

Years later, I, by now a young man, lived in an apartment with my wife and a puppy. My wife and I told the puppy that we loved him. I had never said that to a dog before, but it now seemed a natural thing for me to say.

At first the puppy was very independent-minded, even somewhat standoffish. He relied on my wife and I for food and trips outside, not love and affection. He tugged and pulled and fought against his leash. He was more interested in his food and his toys in and of themselves than in us, the people who gave them to him. But soon that stage had passed and the puppy was growing and developing a personality. He herded my wife and I into bed at night, encircling us and lying across the floor to block our retreat, monitoring our progress as we moved from the kitchen to the living room to the bathroom and then to the bedroom. He jumped into bed with us a few times – checking on us, grooming us a bit, making sure we were down for good – before settling into his own dog bed on the floor.

The puppy followed me to the bathroom in the middle of the night and watched as I peed. The puppy waited, inquisitively cocking his head, then plodded back to the bedroom after me when I was done. Through the apartment's side window, the puppy watched us leave, his front feet perched on the window ledge. He greeted us at the door when we returned, his tail wagging, his ears pressed back, a frisky bundle of tightly wound joy.

The puppy didn't bark very much at all, though lately when unknown people made sudden moves – emerging from cars, opening front doors with a bang – toward my wife or me, the hair on the back of his neck would bristle and he would growl and bark. It was especially surprising when he first did that, because the last time we had heard the puppy bark, his voice had still been squeaky and small. And now, as if by magic, it was deep and imposing.

Usually, though, the puppy's communication was silent. He wagged his tail, curled into the contours of our laps as we squatted to pet him, licked us affectionately, batted his paws playfully in our direction, dropped a tennis ball at our feet, ran through his repertoire of tricks to please us and to be noticed – *up, sit, shake, lie down, roll over, get in your cage.*

The puppy possessed the last of the rugs that had belonged to my childhood dog. That first dog had been given to play with, at one time or another, everything from fuzzy toilet seat covers to old towels to this last one, a carpet remnant left over from when my family had redone the living room. We had referred to all these as rugs. "Get your rug," we would tell the dog, and he bounded into the living room to retrieve the toy and returned to play tug-of-war with us. My mother had given the new puppy the leftover carpet scrap, plus a bed that had belonged to the other dog, as a present after my wife and I went to the pound and got the new puppy.

Besides telling the puppy that I loved him, I called the puppy "mister." That's what I'd always done with male dogs, called them "mister," a trait I supposed I'd picked up from my parents, since they'd said the same thing to my childhood dog. And I found myself doing the same with the new puppy. "Come here, mister," I'd say as we both sat on the floor. And the puppy would run over and lick my face.

I asked my wife one night if she thought dogs loved people in the same way that people love people.

"I don't know if it's love," she said. "I do think they feel secure and protected, and they want to protect their families in return."

It made sense, but it also made me wonder how different that really was from the love people feel toward each other. Except that people have language with which to complicate the matter, as well as some sort of desire or need to do so.

A friend of mine was incensed whenever he witnessed or heard of some people's costly, over-the-top obsessions with dogs: doggie play groups, expensive mobile dog-grooming services, high-priced dog walkers, AKC-registered puppies selling for hundreds of dollars while dogs at the pound were put to sleep by the dozens.

"It's ridiculous," he often said. "People care more about dogs than they care about each other."

I thought that, perhaps for my friend, the issue of money in this case clouded the issue of love. Sure, people who lavish their dogs with extravagant presents might be the same kind to lavish others with things, or to expect to be lavished themselves, in order to fulfill their ideal of love and belonging, some sort of insecure notion that made them equate things with feelings. Be that as it may, that observation said nothing about real love and compassion. I wondered if there weren't perhaps something to the notion that dogs care more about people, at least more honestly and unconditionally, than people often care about each other – and that people understand and respond to this, although maybe unconsciously. Dogs appreciate you all the same, stuff or no stuff, unlike some people. Dogs don't expect to be lavished with things. Dogs love their owners whether they live in a mansion or a mobile home court.

Maybe humans are unnecessarily complex, I would think as I played with the puppy on the floor of the apartment. Or not truly as complex as they like to consider themselves. With vocabulary, imagination, and empathy, it seemed as though people had the potential to help each other just as much as to hurt each other. But in my experience, people seemed more compelled to hurt, or to at least complicate things, make them unnecessarily convoluted and difficult. Which is why I suppose I gravitated toward silence and was quietly thankful to have found my wife, someone who wouldn't automatically interpret that silence as discomfort and unease, but rather the very opposite.

The subject of the fighting on those summer nights of my childhood boiled down to communication, namely my mother's assertion that my father failed to communicate. My mother would yell and my father would remain silent, occasionally nipping back when things got too sharp or personal, like an aging, otherwise tolerant dog that has suffered one affront too many. On those occasions when my parents fought, I felt more like my father but more sympathetic toward my mother.

My father traveled for his job, and when he would return from his months-long absences, he would be distant and solitary. My mother faulted my father for not getting with the program, for still acting as though he were traveling, for not letting her know what was going on at work, for not inquiring about his children and her own work, for not taking the initiative by suggesting we all go out to do something. My mother was a busy person, even when she wasn't at work, always refinishing furniture or canning vegetables or landscaping or gardening or mending clothes. I don't think that I ever saw her really relax. It seemed to me as though she were overcompensating for something. I could see how my father might be daunted by the whirlwind. I myself felt embarrassed and lazy sometimes for wanting to walk in the woods or read a book or go do something with my friends. And I could see, in turn, how my mother could look upon my father's distance as some sort of rejection.

"You don't communicate ..." my mother would say to my father. It made me wonder if she were missing the point, that maybe there were things in his life that he couldn't communicate in the usual ways.

"You don't understand ..." my father would say, and I thought that maybe he wasn't trying hard enough to make her understand, or was perhaps taking the wrong approach.

It occurred to me that my parents had different ideas about marriage. But I wondered if that weren't necessarily the critical thing, that instead not understanding that they each *could* have such different ideas was. Each didn't really seem to grasp what the other one wanted and needed and what he or she was willing and able to give in return. It was a two-way impasse: He needed space and she needed closeness, she needed activity and he needed contemplation, and neither could incorporate the other's need into his or her personal ideal. I understood this in the way that children do, more open-minded than adults but with fewer words at their disposal to define – and thus limit, oversimplify – an idea.

Usually, my dog was in the middle of household activities, keeping tabs on the various members of our family. He would roam back and forth in the house, settling down in an intermediate position where he could keep everyone in earshot. But on those summer nights when the fighting began, the dog followed me outside, or scratched on the door until one of my parents ushered him out to join me. And the dog would sit there with me – in the yard, on the porch, beneath the picnic table – resting but alert, mildly alarmed but confident, pricking his ears in the direction of the altercation and then darting his eyes back toward me.

As a young man looking back on those nights, it seemed to me in hindsight that the fireflies were always floating in the humid air. One of the neighbors was always grilling out. The windows in the house were always open and the lights were on, so the inside and outside noises and sights and smells would merge there around the perimeter of the house. On the edge of that convergence, I used a stick to draw pictures in the flower beds or tried to read a book by the porch light or plucked blades of grass one at a time from the dew-dampened lawn. I did not cry. I just felt empty and confused.

On one of those many summer nights – there seemed like thousands at the time, though looking back later, I knew there weren't nearly so many – I gazed down at my dog and remembered a time when I'd been unkind to him. The dog had been dozing under a tree on the lawn, sprawled in the shade on a July afternoon. I had some friends over, and we boys had lighted strings of firecrackers next to the sleeping dog. When they exploded on three sides of him, the dog awoke with a start and let out a frightened yelp. He immediately ran to me and cowered between my legs, shuddering, his brown eyes open wide, looking confused and forlorn, looking to me for protection.

Recalling that moment several years later – and many years before I had the new puppy with my wife – on a warm Ohio summer night outside among the fireflies and the shadows and the barbecue smells, my dog watching over me, I felt secure. And ashamed. Inside among the lights, my parents were airing their perpetual grievances. The dog was casting watchful glances at me, the way my puppy would later do as he herded me to bed as a young man. I thought at that moment that the truest form of understanding was knowing – and being okay with – the notion that you would never truly understand. Yet being willing to surrender some of that certainty as you tried your best to understand nonetheless.

I reached down to the dog and ruffled the hair on his head and gave him a hug. The dog wagged his tail and licked my hand in response.

"I'm sorry," I said to him. "I'm sorry, mister."

international

This, *this* is what we mean when we say you are wrong.

"*... just about anything*"

Where is it that you are from? Oh, yes. The United States. Yes, I
know the United States. I lived for year and a half in Danbury.
Connecticut? No. Danbury is in New York. Yes, yes, I am from
Cuenca. Yes, there are many of us from Cuenca living in New York, mostly in
Queens. The years I lived in New York were 1994 and 1995. I worked there
long enough to pay off this house, which I had bought on credit. Indeed, there
are many foreigners living here in Baños. They have opened up businesses.
They own restaurants, hotels. No, it is not so difficult for one to buy land in
Ecuador, you just need to first purchase the property and then you can apply for
residency. Owning property, it is easy to live here and run your business. Or you
can find someone local who can purchase the property for you. But you must be
careful. To be successful, you must be nice to everyone. Many foreigners have
moved here, and many of them failed because they did not make friends. My ex-
husband is from Sweden; he moved here with his savings, so he had that money
to spend, but it never quite seemed as though he fit in. And then he spent all his
money and afterwards depended upon me. It is important to have friends, but
you must be careful whom you trust. There is a German family here in Baños
who came here with nothing – the man, his wife, their children, some luggage –
and began to sell fresh bread on the street and now they have a house. One girl
from Baños married a man from Holland and they live here, she teaching

Spanish to foreigners and he teaching English to people from here. There was an American, now dead may he rest in peace, who owned the hotel by the baths. You've been to the baths? Yes, the large brown hotel. And there are two young men from Argentina, young men with ponytails, one dark-haired, one blond, they own a restaurant, perhaps you've seen it. An American owns Café Good and it's always full of people. The Argentines say that they won't get girlfriends from Baños, that they want ones from far away. And that's a good idea. Because people here, you've got to be friends with them, but you can't trust them too much because they'll pull a fast one on you. In the United States, people liked me and got along well with me, and why? Because I was sociable. I was nice to everyone. But I didn't like it there. No, it wasn't the cold, you get used to that, one can learn to live with just about anything. But there, there you have to be careful of what you say, and the Dominicans in the factory were mean to me, they even hit me sometimes. And Dominicans won't help out anyone else, not Ecuadorians, not Colombians, not Argentines. And I sewed nurses' caps and there were supposed to be twenty-five in each bag but the Dominicans – they had keys – they'd come in and take some out, so my bags would only have twenty-one, twenty-two, twenty-three caps in them, and they said I'd miscounted, and I said, "No I did not." I am a woman with credentials, right there is my certificate in sewing. I sew, I design clothes. I'd like to start a little shop. I would like to sell some land and build a hotel here, perhaps with a sewing shop on the bottom along with a little place to eat. I have land in Cuenca. It's cheap there. Thirty hectares with a house are $15,000. And I would like to sell some of my ancestral land so I can start a hotel and there are seven of us children, but three of my brothers live in the United States. There are lots of really nice houses around Cuenca that people ordered built while they were working in the United States, but now the houses are for sale because many people decided to stay in the North. It's hard to live in two places and then to have to choose, but me, I got out of the United States as fast as I could. I worked enough there to pay off the mortgage for this house and then I left, but lots of people stay in the United States or in Spain where they have begun to go recently to seek work, even though there's money here that could be made, and if it weren't for six years of divorce proceedings I might be doing pretty well for myself. My son is twenty-one. He is a student of medicine in Ambato, only three semesters ago did that university open, before he lived in Quito. It's very expensive in Quito – one must pay rent, transportation, so many cars and so much congestion and craziness. Here, it's much more peaceful and my son gets up every morning and goes to school on the bus and comes back here at the end of the day, but they are long days because medicine is difficult, very difficult. And meanwhile, my Swedish husband, he for whom I had vouched, whose name I put on this house – which I was working to pay off – so he could have residency in this country, while I was away working in New York he'd taken up with another woman and had a child. And that's not fair. In New York I was there less than one week and already I was trying to speak English. I would arrive at the factory and say, "Good morning, everybody." And the Dominicans, they asked me, "Why are you speaking English? You don't know English. You need to speak Spanish." Six years of divorce proceedings. I won in Ambato, and he appealed it all the way to Quito because he wanted to keep this house that was not his in the least, except for the fact that I had been kind enough to put his name on the deed. Do you know how much six years of lawyers cost? I could have set up a hotel already. And a little place to sell meals. And living alone can be so difficult. But I haven't found another man yet. I don't want just any man. What for, so he can up and leave me for another woman? I want a man that's worth the while. A serious man. A man who will commit to me for life. There I was, working, doing hard work in New York supporting my husband and son and paying off this house, and what does he do? It's not right. I blame her more than him, but they're both in the wrong. And now I hear that he's left her and is living with another. Living alone is hard. So much work and you never get to go anywhere ...

By the time the woman had finished repairing the frayed backpack strap, her face was sweating in the glow of the sewing lamp. The lamp sat upon a table, which stood behind a glass counter and in front of a concrete wall. The wall was filled with pastel bathing suits for sale and family photos and the woman's degrees. And at some point between finishing the strap and accepting our dollar, her face softened and her chattery voice faltered and she was crying, tears from her eyes merging into the sweat from her cheeks and forehead, her words colliding with her sputters, and she was thanking us and we were saying goodbye and only after we had parted did we truly realize the weight of her heartbreak, as though it had followed us out the door along with the vision of her sitting behind her sewing machine in the bottom floor of the house she'd bought on credit, which she had paid off by sewing nurses' caps in a faraway land. Sitting behind her sewing machine, softly sobbing, a woman whose name I never knew.

dominance

A t the dog park, a woman in a business suit carries on a cell-phone call about a conference call. Her voice is assertive, her posture aggressive, she stands against the wire fence as though facing down marauding hordes of bureaucrats.

"It's not *rocket science*. All you've got to do is look at the GSA price list. We need to get him on the conference call."

Around her, all is dust and drool and flashing fur and rolling and wrestling and retrieving. Dogs sniff and piss and wrangle each other by the scruff of the neck.

"It's the pricing. It's the pricing. I don't mean to bring you in on all this. You're the voice of reason. Exactly. *Exactly.* It's *Jack.* That's the biggest part of the problem."

Out of her sight, her finely groomed Pomeranian mounts, thrusts his furry pelvis against, a bewildered beagle.

at the top of mt. greylock
(anywhere but here)

This is a long story, I tell Cathy when she sits down across from me at the coffee shop. Maybe you wanna hear it, maybe you don't. But it's something that's been bothering me. That's what I tell her. It's the first Sunday morning in September and we're about to drink some coffee.

"Well, let's hear it, then," she says. "It's a long weekend, so your long story won't eat into my free time as much as it normally would."

"It's actually some *things* that are bothering me," I tell her. "Lately, the bad stuff seems to be all connected. Like it's rooted in something. You know? Like the bad things are happening for a reason. They're not the same things, but they're like – cousins, you know? They're all related somehow. Does that make sense?"

"No, not really," she says. "Maybe you should just tell the story, or we *will* be here all weekend."

"So the other night I bartend at this wedding, right? Friday night. I found the job advertised on the Internet ..."

"That's never a good start."

"Well, no. No it wasn't, as a matter of fact." But I don't dwell on this and instead proceed with the story.

It was a clusterfuck, is what it was. One big fucked-up, acrimonious mess. So I get to where it's at, you know, which is this fancy high-rise apartment building just across the river from DC. Turns out that the girl putting it on for the bride lived there, so they could use the penthouse social room for free. Well, she used to live there, anyway; her boyfriend still lived there, she said, but she didn't – though they were still together, she pointed out to me. Even though they didn't live together anymore. Like I give a shit, you know? But at first I was kind of impressed, you know – penthouse and all. But I get up there and this organizer girl is running back and forth like a crazy fool, saying how nothing's ready and that she quite frankly doesn't give a shit that nothing's ready and that she quite frankly doesn't even like the bride very much. I don't even know how to describe it. There's a few other girls sitting around – not really girls, I shouldn't say that. Young women. Early or mid-twenties. One girl's sitting, looking at this bunch of flowers she's got, which she's supposed to be turning into some sort of decoration. Just looking at them and thinking about how nice the arrangement will be when she's done, which is looking to be never. Another girl's just kind of sitting there, staring at me like she's a horse and I'm a bucket of oats or some shit. The photographer is wandering around, like she's walking on air and not really in touch with reality; she tells me she doesn't really know the bride, though she went to her bachelorette party and she's taking the pictures as a favor. So she kind of knows her, you know, but not really; I think the photographer was pretty stoned. Anyway, it's after 6:00, and the wedding's supposed to start at 7:00.

I should mention that I saw the ad looking for wedding help – and responded to it – maybe two weeks before the wedding itself. So you can see that there wasn't exactly a lot of forethought to the whole affair. And I probably made a mistake when I told the bride I had bartending experience. The ad was looking for "people (perfect for students and interns!) to help serve drinks and desserts at my wedding." I should've just played dumb and left it at that, just done exactly what they told me to do when they told me to do it – and nothing more.

There was this air about the bunch. I could smell it immediately. I know the type. You know the type. Privileged transplants to the DC area, you know, who think everything's supposed to work out for them here in the halls of power. And this wedding was no different, despite the fact that they had a wedding to run and that the wedding started in an hour and the room wasn't decorated or set up or anything and the organizer girl is running around like an upper-crust gerbil on methamphetamines, flailing her arms very important-like and saying how she doesn't care about the bride. And here I was in my tuxedo to lend an air of formality and professionalism to their last-minute waltz through fantasyland.

The organizer girl, she's like, the reception doesn't start 'til 7:30. Right after the ceremony. So maybe, she suggests, I could just go downstairs to the mall and eat a sandwich or something and come back for the reception part, which was all being held in this same room. And start setting up as soon as the ceremony was over and stuff.

Wait a minute, I say. Being all professional, though, you know, like I was assessing the situation and how I could best be of service. You really want to have your bar set up as much as possible, because your guests are going to want to have themselves a drink as soon as it's all over and they start mingling and all. And it wouldn't be particularly professional or classy to have me lugging bottles and ice and cups and everything across the common area in front of the guests once they've begun talking and all, and them wanting a drink right then and there and watching me getting ready to eventually serve them the drink that they'd really like to have in their hand right at that moment, you know. You want a feeling of everything being all laid out, waiting for them. That's what the guests expect.

Okay, says the boss girl. Let me show you what we've got, and you can set it up how you best see fit. So she leads me to the service kitchen, which was way across the room from the bar – and to begin with, the bar was just a few tables with plastic tablecloths over them. Low tables, so I had to stoop all night. You know how when you go to an elementary school and everything seems miniature: low sinks and toilets and little chairs and posters hung at waist level. That bar, if you wanna call it that, would've been fine had I been tending it while sitting down. And the only space I had to use as a prep area was this little ledge that ran alongside the windows behind the bar. Little ledge about four inches wide. And the situation in the kitchen was worse than I could've imagined. There were a few bottles of booze, not nearly enough for that sense of pampered abundance hosts usually want to get across; some of them were already open, too, so it was more like a feeling of thrift-store sloppiness. The only bottle of whiskey that they'd brought held about enough for four drinks. Four drinks, I shit you not. They'd bought three cases of beer and some wine and champagne. And a few bottles of mixers. But they had just then put all that shit in the fridge – which wasn't a very cold fridge anyway – and it was warmer than my fucking mucus on an August afternoon.

Right then and there my mood sank. It was riding the fence already, but right then and there it just belly-flopped. She had no big tub to keep the beer and champagne and white wine on ice. I mean, what the hell was I supposed to do – run back and forth to the lukewarm fridge every time somebody wanted a cold beer or a glass of white wine? And the only receptacle for ice she *did* have was a little punch bowl; and no scooper, at that. No pitcher for water, which people are gonna want once they've had their fill of drinks. No rags or cloths. No drink straws. No garnishes. No wine key; luckily, I brought my own. Two of them. And do you know what I ended up using for drink straws? Some dude went down to the Dunkin' Donuts and swiped a bunch of coffee stirrers, which I cut in half with my pocket knife.

Cathy has been fumbling in her purse, looking for her cigarettes. I realize that she's a little impatient and probably isn't entirely paying attention. My stories can take a while to get where they're going. Mainly, I suppose, because I'm not really sure myself where they're headed; I mean, there's something important afoot beneath it all, but I'm not really good at isolating what it is. You know? Like those Magic Eye posters; I never could do those things worth a shit. She's found her cigarettes and lights one. Her face looks tired, her eyes still kind of hibernating. I figure I might as well have a cigarette, too. Maybe that will create some solidarity between us, like we're in this together, like this story is something that matters enough for us to discuss while we're smoking cigarettes and drinking coffee. You know – together.

"Listen," I tell her. "I guess this doesn't seem like it's going anywhere. But it's all connected. There's something deep here. I got home after all that crap the other night, it must've been 1 a.m., and I couldn't sleep. I just paced around. Went down to the gas station and sat on the curb and drank a Hawaiian Punch and smoked about ten cigarettes. I sat there in the parking lot, you know, and parts of the parking lot were lit up and parts of it were dark. And I sat there in the shadows on the edge of everything, and a few people walked in and out of the little store. And I couldn't help thinking that there's something about people that pokes its head up sometimes in different spots. Like the Whack-a-Mole game at Chuck E. Cheese's. It's the same thing, but in different places. And if it would just stay put I would understand it all better. And maybe be able to do something about it."

"That's just human nature: to try to make patterns out of isolated events," Cathy says to me. A little too snippily, if you want to know the truth. "It feeds our sense of self-importance, which is probably just a slightly refined version of some animal survival mechanism. That's how conspiracy theories take hold."

Well anyway, I tell her – the snidely organizer girl – that that beer and wine are in need of some serious first aid. They've gotta be in some ice water to get them chilled quickly; even if the fridge was cold, none of that stuff would get chilled in time by just sitting there. And we'll need a big tub for that, which we'll need anyway when it comes time to serve the drinks at the bar. She says no problem, though she doesn't seem too concerned. So we go downstairs to get ice, down to the mall below the apartments. She gets money for the ice off the bride's stepfather, who's hanging around the space. She asks me how much the ice will cost. Like I know. You know? And she grabs the photographer, yanks her away from her kind of stoned wanderings, who's supposed to follow the bride and groom from the hotel they'll be staying at that night to the wedding itself. So we get down to the mall level, and the organizer chick points the stoned photographer chick in the direction of the hotel that's right down there. Only she realizes that it's the wrong hotel, that the hotel she needs is the one at the *other* end of the mall – which is like ten blocks away, closer to the airport. The mall's narrow and is laid out lengthwise below all those high rises. And the photographer needs to be there like, at that moment. But the organizer girl just shrugs her shoulders and sends the photographer off through the mall. And gives her a little smile and a pat on the back.

So then us two go into the drugstore that's down there to get ice. Only they don't have any ice that day because their freezer isn't working. So we go to the wine and beer store. And the bags of ice they have are small, and we have to wait while this guy fills them up one at a time way back in the back of the store, where the ice machine is. So I'm running back and forth with these bags as quick as the guy can fill them, putting them on the counter so the checkout lady can ring them up and put them in plastic bags for carrying. And we pay for the ice and lug the bags all the way back up to the penthouse. And this organizer girl can't stop talking about how she really doesn't care how all this turns out. Don't worry, she tells me, just do the best you can do with what you've got. I'm not worried, she says, I don't really even care. Though I *am* worried, because I can't justify doing a half-assed job to dozens of people who don't know I'm under instructions to only worry about doing a half-assed job. I mean, shit, I haven't even met the bride yet, and she's the one who hired me.

So I get the bar set up as much as I can, given the time and material constraints. I find a Styrofoam cooler that's lying on top of some shelves in the kitchen – one of those kinds of coolers for steaks that people with money order in the mail – and set some beer to chill and arrange the cups and napkins. It's hard to make half-empty liquor bottles, plastic cups, and paper napkins look classy on top of a wrinkled plastic tablecloth. But I tried. I tell the organizer that her liquor situation isn't exactly abundant, but she just shrugs and ignores me.

And then it's time for the wedding. So I stand in the kitchen with the door closed while the ceremony goes on. And then the organizer pops her head through the door, looks at me, and says, "Serve drinks." That's all she said. Of course, all these people are already hovering around the bar. Wedding vultures. Youngish people who love free drinks but who also try to act all grown-up and important and serious and distinguished. Like little kids playing house. They're already yakking about politics, about elections and polls and focus groups and lobbying strategies. Sometimes I catch a word like "underprivileged" and "disenfranchisement." "This may be the beginning of the end of the Bush presidency," one of them murmurs – with grave certainty, as if to suggest, *Take it from someone who knows about these things.* This was a political wedding, you see. I mean, this woman who got married, I looked up the Web site of her company; it's a "message strategy" company that works with Democrats. As far as I can tell, it's a PR company for PR people. How to make the lies you want to tell ring more true, or something like that.

So I start to serve drinks, and already people are scoffing at the amount of whiskey and the lack of garnishes and the fact that I'm pouring out of these big, clunky, half-empty plastic jugs of booze, with no pour spout or anything. And because there's still no pitcher of water, which I've been told is on the way. All I signed up for was to serve drinks. And these people are giving me looks like I was the bar *organizer* and I was cheating them, you know, not bringing garnishes and stiffing them on liquor. Some guy even muttered as much to himself, though loud enough that I could hear. Something about getting ripped off. I wanted to say, *Hey, don't hang me, man. It's your friends who are stiffing you. They might as well have charged at the door and made you bring a covered dish and chip in for the honeymoon and shit.* That's really what they should've done, actually. At least that would have been honest.

And pretty quickly off the bat, do you know what this one smart-ass motherfucker says to me?

"Do you know?" I ask Cathy, who I know doesn't know.

"No," she says. "What did he say?"

"He says, 'Do you have a tip jar?' And I say – this was still toward the beginning of the night – I say, 'Not yet, but you're welcome to start one.' And I pointed at some clean cups that were sitting on the bar. And he looks at me, and he says, 'That's all right. I don't have any cash, anyway.' And then he grins at me and walks away. With his fucking drink in hand."

"He said that?!" Cathy says. I knew that last bit would catch her attention. "That's tacky."

"Hell yes it's tacky."

Then this big guy with a greasy grin on his face sidles up to the bar. I pour his drink. He takes a big slurp and pushes it back at me. "Can you help me out with a little more vodka? I'm in a pretty deep conversation, here," he says, trying to sound desperate while he smirks in this self-important way. "It's getting pretty emotional."

So anyway, to make a long story short, I work my ass off. I keep as much beer as will fit chilling in that little cooler. I make drinks left and right. There's only one tiny little garbage can for the whole space, and I end up emptying it the whole night whenever it fills up so it doesn't look unsightly. So in between making drinks, I'm running back and forth from the bar to the kitchen. Occasionally one of the organizer chicks – more have suddenly appeared, and I don't even know their names – will ask me if I need anything. Sometimes I tell them and they bring it to me. Sometimes I tell them and I never see them again until they're ready for another drink.

After a while, I guess word got around from some of the heavier-drinking guests to the organizers. One of the organizer chicks, who hasn't spoken to me all night, comes rushing up to me and says that she understands we're out of whiskey – insinuating by the tone of her voice that it's my fault – and we're low on some of the other boozes. Well, yes, I said. That's what I warned about at the beginning. Well, she says, try to push the beer, try to push the beer. And all of a sudden, four or five organizer chicks start rushing to and from the kitchen, cradling bottles of beer in their arms. Bottles of lukewarm beer that they just plunk on the table. I mean, my little cooler's all full; there's at least fifteen beers in there, and I've been sure to keep them ice-cold and refill the cooler every chance I get and everything. I look at these chicks as they're rushing back and forth. I tell one that I don't have room for these beers and that it looks incredibly tacky just to leave them sitting out, that the real problem is we're out of whiskey and people are wanting whiskey. This girl looks back at me and says just to leave the warm beers on the table, that hopefully people will just grab them and forget about the booze. And then she leaves, and I try to hide the beers under the table. And while I'm doing that, some dude grabs a couple, opens one, and glares at me. "These are *warm*," he hisses.

"I felt like just leaving and letting it all disintegrate into chaos," I say to Cathy. "Maybe accidentally spilling the rest of the liquor before I left."

"Why didn't you?"

"Because then I would be the bad guy. I would be the one who ruined the wedding."

"Maybe not. Maybe the bride knows what a shitty job her friend did."

"But her friend orchestrated it so she couldn't take any of the blame."

"Maybe you think too deeply about these things ..." Cathy offers. She's started on her second cigarette.

"But she wanted it to be classy. That's what I'm saying. That's where the disconnect was. This girl doesn't do a fucking thing, says she hates the bride, but still all these friends are there and she wants it to be fucking seamless and professional. She wants them to stroke her ego and tell her what a good job she did on such short notice and with such limited resources. How good of a friend she is. They weren't *nice*. They weren't *genuine*. That's what bothers me the most. Goddamn I fucking hate people."

Just this one old man treated me like a person. He was the grandfather of either the bride or the groom. I don't know which. I never really even talked to the bride. This older guy chitchatted with me a bit, gave me a smile and said thank you whenever he came back for more cranberry juice. And once, after I refilled his glass, he picked it up off the bar table and as he did, he kind of sloshed a little cranberry juice on the cheap plastic table cloth. And he grabs some napkins all urgent-like and tries to mop up the bit that he spilled. I tell him, I say, "Don't worry about it, sir. Let me clean that up. I've already got stuff spilled on my sleeves, so it won't make any difference to me." And he smiles at me, his glass shaking in his hand, and there was a look of gratitude, but also some kind of defeat, in his eyes. And he holds his cup with one shaking hand and reaches into his pocket with the other shaking hand and puts a couple of dollars in my tip cup (Which I'd started myself by throwing some quarters in a cup. You know, to give people a little hint.) "Thanks for not losing your cool," he says to me, trying to smile.

So the night goes on, you know, and they serve cake and I pour champagne. And pretty soon it's winding down, thank god. I run around picking up garbage. The main organizer chick shows back up. I realize I haven't seen her since the beginning of the night, since I poured her a screwdriver and she asked if I needed anything at the moment. Then she was gone, and it was these other organizer girls who'd been helping out. Supposedly helping out, anyway. But the original organizer girl is back now, and she's really drunk. She's wandering around aimlessly, but she's kind of shouting as though she's trying to get things in order. One of the organizer girls, who's cleaning up what's left of the cake, looks at another one and wonders out loud where the head girl has been all night. I kind of wonder that, myself.

Pretty soon most of the guests are gone and we're picking up garbage and shit. The main organizer girl comes up to me and asks how things went.

Well, okay, I tell her. I mean, I made the best of things. That's all you needed to do, she says. Though, I tell her, I was honestly a bit surprised by the tip situation. I mean, I made seven bucks. Plus the quarters I threw in there at the beginning, which don't really count. She looks at me kind of puzzled. I'm telling you, she was wasted. And she hadn't been there at all the whole night, once things got rolling. Where was she? That's what I want to know. She had that strange exasperated look that people get in their eyes when they're trashed and think you're wrong and are wasting their time. I tell her that, frankly – being pretty liberal and all myself – I was a little shocked. I'd worked at the inauguration, you know, at one of the balls, and the Republican VIPs who I was bartending for – the VIPs whose drinks were absolutely free – didn't tip worth a damn. I'd expected a bit more from the progressive types, I told her. Maybe they might have a better idea about the service industry and the kind of stuff people have to deal with. She looked at me as though I'd just demanded her first-born kid or some shit. I mean, damn – she was *trashed*.

"I don't see how we should be any different than they are," she told me. Spat at me, really. "Both parties are all the same now, anyway. Don't you know that? There's little to distinguish them. So how else was the night?"

To be honest with you, I tell her, I'm not sure you realize how hard I worked for you people. I mean, this could have been a real disaster. You could've just as likely gotten someone to agree to this job and then not show up. Or someone who couldn't think on their own. And I busted my tail for you people, I tell her. I wanted to impress to her what a half-assed job she'd done. But even though it was her running around saying how she didn't care from the very beginning – until she disappeared, that is – I also don't think she was capable of considering the fact that she *could* be in the wrong. Sometimes I wish I could speak in a special tone of voice, you know, that would cut through walls of bullshit people surround themselves with and make them understand. You know? Like ethical telepathy or something. But she just says how appreciative she is of the hard work I did. Everything ran very smoothly, she assures me, and the guests were very happy. I want to ask her how the fuck she knows. How the fuck.

Then, when I'm carrying leftover stuff out toward the elevator, this other organizer chick asks me how the night went. All right, I say. I'm trying to avoid a confrontation, which I know will happen if I don't ignore these people and get the hell out of there. By the way, I tell her, I got some blood on one of your towels (They'd finally gotten around to giving me a couple towels.)

"What?!" she demanded.

Look, I tell her, I'm sorry. I had some hand sanitizer that I put on my hand as soon as I realized it was bleeding. I wrapped some napkins real thick around it, and it didn't bleed but for a second. It wasn't a deep cut. You know how bottle caps make those little gouges in your fingers. I'm sorry about the towel.

"It's not the towel," she says. She's drunk, too. Drunk and reminded of how intelligent and compassionate she is. "I'm alarmed that you got hurt on the job and you didn't say anything to me. That's very worrisome. I mean, we're *very much* supportive of OSHA regulations. We're all liberal Democrats here, you know."

"That's funny," I tell her. "Because your friends sure didn't tip like liberal Democrats."

"What's that supposed to mean?" she shoots back. "I was glad to see," she says, "that you put out a tip cup. That's good to see."

"Well, your friends didn't seem very appreciative. Apparently I didn't do a very good job. About seven dollars' worth of a good job, since that's all they tipped."

She frowns then – for just a second, though, but long enough for me to know that I've got some leverage.

"Well," she says, regaining her drunken pride and all, "I don't see how that makes any difference. I'm sorry you think our friends our cheap. We were working on a tight budget here. We're all young, you know. We don't have much money."

"Neither do I," I tell her. "But if I go out, then I damn well make sure I can afford to tip. Especially when the drinks are free. It's just disheartening to hear these people talk about progressive causes and all, to hear them talk the talk but not walk the walk. I'm not here at midnight just because I felt like helping out with your last-minute wedding. Maybe your other friend's right. Maybe the parties *are* the same. Maybe Democrats don't feel any obligation to actually care about people. Maybe it's because of the so-called liberals in this town that my regular job, at a company with a government contract, is a union gig that doesn't even pay a living wage."

She got real stern then. Real, real mad.

"Don't you *dare* accuse me of not being liberal!" she said. Really, she spat it. Very venomously. "I've worked on two presidential campaigns. *Don't you dare!*"

And she spun on her heels and stormed away from me. Far, far away. Out of the room and down the hall. I swear, I've never seen that actually happen before. Maybe stomping around in little circles, all mad and in a huff and stuff, you know. But I thought people only actually stormed out of the room like that in movies and shit.

"Maybe you found an excuse to be mad at the event because you didn't like the people who were there? Or because you didn't make good tips?" Cathy says. She's trying to extract some meaning from my story. Usually with her, though, that involves trying to figure out what's wrong with me that would make me think there's something wrong with something or somebody else. Cathy and I, we tried dating for a while. But it just didn't work out. I don't remember now whose fault it was. Though some people would say that if I don't remember, then chances are that it was mine.

"I'm through keeping my mouth shut about all this hypocrisy," I tell her.

"You already don't keep your mouth shut. That's why you can't keep a job. Maybe you just felt duped," Cathy says. "I mean, she was looking for people on the Internet a matter of weeks before the thing was to take place, right? That isn't exactly a recipe for success. You just hold people to standards to which they aren't willing to hold themselves. Then you get pissed off because things don't work out like you want them to."

"I don't understand people in DC. 'Our Nation's Capital.' Especially the young people," I say. "They've got their little tribes, their so-called 'friendships' that seem pretty goddamn fake and opportunistic, if you ask me. The talk you hear on the train and shit. You know how people sound when they're pretending to be friendly with and interested in each other? Like there's a tone of voice you use for strangers, and one you use for real friends, and then there's that tone of voice for people you pretend to know and like and value, yet who are essentially complete strangers for all intents and purposes?"

But there's more, I say. More to the story, that is. Cathy kind of sighs and starts herself another cigarette.

So the next day, which would be yesterday, I'm at the Eastern Market, looking through one of the used-book stalls. A sign in one of the bins says, "New arrivals – $3.50 each or 3 for $10." Except the book that I want was in a different bin, and it was marked $2 on the inside. So I take that one, then one of the other books in the first bin catches my eye. So two books, $5.50, I figure. I went to the guy to pay. I show him the books, you know, and he says, "Seven dollars."

"Oh," I said. "This one says two dollars on the inside."

So he storms around to the outside of his little canopy and grabs at a sign that's hanging out front, yanking it back toward me so I could read it. "'ALL BOOKS – $3.50 each or 3 for $10,'" he says – which is just what the sign says, too – in a voice that was kind of resigned and more than a little angry.

"Oh," I said. "I just thought, since it said two dollars." Usually, at used book stores and book sales, it's the lowest price marked, you know. At least that's what I thought.

"That's probably what I paid for it," he says back, kind of snapping a little.

"Oh. That's a good profit margin."

The question that I still have is this: Did I have iciness in my tone? I didn't intend to, but I can imagine I could've. I mean, I was disappointed, but not mad. I mean, it wasn't a bad price. $3.50. Brand-new condition, you know. But whatever. To be honest, I was thinking about how nice it would be to make a living buying books at yard sales and library fundraisers and reselling them at flea markets and fairs and festivals and whatnot. How nice it would be to live out of a car filled with books, driving down country roads and visiting all kinds of college towns and staying in campgrounds and little motels. Just buying books and selling books and traveling around and stuff. Thinking how nice that would be, and like usual, a voice snaps back from inside my head: *How?* How *would you do that?*

Meanwhile, the book seller looks as though he's been struck by lightning or something. Just quivering with rage. I mean, his face is all bunched up and his chin is shaking and he's, like, stabbing me with his eyes. As soon as I said what I said, it was like all the life went out of the air in front of him. Like my words had created a vacuum or something – *whoomp*! Then there was nothing but the icy, lead-filled air in between us.

"It is *not*," he says to me. Referring to the profit-margin comment. "I'm workin' my ass off here!"

There was this long and awkward moment; I look at him blankly, you know, not really willing to let him get to me. Trying to show that I meant no offense and all. He kind of holds the books back, menacingly. I hand him my money. He stands there with the money and the books for a split second, longer than someone usually would once they've got their money, you know, but then he hands me the books. He didn't put them in a bag or anything, though. He just took the money and turned his back on me.

"Okay," I said. "Have a nice day."

"Maybe they're in the process of reconciling their dreams with reality," Cathy says. She's talking about the wedding people. "People can sometimes come up short during that awkward period when they're forced to adjust their expectations, to try to forge a comfortable, doable, personal version of the American dream. Something like that."

Cathy's too calm sometimes, too rational. Almost in a forced way. I could take a jab at her about her own dreams being long since shattered, how she just acts overly calm and removed in order to refrain from being overly emotional. I could take a jab, but I refrain.

"Is that what the American dream is?" I say instead. "You realize that life is all about getting shat upon, so all you can do is shit on as many other people as possible to improve your ratio? The goal, when it's all said and done, is just to have shit upon more people than have shit upon you?"

"I don't know if that's what the American dream is."

"Come on! Cars, houses, computers, cable TV? Strip malls and jet skis and SUVs and high-speed Internet access? Timeshares on the Outer Banks? Power and influence and self-importance? Tell me that's not a selfish kind of existence to aspire to. The only reason we can sit around and get fat and lazy and complacent – as a people, I mean – is because somewhere out there in the world, little kids are slaving over sewing machines and coal miners in Third World countries are risking life and limb in substandard conditions for pennies a day!"

I was worked up by then, as maybe you can see.

"I think all this is just padding," Cathy says to me. "Padding and ranting to cover up and justify the fact that you're worked up. And maybe you have reason to be. But maybe you should also just forget it."

"What do you mean, forget it?"

"You feel bad because you might've placed that book salesman in a situation similar to that in which you yourself were placed by the people at the wedding. I mean, you probably would've just shrugged your shoulders at him about the price thing and kept your mouth shut if you hadn't been stiffed the night before. And you sympathize with him because, though he snapped at you, you know that there must've been more to it than just you. He'd probably heard the same thing from tourists all summer long. And you had no way to know that. And really, those girls throwing the wedding have no way to know how rude they are. People just don't realize those things ..."

"So it's hopeless for me to even try to say anything? It's kind of an impasse, you know? You keep your mouth shut, and people take advantage of you while all the while thinking they themselves are fucking peachy," I say. "Or you speak up and people think you're an ungrateful asshole.

"I mean, that girl was probably right. There isn't any difference between Republicans and Democrats," I continue. "When's the last time you overheard people in DC having a conversation about truly philosophical things, like the meaning of democracy and freedom and fairness? It's always these inside-baseball, horse-race conversations about polling and strategy and message and shit. Just the other day, I heard someone call voters 'consumers.' Everyone looking out for themselves, and pretending to care about their little tribe of so-called friends."

"You need to get involved more," Cathy says. "You just stew and get worked up, and in the end you don't really do anything about it. Maybe you're like that girl. Maybe your life lacks real substance, so you have to make a small deal like this into an epic debacle. You should join a community organization. Or maybe you should try going to church. A lot of people go to church to feel better."

"And do what? Say they're sorry for all the mean things they've done to people that week, fork over some cash, nibble on some cookies and sip some coffee, and then go back home to make people feel like shit all over again?"

"Well, I mean, we're only human. You're not going to be a hundred percent nice to people a hundred percent of the time. You just do the best you can do on any given day."

"But a lot of people don't do the best they *can* do. They do the best they *feel* like doing. The best they feel is necessary. Which isn't very fucking much, I'll tell you that," I say. "I don't know. Maybe it's my job. Maybe it's getting to me. Maybe it's this place. 'Our Nation's Capital.' Maybe I need to move."

"I've heard that before," she says. "I thought you said you finally realized that moving around all the time wasn't helping you out any."

"It's different now, though. I realize that moving doesn't solve *everything*. It's gotta be, like, a holistic approach. Moving plus attitude awareness equals happiness. It's different now. It *would* be different now. If I moved again, that is."

"Okay. Whatever. Where are you gonna go, then?"

"I don't know. Anywhere but here. To the top of Mt. Greylock, maybe. Anywhere but here."

"Where?"

"To Mt. Greylock. The tallest peak in Massachusetts. It's beautiful. It's near the border with New York. Rolling green mountainsides and quaint little valleys in the shadows of the slopes. All kinds of cool shit like that. The Appalachian Trail goes across the mountain. There's this observation tower way up at the top. For some reason, I can't stop thinking about it lately"

"You've been?"

"Hell yes, I've been. It's beautiful. I keep thinking about this guy we met. Well, we didn't meet him, which is maybe why I envy him and covet his job. Since I didn't meet him and didn't see him doing his job. So I can turn his job into an idealized version of what it probably is. His name was Joe. We got to the state campground, which is just down from the very peak of the mountain. And there was this little hut made of plywood, which is where you were supposed to check in. And it was closed. And there wasn't any honor box, you know, where you could do self-registration. So we called the number for the visitors' center, which is just uphill from the campground. And they said, 'Well, Joe should be around there somewhere. It's his job to check you in.' And we waited around. And we drove through the campground and out onto this little turnaround right on the edge of the mountain. And we sat there, you know, and smoked a cigarette and looked at the mountains and the shadows of the clouds on the treetops. All that stuff. And then we drove back, and still no sign of Joe. So we just pitched a tent in one of the sites. And the next morning we flagged down a ranger as he drove through, checking for tags. We figured we'd beat him to the punch, you know, 'cause he was there checking to see if people had paid. And we told him that Joe wasn't there the night before when we'd wanted to check in. He shook his head, you know, and said, 'Damn kid. Probably out somewhere screwin' around.'"

"So you want a job where you don't have to do anything."

"No way. I want Joe's job, and I intend to do it well. He didn't know how good he had it. I mean, he probably manned that little shack all day. Sold some firewood, passed out maps, gave directions. Or he was supposed to, anyway. And I could camp just behind the little shack, or somewhere just off the Appalachian Trail. And I'd work in the campground during the day, maybe read a book or listen to the radio when it wasn't busy. And at night I'd hike around or watch the sunset or go up to the observation post. Maybe trek down to the bottom of the mountain, you know, and have a beer. Quaff an ale in some tavern in some New England village. You know ..."

"Listen," Cathy says. "What it all boils down to is you just feel bad about losing your cool."

"Well, not—"

"Okay, so you feel bad about not being able to make your feelings completely known so the people at the wedding could understand why you might have reason to be unhappy."

"You never really have time to say everything you need to," I say. "Or people aren't willing to take the time to listen. Is that why everyone's so short with everyone else?"

"You shouldn't worry about it. Those people probably won't even remember you by next week. Hell, they probably don't even remember you now."

"People *don't* remember things. That's part of what makes me mad, because I have trouble forgetting. Like, I remember this one restaurant I worked at, right? And one of the bus boys only spoke Spanish. And I practiced my Spanish with him and we got along real well. And one day he asks me, kind of timid-like, if I would point out to the owner that his last check didn't have all his hours on it. So I point it out to the owner. I tell the guy that Diego's check only has X hours, when he's pretty sure he worked Y hours. And the owner completely ignores that question. Instead, he tells me to tell Diego how to look on the computer system to see how many hours he's worked for the current week. So if he's ever curious about how many hours he's worked, he can just check on the computer. No word about the hours on his paycheck maybe being wrong. The guy acts as though he'd been asked a different question. Dodged Diego and me in the process. That guy, he had microphones all over the restaurant. Not just video cameras, but microphones! He'd sit in the office downstairs or he'd go home and he'd listen. And all the servers would whisper and point at the microphones and want you, I mean me, to whisper, too. And on Fridays the guy got in the new wine. And he'd have tastings with some of his buddies. And I don't mean two dozen of his closest friends. I mean like two, three other guys. And they'd go through four or five cases of wine on a Friday afternoon, and then the dude would wander around the restaurant for the rest of the night. Drunk. And he'd hover and leer and get in the way. And snap at people and stuff. I mean, it was weird. Creepy, really."

"Uh huh ..." Cathy's not really paying attention anymore. I can tell.

"Someday I'm gonna write a book," I tell her. "It'll be called *Tales from the (Sub)servi(en)ce Industry*. With 'Subservience' spelled with parentheses around the 's-u-b' and the 'e-n,' so it can either be 'subservience' or 'service.' You know?"

"I know. I get it," she tells me, rolling her eyes and stabbing out her cigarette kind of violent-like. "You know, this has really ceased to be a conversation. It ceased being a conversation a long time ago."

"I know," I tell her. "I know. I'm sorry. Thanks for listening to all my bitching."

"Sure," she says. "Whatever. Anytime."

Back when I worked at this bar in Athens, to get to work I used to walk downhill, past some houses and shops and restaurants, and then across this big vacant lot and to the back of the restaurant and bar where I worked. Athens, Ohio, that is. I've never been to Athens, Georgia, though I've heard it's nice. But anyway, I would walk to this place where I worked as a bartender. And I remember it being fall, and the weather was getting colder and the leaves were falling off the trees. And as I walked across that vacant lot on my way to work one afternoon, I can remember thinking how winter was on its way and the snow would soon be falling. And I remember thinking how kind of romantic and idyllic it would be, once it was wintertime, to turn off the lights after a long night's work, to close up the bar after everyone was gone for the evening, and then walk back across that vacant lot while the snow was falling all around me. Going back up the street, you know, and passing the other lighted establishments that would still be open. The place I worked at usually closed about midnight on weeknights, since it was more of a restaurant than a bar. And maybe, I remember thinking, I might slip into another bar for a quiet after-work beer. Maybe sit by the window and watch the snowflakes falling outside. I can remember thinking how nice that might be. But I can never remember actually doing it, even though I stayed at that place nearly another year, and I certainly walked to and from work through plenty of snow. But I can't remember ever actually stopping off for a beer after work and watching the snow and feeling peaceful. Only wishing for the chance to do so, very much looking forward to it.

And so I'm kind of lost in thought while we sit there at the coffee shop and I wonder what to say next. I sip at my coffee. Which tastes pretty good, I'll admit. But I can't help but think that it would taste better if I were sipping it on a rock outcropping atop a mountain, you know, looking down upon the peaceful valley below.

Just maybe there and then things would be better. At least better than here and now.

Shit.

honor guard

Ll kinds of hot tail walkin in and out of here every day, man. Man, you won't believe the titties I've seen here. Fuckin boobs all over the place. The way these women dress for the funerals. Just today, there was a funeral down in the Iraq section, so there was all these fuckin hot young women, twenty, twenty-one, comin over to console the widow after the funeral. Like, yeah, right, they don't even know her – they're just tryin to get close to me, you know? I mean, all the time, these girls are lookin at me as I stand there at attention – cause I've got a lot of medals on my chest, you know, and we stand there at attention and salute the family one more time at the end. They don't even know this fuckin woman, and all the time they're standin there afterward, supposedly consoling the widow, and they're really just lookin at me, gettin close to me. That's what they wanted; you know they wanted it, cause the limo pulls away and the funeral's over, and they're still standin there, lookin at me. They're wearin these skimpy little fuckin dresses. All these dresses, man, the real low, V-cut dresses, the kind you've gotta glue the boobs onto. No underwear half the time. Fuckin boobs and pussy all over the place. I usher up at the chapel sometimes, you know, and once this fuckin eighteen-year-old niece comes in with her aunt and uncle. She gets out of the car and her dress was all bunched up and you could see it all – ass, titties, everything. Thin little V-cut dress, hiked all the way up, and she starts walkin to the chapel, doesn't even notice that her ass and twat are hangin out all over the place. Just fuckin showin it all off, man. Finally, her aunt comes runnin up behind her and pulls the fuckin thing down. Me and my buddy and the chaplain are standin there, right, and the chaplain – you know, he's got a wife and two kids and he's like, a fuckin priest and shit – the chaplain just looks away, but me and my buddy are like, *Fuck yeah!* If I could, I'd just go back, just once, and give her a good fuckin two-finger dip as she passes me by. I swear, man. Just once. Right up the twat. Fuckin pussy hangin out all over the place. If I could just go back and give her oil a little check. Two fingers right up her slippery little hole. It was the kind of dress, you know, made out of the sheer black stuff. Looks like pantyhose. See all of it, see through that fuckin thing. You ever see Colonel _____'s wife? Fuckin A. Fuckin hot blonde. Bout fifty years old, looks like she's twenty-five. Fuckin hot. Once, she's bent over layin these flowers, and I see right up her short little skirt, see that fuckin black thong huggin her cute little ass. Fuckin hot as hell. That tight ass just hangin there, right in front of me. Twice, two funerals in a row, I swear to you, I saw tits. Saw everything, man. The wind comes blowin through, and these two sisters are just kinda sittin there, and the wind whips the tits right outta their dresses. Right at the same fuckin time. And this young widow, I swear, the very next funeral, she's just kinda standin there watchin things go by and she's holdin her baby. And she's got no bra on underneath, and the kid just rips down her blouse, cause it's hungry, you know. And it rips down her blouse and this nice round titty comes fallin out. *Beautiful.* God, all the tits you see in this fuckin place. You ever see the woman works downstairs in administration? Hot little brunette. Well, we had kind of a thing goin on cause I was separated from my wife at the time, you know, and I would've asked her out. And the only reason I didn't ask her out was this guy who works there tells me it probably wouldn't be a good idea. I mean, she's a GS and I'm just a PFC in the fuckin Army. It wouldn't look good, you know, he says. But God, all the fuckin tits. I seen more tits here than you would ever believe.

the traveler and

the tavern keeper

"Hello, stranger," said the Tavern Keeper kindly to the Traveler.

"Hello, friend," said the Traveler kindly in reply.

The Traveler drew a clay pipe from his leather satchel. The Tavern Keeper drew a pint from the wooden keg behind the bar. The Traveler pinched tobacco from his pouch and packed the pipe with care. The Tavern Keeper placed the pint atop the bar and handed the Traveler a taper with which to light his pipe.

The Traveler nodded in thanks as he drew upon the pipe. The flame from the candle embraced the tobacco, which crackled as tiny leaves under fairies' feet.

The Traveler exhaled languidly. Smoke crept in wisps up the stone walls of the tavern and gathered in the wooden rafters above. The weary Traveler gathered his strength bit by bit and the tired Tavern Keeper gathered his thoughts in his slow and methodical fashion.

"What brings you through these parts?" the Tavern Keeper said at last.

"The road and its bends and its curves," the Traveler said in reply. "Lately I travel less and am led more."

"Led by what, if I may?" said the Tavern Keeper, for the minds and customs of travelers interested him greatly. And though he never succeeded in understanding them fully, he labored to nonetheless.

"What by, I cannot precisely say," the Traveler said after a draught of ale and a moment of thought. "By the wind and the sun and the snow and the dew. By the pathway seen and unseen. By the hand of providence and the claw of fate. By the clouds and the stars and beyond, by the earth and the rivers and below."

"Tell me of the World," the Tavern Keeper said. "Recount to me what you have seen."

The Tavern Keeper was not ignorant of the World, of course. He knew perhaps more than most, talk as he did with travelers every day. Yet he never tired of listening to their tales.

"I have seen the cities and the sea," the Traveler said. "I have rounded the inland oceans and crossed the ice fields at the continent's edge. I have stood upon the cliffs of the north and strode across the plains of the south. I have traversed the deserts and the swamps. I have ascended the mountains and slept in their highland meadows. I have wound my way through the valleys and across their fertile plains. But never, I believe, have I come upon this town before. It seems to me a pleasant place."

"It is, in its fashion," the Tavern Keeper replied. "It is my home, the only one I have known. Folks are friendly here. Work is plentiful. We never want of provisions, nor of tasks necessary to procure them."

"Surely that is not all," the Traveler said, sensing reticence on the part of the Tavern Keeper to speak of his people and of his place. It was a reticence he found not uncommon among those in towns.

"No, I suppose that is not all," said the Tavern Keeper. "It *is* all, in its way – and by being so, it is not. I have tried to travel, yet I have never made it more than three days' journey from this place. I become anxious and timid, and thoughts of home accompany my every step. So you are right, there is something that draws me back and keeps me here. Something in the rhythm of the seasons and the passing of the years. Of being centered in one place, watching the world slowly move about me, observing it change in ways that are dramatic in their smallness. There is fraternity here, there is security. There is family in the streets and comfort in the streams. There is understanding and care. There is warmth in the walls of the houses and support in the roofs. The square is our heart and the streets are our lungs. We move about the nearby fields and woods with intimate ease. The hills surrounding the town are like a baby's cradle: sturdy and familiar and reassuring. Though from time to time I dream still of taking to the road."

"I have slept in caves and in castles," the Traveler said. "I have worked for pennies picking crops and made pounds of gold buying and selling at the great bazaars. But ..."

"What adventure!" exclaimed the Tavern Keeper.

"Adventure, to be certain. As well as long stretches of tedium," the Traveler said. "At times I would cherish the certainty of knowing what the next day will bring."

"Ah! How I might cherish the surprise of not knowing what it will bring," the Tavern Keeper said. "To know the rhythm of life, to feel it in my bones – the flow of water, the habits of animals, the customs of my fellow townsmen – is gratifying, to be sure. It is wondrous and it is profound. But on the worst of days it becomes boring and predictable."

"The life of the road is not without its perils and drawbacks, of course," the Traveler said. "There are storms of sleet and rain, beasts that inhabit the caves. There are the constables of the law – or so they dub themselves – warped by greed and avarice, assessing tolls and fines at will. There are specters that haunt the skeletons of demised villages, marauders and highwaymen who pillage and plunder. The best of friends may keep your company for only a day ..."

"But to make a best friend in a day, when in town trust is earned in increments of years and generations!" the Tavern Keeper interrupted.

"... food may be scarce or nonexistent," the Traveler continued. "I wish it were in my temperament to settle for a while. Each time that I stroll into an attractive town I am struck with a pang of sadness. I yearn to stay there, to rest and absorb its constancy."

"There are drawbacks to a town, too," the Tavern Keeper said. "In security and comfort there is sameness."

"In discomfort and uncertainty there is sameness, as well, though a sameness that differs each day," the Traveler said. "Change can also attain a level of predictability, which can be exceedingly taxing. I have longed for the capacity of stationary, infinite contemplation, the ability to feel at home in a single place. But alas, I have not the temperament."

"Towns are not without their thieves and villains. The worst of enemies may be your neighbor for all the life long," the Tavern Keeper continued. "In close friendship there lies the seed of potential jealousy. When living in such proximity, disagreements and distances loom large and omnipresent. Familiarity, I believe, can often impede true knowledge and understanding."

"But it is just as well that you live where you do," the Traveler said. "You will age among acquaintances and die among friends and your spirit will reside in a place where it belongs."

"Perhaps my soul would prefer to wander and rest where it may," the Tavern Keeper said. "As yours perhaps will."

"I have a fear that rest may be sparse in the traveler's afterlife," the Traveler replied, "that wandering may predominate over resting."

"Permanency may be no more comforting," the Tavern Keeper said. "Imagine how close the souls of this town may be if they are all anchored here for eternity. The village is crowded enough with the living. When I think upon such things, it redoubles my nagging wish to take to the road ..."

"And when I rest at an agreeable establishment such as this in an agreeable town such as this, how my desire to remain a while is rekindled ..."

"We are perhaps more alike than not," the Tavern Keeper said.

"Perhaps. But many tavern keepers are suspicious of us travelers," the Traveler said, "though we provide the bread for their tables and the thatch for their roofs. They are suspicious of roads and what they bring and the World and what they feel it means. And suspicious of travelers by extension, though without the roads and without us they would not thrive."

"Many travelers are suspicious of us tavern keepers," the Tavern Keeper said, "though we shelter them from the wind and fill their bellies with bread. Suspicious of towns and taverns and traders, though all make the traveling life possible. There is no road without towns, no leaving without arriving."

"You speak the truth," said the Traveler. "I do feel as if I carry with me a piece of every place in which I have set down my roots, however brief they may be."

"Likewise," said the Tavern Keeper, "the World comes to me, in its way. I feel that I understand it better than others here, for I experience it at least in passing, a bit of each passing traveler remaining with me."

Outside the tavern, dusk was descending. The town – the cobbles of its streets, the stones of its walls, the thatch of its roofs – was all aglow with gold and crimson. The autumn breeze scurried down from the hills. The leaves atop the trees in the streets and the square rustled with brittle uncertainty. Children rushed home as candles blinked into view through translucent window panes. Women bore water from the nearest stream up the winding pathways leading into town. Men trudged the streets bearing tools and crops and game, conversing in relaxed and tired tones.

From his pouch the Traveler produced a bottle of strong spiced liquor from across the sea and offered the Tavern Keeper a drink. In turn, the Tavern Keeper uncorked a small clay jug of barleywine. They traded drinks for quite some time while around them the air grew close and outside the tavern the night grew dark. The flames and embers of the fireplace danced and glowed and crackled. The Traveler packed his pipe once again and the two shared the smoke in the low candlelight of the wooden bar.

When at last his time to retire was upon him, the Traveler shouldered his satchel and stood to leave the building, heading for the space in the stable he had rented for the night. The Tavern Keeper offered him a mat before the hearth; the Traveler thanked him but declined. The two men clasped hands in the shadows of the tavern, the Tavern Keeper's strong and hefty paw surrounding the Traveler's tough and sinewy fingers.

As he slept beside his wife that evening – as he slumbered in his bed in the house in which he was born, with the beams his grandfather had hewn supporting the roof that divided him from the stars – the Tavern Keeper dreamt of castles on cliffs and caravans meandering beneath mysterious skies. As the Traveler slept alone in a rented bed of straw in the stable out back, with a thin and unfamiliar wooden roof between him and the stars, he dreamt of a quiet town and a pleasant cottage and an abundant garden in a future where he knew no restlessness.

In the morn, each man awoke and returned resolutely – yet reluctantly – to his world.

sack full of genocide

In the Gnadenhutten massacre museum, the three critical display cases go almost overlooked, their charred corncobs and pottery shards and fish hooks and buttons – all that's left from when they excavated the two buildings where ninety Christian Delawares were bludgeoned and then burned and then abandoned more than two centuries ago – overwhelmed by unrelated arrowheads, some local guy's collection of bright polished stones, rusty farm equipment, moldy photos of train yards, an amateur oil painting of a canal boat, and for-sale trinkets of tin soldiers, plastic crosses, and toy bows and arrows.

At the end of the visit the caretaker casually produces a bulging plastic bag and hands me a piece of mass murder, a scorched chunk of chinking – mud and horsehair and clay – "left over" from the excavation, along with a pre-printed pea-green card that explains the significance of it all.

mr. smith's place

Now there's a real hermit for you, J.R. says. He used to walk the country roads in rubber boots, a black flowing coat, a wide-brimmed black hat. He didn't believe in owning things, things like cars. He never had indoor plumbing. The first time I met him, I was seven or eight. My sisters and cousins took me back down the overgrown lane that led to his cabin. Even then it was run down, dilapidated. We crept closer and closer to the cabin when all of a sudden the door banged open and out he stepped in his long flowing coat and white, tangled beard. We ran.

"Come back!" he cried. "I won't hurt you! Come back!"

So we turned around and walked back. And he made us tea and we sat in his cabin with him. We sat there for hours, and he told us stories. He had lived in that cabin all his life. He'd never left, except to go to war when he was young. The cabin walls were covered in murals he'd painted of the Roaring Twenties, of canals and railroads. Mr. Smith was a collector. He had pieces of this and parts of that, and stacks and stacks of old newspapers.

I'd never heard of him until that day, but afterwards I seemed to see him frequently, trudging down the country roads on his way into town. Finally, when he got too old to take care of himself he moved in with his sister, who lived a few roads over. I don't know what ever happened to him. I wonder if he's still alive.

My cousin said he saw people over there not long ago, on the road near Mr. Smith's place, dragging a bunch of things through the woods, loading them onto trucks. My cousin said he walked back there a few days later, said the cabin was still there – but barely. And outside of it were Mr. Smith's newspapers, enormous piles of faded newspapers, the wind lifting them one by one into the trees, into the winter sky.

christmas on the rocks

D owntown Reliance, Ohio, embraced Christmas Eve like a little boy forced into an awkward and unwelcome holiday hug with an obese great-aunt reeking of well-fermented halitosis, mothball-dusted velvet, perm solution, mentholated Misty Lights, and decaffeinated Folgers spiked with saccharine, non-dairy creamer, and peppermint schnapps. That is to say that impending Christmas seemed an awkward fit with the town I call home. But that is the way it had always seemed to me, ever since I gave up running away to exotic locales (At least, as exotic as I could afford at that particular moment in time; one year it was Steubenville.) every Christmas and instead resigned myself to hunkering down for the holidays in the little post-industrial, bucket-kicking burg.

Everyone had already left the newspaper by the time I turned off my computer and announced the work day's end with a sloppy, reverberating fruitcake fart that really did have layers to it: a few dates here, some raisins there, several walnuts sprinkled about, a candied maraschino cherry thrown in for good measure. Everyone had left except for the intern, that is, an over-eager little turd who thought himself bound to be the next Bob Woodward but who I knew, statistically, would more than likely end up selling insurance or writing for some trade magazine like *Wash Basins Monthly*, one of those slick rags that turn a profit by telling an entire industry how innovative and wonderful said industry is, the ones that sell their covers to the highest bidder.

The intern kind of peered quizzically through the newsroom shadows at me, as though surprised to encounter a fart – an actual, true-to-life, *authentic* fart – in this wide and always surprising (and perhaps slightly quaint and most certainly more than slightly disappointing) world that lay beyond the pearly gates and ivory towers of academia.

He was pretty indignant – though he tried stoically to disguise it, lest he be thought naïve – when he discovered, after emerging from the confines of his private-college utopia to pay his dues at our little haven of First Amendment bliss, that in the real world councilmen really did take bribes, that police chiefs did provide protection to illegal bookie shacks, that city managers did skip town after embezzling hundreds of thousands of dollars, that health inspectors did trade strategic oversights for sexual favors, that abused women really did profess love for their crack dealers – and, to top it all off (indignation of all indignations!), that local newspapers frequently didn't do anything to publicize these facts (Why should they, after all, if everyone already knew about them, anyway?) and that even if the papers did print such stories, they wouldn't make a goddamn bit of difference because nobody fucking read newspapers anymore, anyway.

He meant well, though. I had to give him that. Though I wished at that moment that I could remember his name. Just to be nice, since it was Christmas Eve and all. In the grand scheme of things, though, I didn't give a reindeer's wrinkled ass what his name was.

"So aren't you going home for Christmas?" I called across to him.

I think that I startled him, because he jumped a little at the sound of my voice. He was probably still basking in the majesty of my authentic fart. He was also probably a little shocked, since I suppose that I hadn't addressed him all day, even though for the better part of the afternoon we'd had the newsroom to ourselves. He had been busy working on some Big Story that had him all enthusiastic and righteous and pacing back and forth and furiously working the phone. I'd been writing about the local Rotary Club's Christmas caroling endeavors (a story slated to run the day after Christmas, since we didn't publish on Christmas Day).

"I'm Jewish, actually," he said back to me through the lengthening late-afternoon shadows.

"Oh," I said. "I'm sorry."

His quizzical stare shifted a bit more toward the glare end of the spectrum.

"I didn't mean to say I was sorry," I said quickly. "Not *that* kind of sorry. I mean, I'm sorry I assumed. I mean ... Hell, I'm an atheist. I don't give a goddamn either way. You could spend Sundays wearing a G-string and a Technicolor beanie and worshipping Satan's chambermaid for all I care."

"You know, they say God is a more significant concept to an atheist than to a believer," he said in return. "That, in a sense, atheists believe more in God – in that they spend more time considering the very notion of God, or the lack thereof – than most believers, who substitute faith for speculation."

"Who's 'they'? College professors who don't do anything all day but navel-gaze and boink co-eds? Professors who then have to take a sabbatical every few years because they're so mentally exhausted from the grinding and rigorous routine of the academy?" I said. "Though I guess they probably don't call them co-eds anymore. Last I heard, there were more women enrolled in college than men. So maybe the Ednas are really the eds and the Eds are really the co-eds."

He actually laughed at that one. It was a quick laugh, though, and he'd soon retreated into the safe and smug confines of his Bob Woodward costume. Next thing you know, I thought, he might get crazy and cut himself a fart of his very own.

"I'm not really a practicing atheist," I said. "I don't spend my spare time trying to debunk the myth of God. I'm such a cynic that I lack even the conviction to actively disbelieve."

"So ... um ..." he began to reply. I could tell he wanted to try out some small talk but was drawing a blank. "What *do* you believe?"

"I believe I'll have a cigarette," I said, and fished beneath the stacks of papers on my desk for my Lucky Strikes. "Want one?"

He shook his head, then gave a little involuntary two-shouldered glance into the void behind him, as though making sure his mom weren't around to hear him even being offered a cigarette by a lecherous old reprobate like me.

I found the matches and the cigarettes and I lit up a Lucky. I tossed the still-smoldering match into the wastebasket, which sent a visible convulsion through the intern as he no doubt imagined all his dues-paying being engulfed in a Christmas Eve blaze started by a half-crazed sixty-year-old scrooge.

"Can you smoke in here?" he asked.

"Well, I'm not having much of a problem thus far. I'll let you know if I need some help, though. Would you like some whiskey?"

"Um ..." he said.

"Come on," I said. "We'll pretend it's the 1950s, the world is black and white, suburbs are all the rage, reporters get drunk with their sources and the sources have affairs with their secretaries, and whiskey and cigarettes are good for us."

I opened one of my desk drawers and pulled out the bottle and a couple of tumblers I'd swiped from some hotel somewhere. I poured us each a double and I carried them across the newsroom toward him. As I weaved through the desks and computers and printers, I was enveloped in the supernaturally still feeling that a newsroom has about it when it's empty and the day's commotion has evaporated. That feeling of shiftless, unanchored yearning seemed always more severe in the cramped confines of the *Reliance Record*, given that, to begin with, the office was never more bustling than a sloth on a sunny day. So instead of feeling as though the place were inhabited by restless ghosts, it always felt more like the ghosts of ghosts were slowly starving to death in the corners.

I handed him the whiskey and he took a sniff of it. Then he eyed me. Then he took another sniff.

"It's cold out," I said. "This shit'll de-ice your engine. Ho, ho, ho."

"I don't know," he said hesitantly. "I'm not much of a drinker."

"Neither am I," I said. "This will only be my third glass so far today."

I clinked my tumbler against his and then gulped the golden poison and chased it with a drag on the cigarette. He took a hesitant little sip, then shuddered uncontrollably from his head to his ass, like a dripping dog shaking off after a bath.

"Hold on," I said. I went out to the hall and put fifty cents in the Coke machine. I brought him back a Coke, which I opened and poured half of into his glass. "Try that," I said, also handing him the rest of the Coke.

He took another sip, a bit less hesitantly.

"That's not so ... bad. I guess..." he said.

"Learn to like it," I said. "It takes the edge off the world. Makes the bitter pill a bit easier to swallow."

I threw my cigarette butt on the ground and put on my coat. The intern leapt to his feet and dashed out the glowing butt with some of the Coke that remained in the can. I was pretty impressed to see, though, that he saved the liquor, which jiggled in the glass in his other hand.

"Well, have a nice night, Roger," he said timidly. "Happy holidays."

"Yeah. You too. Ralph," I answered, though I could tell by the look on his face that I hadn't guessed correctly.

I always had fucking hated Christmas.

"Remember when Christmas used to mean something?" Wade said to me from his bar stool even before the sleigh bells on the door had ceased jangling and before my eyes had even had a moment to adjust to the dim light inside.

"That's just something old farts say," I shot back in his direction, even though I had yet to successfully make him out in the gloom. "Christmas never meant anything. Nothing that we think used to mean something ever actually meant anything to begin with. We were just too young to give a shit at the time.

We're all hedonists at heart. It's just that we turn to grousing and complaining about some nonexistent nostalgic yesteryear once our merrymaking machinery gets a little rusty."

"Well, I remain a hedonist at heart and in deed," Earl offered from the barstool beside Wade's. "I'm a love machine."

"I bet you are, Earl," I said as I sat down at the bar.

"The reason I ask is that I was reading your column in today's paper ..." Wade said.

"So you're the one ..."

"Well, there are at least two of us, because Earl showed it to me."

"I did," Earl piped up. "I thought it was very sweet."

It *was* sweet, I supposed. If you were into that sort of thing. Most of my "Roger's Ramblings" columns that dealt with the way things used to be *did* succeed in being sentimental – maybe a bit wistful, even – without coming off as bitter. I kind of liked it that way, to tell you the truth, since it seemed to me as if I were pulling a fast one on people, tugging at their heartstrings with emotions that I myself didn't share.

"It really brought me back to when I was a kid," Wade agreed. "I mean, you made Reliance come alive again."

"Yeah," said Earl. "The big tree. And the train. And the lights. And the concert. And the toy store!"

"Childhood's overrated," I said. "Bah fucking humbug ..."

"Roger Delancey!" Annie scolded me from behind the bar. I hadn't noticed her approach from the back. "Don't you like children?"

"Yes, very much so," I said. "I think they're delicious. Like veal. Only they go better with mustard."

"That's disgustin'," she said as she lashed out with her bar rag so it snapped loudly a couple inches from my nose. "Shame on you. You was a child once."

"Like hell I was."

"Yeah, Roger was born with a Lucky Strike in his mouth, a bottle in his hand, and a nasty wad of thorns up his ass," Earl said.

"Well, what are you drinking, Mr. Thorny?" Annie asked me with a wink. She was about fifty, divorced a few times over, wore the weight of the years beneath her eyes, and had a bit of the hots for me. Or whatever it is you have when you reach middle age. The longings? The desperations? She tried to lean across the bar to plant a kiss on me one night after I'd bought her a few shots. I had no idea it was coming, though, and I doubt I would have reciprocated if I had. So I was lifting a cigarette to my mouth at that very moment and burned her on the upper lip. It sizzled. She shrieked. I felt bad, so I bought her another shot.

"Everything Christmas is only a quarter for the next hour," she added.

"What do you mean, 'everything Christmas'?" I said. "How the fuck do you drink Christmas? Put some pine needles in a blender?"

"No, silly," she said. "Anything that looks or tastes like Christmas ..."

"Christmas tastes like wasted money and unreal expectations," I said.

"Hot toddy, Bloody Mary, Irish coffee, creme dee mint," she rattled off, taking pride as always in her humble attempts to add some variety and class to what was essentially a hopeless hole in the wall. "Cinnamon schnapps. There's some mulled wine ..."

"I'll have a Scotch," I said.

"That's *sad*. You should order somethin' *festive*," she said. "Scotch – that's not Christmas. That don't look nor smell nor taste like Christmas. Just plain drunkkenness. The idea is to get some variety goin' on so this place ain't so sad-and-ordinary feeling. Straight whiskey isn't Christmas at *all*."

"It is when you put a cherry, an olive, and a cocktail onion in it," I countered.

She smiled and waved away my quarter as she poured me the drink. Behind the bar, the Discovery Channel was showing a special on the Holy Land which was interspersed every few minutes with holiday-themed Victoria's

Secret ads. Earl stared intently at these, muttering lewd things (only somewhat) to himself, such as, "I'd love to plant some seeds in *that* Fertile Crescent."

"Nothing says Christmas like boosted busts and beautiful butts," I said to Earl.

"And perverts who get off on lingerie ads," Wade added.

Truth be told, ours were the kinds of lives that country songs were stereotypically supposed to be about – though even if that generalization were true once upon a time, it wasn't anymore, since country songs those days, it seemed, were all about bombing foreign lands in the name of mom and apple pie. Wade had been laid off when Reliance's last steel mill closed down a few years before; he was only two years away from retiring. He was a borderline drunk before losing his job, but he'd since redoubled his efforts – with smashing success. His wife left him when the mill closed. Now he spent a lot of time mowing his lawn when it was warm out and building model airplanes when it wasn't. Sometimes I would come upon him downtown, just ambling about with his hands in his pockets. I knew that more often than not he was on his way either to or from the steel mill, where he would stand out by the railroad tracks and stare at the big, still structure. But I never made mention of this to him. Earl used to work in the mail room of an office building in Canton, but he called his boss "Mr. Wiener" during a heated dispute one day; the dispute was over Earl's timeliness, or lack thereof, so the comment sealed his fate. Now he worked stocking shelves at the Wal-Mart outside of Reliance. His son was in juvenile detention for igniting a tear gas canister beneath the bleachers at Homecoming; his daughter ran away to California with a truck driver named Toad. That was his nickname, really, but no one knew his real name.

"Hey," I said suddenly to Annie, having just thought of something. "Turn that TV off."

"What for?" she said.

"Yeah," Earl said, his eyes not parting from the screen, "what for?"

I walked around behind the bar, snapped off the TV, and started fiddling with the little radio that sat beside some dusty liquor bottles. It squawked and buzzed as I moved the tuner toward the basement end of the spectrum.

"'A Child's Christmas in Wales,'" I said. "They're playing it at 6:30."

"Beluga whales?" Earl said. "*Sperm* whales?"

"No, dumbshit," I said. "Dylan Thomas. Probably the best Christmas story ever."

"Even better than Charlie Brown's Christmas?" Wade said.

"I'd have to say so," I said. "Though I'm rather fond of Charlie Brown, too."

"Yeah," Earl said. "Because he's such a philosophical, defeatist loser."

"I didn't think you was fond of anything, Roger," Annie said.

"Well," I said, "I don't personally *enjoy* it. But I ... respect the craftsmanship."

"You're just a big softie is what you are," Annie said. "You act all mean and grouchy, but I bet you've got a heart of gold."

"Fool's gold, maybe," Wade said. "And that's buried under cholesterol and hardened arteries and tar and nicotine and booze and bad attitude."

"That's about it," I agreed.

I found the station just as it squawked out *"news and classical music."*

"Public radio?" Earl groaned. "*Public* radio?"

"Shut up," I said. "Nobody picks on public radio in my presence. We *will* have words ..."

"You're probably even a member! Mr. Roger the Reject Rebel isn't even badass enough not to pledge," Earl said. "I bet you crumple with guilt when they get on there and do those fundraisers. 'Did you know ... um ... err... know, Carol, that out of ... um ... every ten listeners to this ... err ... station, only ... uh ... one-and-a-half is a member? Don't ... uh ... be ... uh ... one of those other eight-and-a-half people. You ... er ... you'd hate to end up with just one arm, or half a head ... um ... so step up to the plate. Do .... um ... do your part to save public radio.'"

"Shut up, asshole!" Wade said. "I want to hear it, too. My dad used to read it to me." He looked at Annie. "It's real good. You should listen to it, Annie."

So we ordered another round of drinks and settled in to the magical, melancholy cadences of "A Child's Christmas in Wales." The few other patrons scattered around the bar looked at us with annoyance. But to hell with them, I thought. It was Christmas Eve, and I'd offend people if I felt like it. Annie perched herself on her stool behind the bar and looked at me, I looked at the radio, Earl looked at his drink, and Wade stared at the mirror behind the bar. The crisp British voice boomed the story through the speakers.

"One Christmas was so much like another in those years ... " it began. And all three of them were hooked from the start. I watched as they listened and smiled, occasionally grunting or nodding their heads. Even Earl stopped fiddling with the ice cubes in his drink and simply sat still and paid attention. And soon, too soon, it was over: *"I said some words to the close and holy darkness, and then I slept."*

And then there was that moment of satisfying silence when you know something has connected with someone who didn't see it coming.

"That," Annie said, "that was ... Well, it was really somethin'! I liked it a lot."

"I liked the pipes," Earl said. "'Their inextinguishable briars.'"

"I liked the uncles," Wade said. "I'm one of those uncles."

"I liked the presents," Annie said. "And the food."

"I liked the hippos," Earl said.

"And it was Reliance and it was Christmas and there was booze," I said. "And the smog-sprinkled snow tickled the decrepit doorways of the sad somber city. And it was Reliance and it was the Rust Belt and there was booze and it was Christmas."

"And it was depressing ..." Earl said.

"Years and years ago when I was a boy and when there were wolves *and* jobs in Reliance ..." Wade said.

"Dylan Thomas drank himself to death, you know," I said, polishing off my Scotch.

"Humph!" Earl said, then hoisted his tumbler of vodka and peppermint schnapps.

"I can think of a lot worse ways to die," Wade said, sipping his Irish coffee.

"Yeah," Earl said. "Like being eaten alive by a brontosaurus."

"Where the hell did that come from?" I said. *"Eaten alive by a brontosaurus?"*

"Yeah, where *did* that come from?" Wade said. "Everyone knows that brontosauruses were plant eaters."

At that very moment, the bar's door jangled open and in shuffled the saddest excuse for a Santa Claus upon whom I'd ever laid eyes. He wore a pair of Moon Boots, holey red running tights, a fake professional wrestling belt made of plastic, a faded Santa jacket lined with faux fur, and a neon red ski cap with a fuzzy dirty-white bobble on it. The cap was perched precariously across his head. His jacket was about three sizes too small, and the pillow he'd strapped around his belly was peeking out below the faux fur. The only thing that seemed halfway genuine about him was his beard; though that was red, and dusted with flecks of gray and more than a few crumbs from what looked to be powdered donuts.

"Ho, ho, ho," Santa said weakly. "Merry Christmas! God rest ye merry gentlemen."

Santa was very drunk.

"Well hell*ooo*, Mr. Claus," Annie said cheerily. "Pull yourself up a seat. Got any presents for us?"

"Something tells me," Santa said as he teetered toward the bar, "that you kids have been nothing but naughty this year."

"You got that right, Santa," I said with a tip of my glass toward the tipsy old elf. "Especially Earl, here. He's a love machine."

"That's right, Santa," Earl said. "You can cross *me* off that list of yours."

With great concentration and a bit of trepidation, Santa shuffled the rest of the way to the bar and hauled himself atop a stool. It teetered a bit, and for a moment I thought he would plummet to the floor. But he braced his arms on the bartop and steadied the stool. He looked over at Annie as though to place an order, but all that came out of his mouth was drool and gibberish.

"'Scuse me, Santa?" Annie said.

Santa cleared his throat with an earth-rumbling retch that shook his frame and made his eyes bulge and turned his cheeks beet red. He froze like that for a moment, and I was sure that he would choke to death on his own phlegm. But then he swallowed and his face softened.

"Gin," Santa said. "Double."

Santa sipped at his drink, and we all of us sat there, awaiting some pronouncement or explanation from him. But none was forthcoming. In fact, Santa looked as though he might pass out face-first into his gin at any moment, so we politely turned back to our own drinks.

Earl purred at the never-ending cavalcade of lingerie ads. I, too, got somewhat sucked in by all the commercials. Christmas Eve, and you'd think all the shopping was done. But still we were being bombarded by a barrage of fake, sugar-coated nostalgia, concocted and shoved down our throats by twenty-four-year-old Madison Avenue millionaires. Chug some cheap American light beer out of a festive can and suddenly you're in a cabin in the mountains, with noble horses thundering through the crystal-cold streams, a light snow falling upon the boughs of the mighty fir trees, and a nubile young woman expectantly awaiting you in the cabin's hot tub. Sentimental phone calls brought to you by your friendly long-distance provider. Modern families brought together by the latest board game or some new electronic gadget or another. Pizza Hut warms your heart this holiday season. Tramping the snow off your $300 European leather boots and warming up with a mug of name-brand gourmet hot cocoa before a blazing hearth. Bursting through snowdrifts in a Jeep Commander and leaving a

Coke out for Santa Claus. Pine-scented candles and Christmas-colored candy to thrill your senses.

"I went to Canton to go to the mall the other day," I said after seeing the same holiday-themed credit card commercial for the fourth time.

"I'm sorry," Wade said.

"Yeah," I said, "me, too. I went into the electronics store to look for a present for my teenage nephews. The ones in Omaha. It was like walking into a screaming electrified maelstrom. I couldn't take it. I gave up after about five minutes and instead went home and boxed up my entire Encyclopedia Britannica and carted that to the post office and shipped it off to them."

"I went into Starbucks the other day," Earl said.

"You? To apply for a job?" Wade said. "Or were you in the market for a good folk music CD?"

"I'm being serious for once, here," Earl said. "Give me a break."

"You went to the Starbucks out on East Street?" I said.

"That's the one," Earl said. "Out in the strip-mall jungle. I'd just got finished at Wal-Mart. I've always had a soft spot for eggnog lattés."

"Like the soft spot on top of your head?" Wade said.

"And there were all these people in line, waiting to order their festive seasonal drinks. And there was just one girl behind the counter. And she was working fast. *Wham!* She'd measure the espresso. *Whoosh!* She'd steam the milk. *Ker-plunk!* She'd whip it onto the counter. *Ka-ching!* She worked the cash register like an old lady riding out a lucky streak on a slot machine. *Wham bam coffee's here!* But she just couldn't keep up. The line kept growing and growing, everybody wanting their toasty spot of holiday-flavored cheer. And this girl was working the drive-thru, too, slopping the troughs of all the fat pigs who were too lazy to hoist their lardy asses out of their SUVs and actually stand in line to buy some coffee. And the people in line weren't any better. They acted like a bunch of impatient cows trying to get to the salt lick all at once. *Moo moo moo* coffee coffee coffee. And boy, were they indignant! They were scandalized at how slow the line was, and they had no qualms about expressing it out loud. They were mumbling and grumbling and throwing their arms in the air all agitated-like. 'Some service!' this one woman said to no one in particular. 'It'll be spring before we get to the front!' some guy said to me. 'This is taking, like, forever!' this twentysomething-year-old chick said to her cell phone. I tell you, these people were making me steamed like a venti vanilla chai."

"So what did you do?" Wade said.

"I looked around at all of them," Earl said, "and I said, 'It's Christmas! You're all a bunch of dumb cows, and you should be ashamed of yourselves. It's *Christmas*!' And then I farted. I dropped a greasy, delayed-reaction stink bomb right in their midst. And I left. I settled for a pumpkin spice cappuccino at the gas station."

"Crappuccino?" I said.

"Well, not right away," Earl said. "But soon enough ..."

"I walked in on my wife with another guy on Christmas," Wade said from out of nowhere. He'd apparently been chewing on this piece of gristle for a while, weighing whether to swallow it or spit it out. "On Christmas! I bet you think that's the kind of thing that happens only in the movies and in dirty jokes. Well, that's what *I* thought. On Christmas even more so. You sit back for a split second that seems like forever and kind of wonder if this is really happening to you. Because you're so used to a situation like that being the punchline to a ridiculous story that someone else is telling you. It's ... unreal. And there they are doing the boxspring boogie before your unbelievin' eyes. On Christmas ..."

"And where were you on Christmas that your wife had the opportunity to have a 'tween-the-sheets tussle with some other dude?" Earl asked.

"Well, I was here. I think," Wade said. "Or maybe at Sid's Tavern. Either way, I wasn't cheatin' on her."

"Cheatin' on a woman with a bottle can be even meaner'n cheatin' on her with another woman," Annie offered. "At least you don't bring the woman home with you."

"Well *I* wouldn't have brought anyone home with me, anyway," Wade said. "I can't say the same for her."

It occurred to me that after you've lived long enough, you'd probably be hard-pressed to single out any one run-of-the-mill Christmas that you've experienced, packed as your mind probably would be with all the (on the surface, at least) satisfyingly similar, if also rather mundane, experiences of snow and eggnog and comfy couches and fires in fireplaces and nuts and candy and football and a bit too much to drink and people you care about who also care about you. But you'll always remember every cold, jagged detail of the Christmas when your heart got broken. Or when you broke somebody else's. Or both.

"I once went to South America over Christmas," I said, "where at night this guy dressed up in a papier-mâché cow costume and danced around in public. There were fireworks built into the costume. He ran around dancing and smoking cigarettes and drinking from a bottle of cane liquor and chasing people up and down the street, while all the while his costume was erupting in little explosions and showering sparks and firing rockets all over the place. The fireworks would ricochet off the buildings and go bouncing into the crowds. It was nuts."

"What was you doin' in South America?" Annie asked.

"Cocaine," Earl offered. "And a girl named Maria."

"Just traveling," I said, ignoring Earl for once.

Leaving the one-man fireworks display behind, though I did not mention this in retrospect, I wandered around the colonial downtown, where impoverished and disfigured beggars moaned for alms in the street while sharply dressed parishioners made their way into enormous churches lined top to bottom in obscene amounts of gold. I sat down to eat at Mr. Happy Chicken, a Kentucky Fried knock-off. A couple of dirt-smeared children wandered up to me. Assuming they wanted money that they might not get any benefit from themselves, I waved them away automatically, as you become accustomed to doing when you spend time in South America. But I watched, with tears welling in my eyes, as a young couple pulled the children into their laps and the kids proceeded to hungrily wolf down the rest of the couple's food.

Thankfully, the door jingled open again, and Annie's son Eddie stepped into the bar, accompanied by an arctic blast of evening air. Eddie held two pizzas in his hands. His head was tucked into the pulled-up collar of his jacket. Wisps of his shaggy beard peeked above the collar, and strands of his unkempt hair cascaded down from beneath his Jimmy's Pizza baseball cap.

"I don't understand," Eddie said. "You'd think that people would make sure they actually have enough money *before* they decide to order pizzas ..."

He walked up to the bar and plopped the pizzas onto the counter. He took a look at Santa, who had indeed passed out face-down on the bar.

"Better give Santa here first dibs," Eddie said. "He looks like he could use the nourishment."

Annie retrieved some paper plates from behind the bar and started plopping pieces of pizza onto them. She beamed in Eddie's direction. She was awfully fond of her son. He was the kind of son of whom even I would be fond: artistic and easygoing, affable and funny without being annoying, sarcastic without being mean-spirited. Eddie must have been about twenty-five. He rented a corner of an old warehouse by the train tracks, where he slept on a pallet next to a space heater. He made sculptures during the day and delivered pizzas at night.

"What are all you good-for-nothings up to this Christmas Eve?" Eddie asked.

"They're swappin' tales of woe and heartbreak, like usual," Annie said as she delivered me a plate of pizza. "'Cept they're a bit sentimental, it bein' Christmas Eve and all. Though I doubt they'd admit to it."

"I spent one Christmas working for UPS in Florida," Eddie said. "Outside of Tampa. I was a 'jumper,' which means I helped the driver run packages to and from the truck."

He sat down at the bar, and I bought him a beer. He pulled out a pack of American Spirits – hippie smokes, I always said to him, though I never turned one down when he offered it to me – and lit one up.

"It was a strange route," Eddie continued. "It had these huge gated communities, with their own golf courses and tennis clubs and little social halls. These people got mail-order steaks and golf equipment and L.L. Bean thermal underwear. All kinds of stuff. And then there were these little mom-and-pop businesses that people ran out of those little stalls you can rent in industrial plazas. They made candles and T-shirts and customized car parts. Stuff like that. This one woman made a living selling stuff on eBay, I think. She would always have the packages stacked in front of her house for us to pick up. She would peer at us through the barely opened front door while we loaded them, and as soon as we had the last package in the truck she would slam the door shut.

"Most everybody's always happy to see the UPS man. Especially around Christmas, I think. It's kind of like delivering pizzas. I imagine it's like being a reporter – you get to know what goes on at different hours of the day in different parts of town, what goes on behind the scenes, what kinds of things people get delivered to them. Like being a reporter," he added with a smile aimed in my direction, "except that people are always glad to see you."

"Maybe I ought to switch careers," I muttered.

"And I'll never forget Christmas Eve of that year," Eddie said. "The business side had slowed down quite a bit. I mean, the last of all the big shipments had gone out several days before. It seems like we went to a lot of nursing homes and retirement apartments that Christmas Eve. Like maybe these people's kids had forgotten all about them until the last minute, and then rushed them some chocolate or a scarf or whatever the hell you buy for Christmas for someone who you've institutionalized so they can die out of your sight and out of your mind.

"Those places smelled, I tell you. They smelled like disinfectant and they smelled rotten all at the same time. We went into this one nursing home, and there were all these old men and women in wheelchairs kind of just sitting in the hallways or gliding around aimlessly. You could almost see through their skin. And they would look at you without seeing you.

"There was this other place that had a mix of low-income older people and it seemed like people with mental disabilities or something. We walked up to the door and there were a couple people out smoking. We'd seen them a few times before, this man and this woman, always standing outside the apartments smoking Bronco menthols. We had two packages to deliver that particular day. They asked who they were for. We looked at the labels and told them. They said they didn't know those people. 'I can't stand most of the people around here,' the woman said. Then she pointed at her buddy. 'He's about the only one I can talk to,' she said.

"So we go to the door and there's this guy standing just inside the entrance. He was probably thirty, though he looked nineteen. He let us inside. I think he must've been the happiest person I ever met. He just beamed. He opened the door and said 'hi' to us. And he looked at the packages we were holding. 'Do you have one for 206?' he said. I'm telling you, he was so happy. And we looked, and one of the packages *was* for 206; which means one of the packages was for him. He snatched it from us and practically jumped up and down with joy. And I only realized later on that day that he was probably waiting for it. Who knows how long he'd been waiting for that package? Maybe all day. Maybe the day before. Maybe the whole week before. And he was so certain that package would come. And he was so happy to be proven right.

"And then we start looking for the other apartment. We go to the second floor. There was a handwritten sign on the door of one apartment that we passed. It said, 'Ralph died Monday and Edith is in intensive care.' It's Christmas Eve, and there's a piece of paper with that written on it hanging in that musty hallway.

"We find the other apartment and ring the buzzer, and there's no answer. We ring it again and then we wait a while. So we go across the hall to the neighbor's apartment to see if maybe they'll hold the package. This woman's voice answers the intercom, and we tell her we're with UPS. 'No, sorry,' she says, 'that's not me.' No, we explained to her, we were wondering if you would hold a package for your neighbor. So the door cracks open and there's a large, pale woman standing there. She was wearing this thin white nightgown. Her arms and legs were kind of purplish-bluish-colored. And after some more explanation, she agrees to hold the package. 'As you might guess,' she says, 'I never get any packages myself.'

"When we came back down, the man and the woman were still outside smoking cigarettes. We said 'hi' to them again. The guy looks at us and says, 'Hey, guys, I wanna show you something.' We kind of shrug our shoulders in each other's direction, and we let him lead us back inside and to his little apartment. It was nothing fancy, just a living room-kitchen combo straight ahead and a hall on the left that led to the bedroom and the bathroom. You could take it all in with one glance. The living room had Boston Bruins souvenirs on the walls. But he waved us into his bedroom.

"'I collect Snoopy,' he says to us, as though Snoopy was some kind of essence, some elusive thing that had to be snatched up and held onto by magical means, lest it escape forever. Like snowflakes or sunshine or something. 'I got all the Snoopy stuff,' he says. And he showed us the bedroom; there was a Snoopy banner and a Snoopy Sno-Cone maker and Snoopy dolls and a Snoopy duffel bag and a framed print of Woodstock.

"He was so proud, that guy. You could tell that he didn't want us to leave. He wanted us to stay there and bear witness to his Snoopy collection. On Christmas Eve."

Eddie shook his head. He drained his beer mug and pushed it across the bar to his mother.

"Well," he said, "that's enough sentimentality for one evening. Gotta go deliver some holiday cheer. Merry Christmas to all, and to all a good night."

I got out of my stool along with Eddie. I tapped him on the shoulder.

"I'll follow you out," I said. "I've got something for you."

A frigid wind was whipping to and fro outside the bar. A few snowflakes had begun to fall. Eddie and I stood in the little pool of light in front of the entrance. I reached into my pants pocket and pulled out a Zippo. It was some little token the mayor's office had given out at Christmas one year, in the days when cigarette lighters made for perfectly acceptable all-purpose gifts. It had a little picture of the courthouse on it, along with the legend *Reliance. A helluva town.*

"Here," I said to Eddie. "Merry Christmas."

"Hey!" he said, seeming genuinely pleased. He turned it over in his hands. "This is sweet. Thanks, man."

He fished a couple American Spirits from his coat pocket. He gave me one, which he lit for me with his new lighter. The flame held up well in the wind, I was happy to see.

"So what were you doing in Florida?" I asked him as we stood there smoking.

"Girlfriend," he said with a sheepish smile.

"Oh yeah?" I said. "That's the only thing that I ever let lure me to the Sunshine State. Though the last one that really meant anything to me was in Boston. I left her on Christmas Day, in fact. We had our little Christmas together that morning. She was a waitress, and she went to work that afternoon, and when she came back that night I was gone, on my way back to Reliance."

"Oh yeah? Why'd you leave?"

"She wanted to get married."

"And you didn't? I can understand that ..."

"No. Actually, I thought about it. And I really *could* imagine myself growing old with her. Maybe having kids. And I was paralyzed with fear, certain that saying yes would be the beginning of the end. I was scared to death of being content, which I'd always equated with complacency. That was twenty-five years ago."

I left her place that afternoon and drove out to Revere Beach before heading to the highway. As I drove, out the car window I could see all these people rounding out their Christmases. A man, a woman, and a little girl were crouched in the middle of an otherwise empty football field, setting up a model rocket. One family was out on their porch, the mother and father assembling a bike with training wheels for their son, who was leaping around expectantly. A slightly older boy was already on the sidewalk, tooling his own new bike along on the cleared swaths of concrete. A bit down the road, a kid was trying out a new gray skateboard ramp in a bank parking lot. A battalion of children was launching an all-out snowball assault on a massive snow fortress, which was defended by an equally enthusiastic group. The parking lot at the movie theater was full of cars.

Eddie and I were taking the final draws on our cigarettes when I heard the *clang-clang* of the railroad warning bells echoing a few blocks down the street. I immediately threw open the door to the bar.

"Annie! Earl! Wade!" I said. "Bring a bottle! Let's go! It's the last Amtrak!"

The last Amtrak to ever serve Reliance on a Christmas Eve, anyway. The stop was slated to be phased out after the first of the year. It only made sense, too. There was a time when Reliance had been a big way station between the East Coast and Chicago, and Cleveland and points south. A large, graceful depot had once greeted passengers only a few blocks from the then-bustling downtown. But the station had been destroyed during a big derailment in the '70s. Passenger traffic had already begun its decline, and the station was replaced with nothing more than a platform with a little roof on top of it.

Wade, Earl, and Annie came through the door. Wade had a few bottles of beer stuffed into his coat pockets. Earl clutched a pint glass full of vodka and peppermint schnapps. Annie handed me a bottle of off-brand Scotch. Santa, miraculously, also emerged, stumbling through the front door and nearly bowling over our little gathering.

We all piled into Eddie's Escort with the Jimmy's Pizza light on top, and he deposited us at the train station, where the barriers had been deployed and warning lights were flashing amidst the continued clanging of the bells. Eddie gave a toot on his horn and sputtered off, and we clutched our arms about ourselves and awaited the train's arrival.

"'As Christmas neared, each evening's trains increased our anticipation,'" Earl said from behind me. "'They bore uncles and aunts laden with presents and family stories from afar; sons and brothers in uniform, home on holiday leave from the Cold War, having abandoned for the time being their radar posts in the Rocky Mountains and their missile silos on the Great Plains; and always a number of wayfaring strangers, stopping en route to some other destination, or intent upon looking up an old friend separated in distance but not in memory. And we would idle in spacious Buicks outside the station, or go inside and warm ourselves with cider at the bar (the grownups favored Sebring Stout). And we would greet our people with holiday hugs, then proceed back down Main Street, perhaps tarrying to take in the light-bedecked lamp posts or the enormous tree that glistened and blazed before the court house or the oversized model train and Christmas village set up in front of City Hall.'"

"Earl ..." I said gruffly, having recognized the words from that day's newspaper, having turned around to see him reading them verbatim.

Mercifully, that evening's train was pulling into sight, slowing as it approached the platform. I swigged from the Scotch as the Amtrak stopped before us. I could see faces framed in the lighted windows, staring out at the desolate patch of darkness before them. A conductor stepped down from the train. He glanced at us, then at the empty platform. He checked his watch, then stepped back into the train.

No one had gotten off. No one had gotten on.

We stood there, watching the train depart. I took another slug at the bottle. The wind whipped through my clothing, squeezing me with its icy tentacles. I'd been in such a hurry that I hadn't even put on my coat. Wade cracked a second bottle of beer. Santa coughed loudly. Earl rustled his newspaper.

"Well ..." Annie said.

"'And, of course,'" Earl continued, "'there was the parade. A clanging, banging, boomingly enthusiastic melee of holiday sights and sounds. There was Santa atop his sleigh, casting candy into the gathered jubilant throngs of boys and girls. There was the mayor in his three-piece, candy-striped suit and his bright green top hat.'"

"Earl ..." I said.

Earl paused in his recitation. "What say we have our own little parade? Right down Main Street and back to the bar? We'll resurrect the ghosts of Christmases past."

High-stepping his way away from the Amtrak platform, Earl marched us back in the direction from whence we had come. As we proceeded, he gave a guided tour of the Reliance that once was.

"Right here was the pet shop." It was now a pawn shop. "And the bakery." Now a vacant storefront with dust and two broken chairs inside. "And the bank." An optimistic attempt at a microbrewery, gone bust after only a month of operation. "And Melnick's Department Store – 'We've got what you need, in a place you like to be.'" Long since closed, then gutted by a fire, then reduced by a wrecking ball to a still-present pile of rubble. "And Larry's Diner and Delicatessen." A carry-out Chinese place. "And Mrs. Wonderful's Fine Coffees, Candies, and Teas." Another vacant storefront. "And Peter's Pub and Grub." A liquor store.

We paused before the crumbling court house, gazing up at the once stately statue of John Rutherford Reliance, founder and namesake of the city. Some hooligans had gouged out his eyeballs with a hammer and chisel and spray-painted neon pink bikini briefs onto the crotch of his pants. Following Earl's lead, we all settled into seats on the warped and rotting benches scattered about the little plaza.

"Reliance is a piece-of-shit town, really," Earl said dejectedly. "Sometimes I wish that I were living in exile. Then Reliance would seem more romantic. I would be obligated to pine for it because it would be deprived of me by forces beyond my control."

"You don't even vote, Earl," I said. "I'm sorry to break it to you, but I don't think you're very likely to be declared an enemy of the state."

"I can always hope, though," Earl said. "The Man fears extreme apathy. It's only a half a step away from revolution."

"I'm not really Santa Claus," Santa said suddenly, then hiccupped loudly.

"I figured," I told him.

"There isn't really a Santa Claus," he added.

"I know," I told him.

"You do?" he said.

"I'm afraid I'm a disbeliever," I said. "Have been since I was three. I was quite a cynical kid."

Santa's name was really Bob, he explained. He worked in a little factory in Colby's Corners, making tags that said "Made in America" to go on clothing sewn by twelve-year-old girls in various foreign nations. The final assembly of the clothes was done in Guam, but the tags were the only thing about the clothes that were truly made in the United States, Santa said. The tags and the plastic bags used by the big-name department store that sold the clothes.

"My wife lives in Reliance," Santa explained. "My ex-wife, I should say. She's got custody of the kids. I haven't seen them for two years. She got a restraining order against me, back when I was a violent drunk. Now I'm just a drunk. So I came up here to see my kids and give them their Christmas presents. My little girl answered the door. She took one look at me and she started bawlin' her eyes out. 'Sweetheart,' I said. 'It's me. It's your daddy. I'm here to be your Santa Claus.' But she just screamed. And my wife came to the door and she ... she kicked me. I fell down the front stairs and she slammed the door shut. I just left the little bag of presents at the bottom of the stairs and limped my way to the liquor store."

I couldn't think of anything else to do but give Santa Claus a hug. He melted in my arms, blubbering like a baby and slobbering all over my shirt sleeves.

"Listen, Santa," I said. "Or Bob. Sorry; I can't stop calling you Santa."

"It's all right," he said. "It's nice to be somebody different for a change."

"Here's the key to my apartment," I said. "Why don't you head there and make yourself at home? Seems like you could use some rest. And you definitely don't need to be driving your sleigh tonight."

He nodded, looking appreciatively into my eyes. I told him how to get to my place, and he wandered off in that direction. The rest of us wandered back to the bar. Wade excused himself soon thereafter. He was off to watch *It's a Wonderful Life*, he said. That left me, Earl, and Annie, plus a half-dozen other lost souls scattered throughout the bar; luckily, they hadn't burned the place down or run off with the liquor and light fixtures while we were out galavanting around Reliance. I'm not sure why, but I suggested to Earl that we head out to Wal-Mart.

"I'm sure you don't get enough of the place, Earl," I said.

Truth be told, Wal-Mart was one of the few places left in Reliance where you could go after 9:00 at night. Besides the bars, anyway. And Taco Bell. There were no coffee shops. Unless you counted the strip-mall Starbucks, which I didn't. All the all-night diners had shut down. No one hung out in the town square like they used to. The old movie theater had closed now that there were several super-plexes just outside of Canton.

This time, I remembered to grab my coat. Then Earl and I went over to the newspaper lot, where my station wagon was still parked.

"How much liquor have *you* had?" Earl said. "I wonder if *you* should really be driving *your* sleigh tonight."

"Too much, probably," I said. "Which is just enough, in my book. Besides, I may be drunk, but I'm not bereft like Santa was. That's a deadly combination."

"Yeah," Earl said, "you're just bitter."

But he didn't protest any further, so we drove off in the car, past the vacant storefronts and decaying houses, out to the well-lit, soulless strip-mall jungle, the festering sore on the ass-end of Reliance. The stores were all closed up, save for Wal-Mart, its expansive parking lot lit up like a landing strip. We went inside and wandered around the aisles, bathed in the surreal fluorescent glow and surrounded by the cheap bounty of globalization. Big leering yellow smiley faces accosted us around every corner. Earl said hello to the people he knew who were working that evening. I had half a notion to climb atop the glass display showcasing the latest digital cameras and MP3 players, to squat down and drop a steaming dump right then and there. But Earl talked me out of it, saying that it surely wouldn't win him any points with his co-workers. We finally ended up at the tobacco counter. I asked the kid working there for two cartons of unfiltered Lucky Strikes.

"No filter?" he asked incredulously. "Jesus, man. You're one tough motherfucker."

"No," I said, "just a stupid one."

As Earl and I trudged back through the parking lot, I couldn't resist the urge to shove a wayward shopping cart into another one. They collided with a satisfying metal *crunch*. I took another cart and sent it careening into a light post.

"Fuck you, Sam Walton!" I screamed. "I hope you rot in hell! Fuck you and your super-low prices!"

"Whoa!" Earl said, grasping my shoulder. "Easy, now."

He led me back to the store and sat me down on the curb out front. He fished in his pockets for some change and bought us a couple cans of Mountain Lightning from one of the vending machines outside. We drank them while sitting on the curb. I cracked open one of the cartons of cigarettes and passed a pack to Earl. We lit up and sat there sipping our pops, sobering up in the Wal-Mart parking lot on Christmas Eve.

"You know," Earl said, "I can understand why you're angry. I don't particularly care for this place, myself. If you think having no option but to shop here is bad, you should see what it's like to have no option but to work here. But I've had a lot of time to think about the matter while I stock the shelves. And I've come to the conclusion that Wal-Mart is probably more of a symptom than a cause. Or at least it began that way, anyway. Now it's big enough that it may be a force all its own. Same for the super home-improvement stores and the super supermarkets and the super movie theaters ..."

"But a symptom of what?" I said.

"That," Earl said, "I don't know."

"The past has never been good to me, Earl," I said. "Or I've never been good to it. We're like conjoined twins reaching for the same bottle of milk: either way, we lose."

"Well," Earl said, "welcome to the club."

I dropped Earl off at home, then I swung back by the bar for one more Scotch. Which predictably turned into several Scotches. I tried to make chitchat with Annie. She could tell I wasn't having an easy time of it, though, so she kept a respectful distance, for the most part. By midnight, the glorious dawn of Christmas itself, we were the only ones left in the place. Annie pretended to busy herself behind the bar, but she kept casting sidelong glances at me as she went about emptying ashtrays and drying glasses. Finally, I threw some money on the counter and heaved myself into my coat.

As I left the bar for the last time that night, Annie called out to me.

"Roger ..." she said.

I cocked my head back for a split second.

"You don't hafta go home, y'know" she said. "Least not alone, anyway."

I could, truth be told, think of far more unpleasant ways to spend the holiday than in her company. Which is why I shoved open the door and trudged into the frigid, lonely world without a second look back.

The walk back to my apartment took me through several forsaken alleyways and across the sad expanse of Sodgrass Park, Reliance's own little half-acre of hell, with more rapes and knifings per square inch than any other similarly sized slab of land in the continental United States. I crossed the street on the other side of the park and approached my apartment building. Outside, a figure lurked in the shadows, its face shrouded by a hood like a cloak-bedecked Ghost of Christmas Future.

"Merry Christmas, sir, can I int'rest you in some hol'day cheer?" The words came from inside the hooded sweatshirt. "Gots coke, crack, hash, meth. Good stuff. Gots some o' that eks-tuh-*see*."

"No, thanks, Cecil," I said, recognizing the would-be ghost immediately. "I'm about as ecstatic as I care to get."

"Oh, it you, Mister Roger," Cecil said, stepping in place from one foot to the other and blowing fiercely into his cupped bare hands. "Merry Christmas alls the same, though, sir. Say, you wouldn't have a dime on you, would you, sir?"

I gave him a twenty.

He took a slug from a paper bag-sheathed bottle that he retrieved from the sweatshirt's pocket. Then he started to softly sing "Jingle Bells" in a harsh, wavering falsetto.

I looked at his gaunt face, his skinny frame swallowed by the enormous sweatshirt.

"Cecil, when's the last time you had a good meal?" I said.

He looked a little wounded.

"I eat just fine, sir. Usually. Only times is tough these days ..."

"Come on," I said, leading him inside and up the narrow staircase to the top floor.

Luckily, Santa had left the door unlocked as I'd asked. He was passed out on the couch, snoring like a bulldozer. Cecil let out a low whistle upon seeing Santa's slumbering form.

"Gonna be some sad kids tonight," he said. "Looks like ol' Mr. Claus done got tired."

I warmed some soup on the stove and gave a bowl of it to Cecil. He thanked me and proceeded to dive in. He'd soon polished off a second and a third bowl. Then he, too, collapsed, falling asleep face-first at the kitchen table.

I made myself a cup of spiced, spiked coffee and proceeded to pace around the cramped kitchen. On the counter next to the sink sat a pile of unopened Christmas cards. The one on top bore a Boston mailing address. I hadn't told Eddie that part of the story, how she had never expressed the slightest bit of rancor at my sudden departure from her life. For several years, she continued to send me letters every few months. And, without fail, she'd sent a card every Christmas since then. I hadn't read any of the cards the last ten years or so. Hadn't even opened them.

I scrounged around in the kitchen drawers for a knife, but then changed my mind and turned toward the window. I opened it and took in the smell of the icy outside air, which intermingled with faint whiffs of woodsmoke and grease and car exhaust. I lit a cigarette and stared out at the alleyways and streets and rooftops, obscured by the wavering flakes of the evening's uncertain snow.

If this were a Christmas story, I thought, I would see the folly of my ways and hurl the pack of cigarettes and a silver dollar out the window and reach for the telephone. The cigarettes would land in the Dumpster and the silver dollar would be snatched in mid-air by an eleven-year-old boy freshly escaped from the evil confines of the county orphanage. "God bless you, kind sir," he'd say. "God bless you, and a very fine Christmas to you, indeed." And the phone call would go through and a familiar voice would greet me on the other end. Or the heavens would part and American Airlines would come forward with a generous offer to spirit me away to reunite with my true love. Or I would win the lottery, buy the newspaper, publish a series of galvanizing articles, and launch a foundation to rejuvenate downtown Reliance. If this were a Christmas movie, I thought, I could at least change the channel and escape the holiday and instead be instantly obliterated by a cyborg sent from the future to prevent mankind's eventual destruction by a race of sadistic machines.

I pulled a chair to the window and sat down. I took a final draw on the cigarette, then cast it out the window. Its glowing tip winked as it tumbled, then was swallowed by the swirling snowflakes. I took another sip of the coffee, then propped the mug and my chin on the window ledge. Around me the room was abuzz with the snoring of Cecil and Santa Claus. My eyelids grew heavy, I sensed the creeping wall of impending restless dreams, and I mumbled some curses toward Reliance, dying out there in the darkness.

And I wept. And, still weeping, then I slept.

the long walk

I sit on the platform at Alexandria's Union Station, immersed in the intermittent hustle and hush of impending rush hour. Brittle leaves dance on rail beds amidst the clean steel scent of a windswept winter afternoon. Commuter trains slip past, fleeting faces framed in the windows. But as I flip through the Amtrak schedule, it is the long-distance lines that beckon me – Boston, Providence, New Haven – to the gray cities of the North, into the bowels of winter. But I am broke and expected back soon, so with my hands in my pockets I trudge homeward, beneath February's bruised blue skies.

Tim Bugansky has been a caddie, newspaper reporter, bus driver, waiter, bartender, tour guide, public information officer, temp worker, and ESL teacher. Hundreds of his articles and essays have been published in newspapers such as *The Tampa Tribune*, *The (Cleveland) Plain Dealer*, and *The Washington Post*. *Anywhere but Here* is his first book of fiction.

www.ingramcontent.com/pod-product-compliance
Lightning Source LLC
Chambersburg PA
CBHW030351020726
47493CB00003B/778